SCARS ON THE FACE OF GOD

CHRIS BAUER

SEVERN RIVER PUBLISHING

Severn River Publishing
severnriverbooks.com

ISBN: 978-1-64875-501-9 (Paperback)

ALSO BY CHRIS BAUER

Blessid Trauma Crime Scene Cleaners

Hiding Among the Dead

Zero Island

2 Street

Scars on the Face of God

Binge Killer

Jane's Baby

with Andrew Watts

Air Race

Never miss a new release! Sign up to receive exclusive updates from author Chris Bauer.

severnriverbooks.com/authors/chris-bauer

To Terry, whose childhood was the closest thing to an orphan's without her being one.

PROLOGUE
APRIL 1909, SCHUETTEN, PA

We heel-toed our way through the kitchen, all moon-shadowy dark this early in the morning, me first, Heinie following real close, past the hearth and the three stoves and around the two butcher-block islands, over to a covered bin. I held the lid open so Heinie could pull out two empty potato sacks. Sister Irene would be up at six to make the oatmeal, so we had an hour.

Heinie was a skinny kid who said he was a full eight years old but I was sure he weren't a speck over seven. The nuns picked him up last year the day after my ninth birthday, after someone seen him wandering the bungalows eating from garbage pails in the middle of the night. His mother was dead on account of she froze stiff in a snowdrift outside the hotel taproom. His father was a tannery worker, except Heinie said his mom never knew which one. I cut him in on a good deal only because he had the guts to lie to me about his age.

"Them dogs been crapping two full days since we last been out," I said, my voice low. "Let's go make us some money."

I tugged at the knob of the heavy back door with both hands till it pulled open. In seeped a door full of night mist that settled thick and heavy on us, tickling my nose with the smell of drying creek mud and plants that rotted in it. We looked through the screen door into the grayness, all mixed in with dark swirls left over from a rain we got overnight.

"Looks creepy outside," Heinie whispered, his eyes big as all-day suckers.

"Night fog," I said. "Came up from the river. That's all it is."

"Yeah, but how do we tell the difference if there's ghosts out there?"

I unhooked the screen door latch and told him to quit bellyaching, then I pulled him outside by the shoulder when he didn't move. We stayed under the overhang of the back porch, potato sacks in our hands, me listening to crickets and frogs, him listening to who knows what. A full moon played peekaboo behind the clouds until it poked itself through and lit up the backyard. The shadowy mist that surrounded the orphanage was now crawling down the slope. If there were any ghosts mixed in there with it, they were heading back to the river.

I hopped down the steps, reached my hand under the porch floorboards, and pulled out two wooden spoons from a ledge. Time to get to work.

First stop was the Schuetten Hotel, opposite side of the road from the orphanage and down a bit, around a bend lined with maple trees. Pale yellow shingles, brown trim, and four rounded corners that looked like small grain silos with windows. Real pretty in the daytime, but now it was all tan and gray, the only light on it coming from the moon. Out front of the hotel the shingles had a shine to them, sparkled up some since this was where the town cobblestones began. Sister Irene said folks often traded in their country smarts for city smarts once they stepped off the dirt and onto the brick, and weren't it too bad their common sense didn't always tag along for the trip.

A puddle of muddy rainwater made trickle-drip noises as it ran through a black iron sewer grate set flat in the cobblestone out front of the hotel. Heinie and me stepped around the grate, our eyes on the empty spaces between the bars, spaces I knew were wide enough for cats and other small critters to fit through if they got pushed hard enough, 'cause I seen it done. We tiptoed past, listening for noises different than the trickle-drips, heard nothing else from underneath. We quickened up again till we were on hotel property.

We started at the far end of the back lawn and moved silent through the grass, our eyes to the ground while we worked our way toward the hotel porch, bending, standing, bending, standing, careful where we tread. This time of year the sun got up about the same time Sister Irene did. A good thing, seeing as how the hotel owner wanted us to work when it was mostly dark and his guests were still asleep. Heinie spied a large pile a few feet ahead of him and hurried his skinny legs to get to it.

Uh-oh. Oopsy-daisy.

"Johnny," Heinie whimpered. "Aw, Johnny, help me."

Heinie's lace-up shoes were a size too big for him, so when his potato sack dragged underneath them the little goof's legs got all tangled up between burlap and leather. He pushed himself up from the dew-soaked grass. The right side of his face was now a brown smear. I got him to his feet.

"Pick up the shit with your spoon," I told him, "not your face. Hold still." Heinie held his nose and gagged, still not used to the dog-shit business. With a few swipes of my spoon, I scraped off most of what was on his face. I untucked my shirt and ripped off the tail, then used it to wipe the rest of the mutt cake off his cheek.

On the hotel's back porch a rocking chair squeaked over a loose floorboard, then stopped its slow back-and-forth. The person sitting in it struck a match, his smooth dark face lighting up behind the flame as he pulled hard at his pipe, the match held fast to the bowl end. Fat Cookie worked in the hotel's kitchen.

"Thanks, boys," Cookie said through little puffs of smoke. "The coins is where they always is." He snapped shut his pocket watch, then went back to his rocking. "Better hustle yourselves up. Forty minutes till your oatmeal."

I sneaked up on a lawn angel that was really a stone birdbath and quick snatched the pennies out of her hand. I waved Heinie into the underbrush; we left the hotel property through a separation in the trees.

We doubled back across Schuetten Pass Road and came up on the church rectory's lawn. Monsignor owned two well-fed bullmastiffs, and with all the crapping they did, the town strays took to dumping here, too. His dog stuff stayed right where it was, all except for a few chunks I flicked into the open window of his horse carriage. I never much liked the monsignor.

On the other side of the maples we slipped onto the grounds of the Volkheimer bungalows, one-story shacks with black-and-white smoke curling out their stovepipes, their front and back doors under hand-painted hex signs supposed to protect the people inside. From what, I never fully understood, but around here there were hex signs everywhere, on shacks and barns and stables, even outdoor privies, except most all the signs were faded and flaking off the curled-up wood they'd been painted on. About fifty German families lived here, the shanties spread out north and west across the railroad tracks along the upper tip of town, and didn't none of them families ever talk much about them hex signs, least not to us orphans or other outsiders.

"Old charms for old evils" was how Fat Cookie once put it, one outsider to another. "Can't rightly say them signs been much help to these folks lately."

Heinie and me traipsed two rows inside the settlement and stepped onto a small square grass patch we hadn't had time to police the last few days. Hot damn. Pay dirt.

We worked the area same as we worked the hotel lawn. A stray came out of nowhere, a rammy little brown-and-white rat terrier that chased us the last time we came through. He leaped onto the back of Heinie's leg, started getting all pecker-happy with it. I grabbed the mutt by his tail and tossed him a good five feet, enough so Heinie and me could get a running start. The rat-dog landed and spun like he was ready to come at us again, except something stopped him; he stiffened on all fours. His bulging terrier eyes narrowed and he growled low like a cornered raccoon, his upper lip curled and showing teeth sharp enough to do what rat terriers been known to do, which was clamp onto and rip apart a rat's head.

"Back up, real slow," I told Heinie.

The hair on the mutt's neck and shoulders rose. It was then I seen something I'd never seen a ratter do before: He took a backward step. He snapped once then stiffened again.

"He's gonna bite, Johnny."

"No, he won't. He's too scared. Keep moving."

"Scared? Ratters don't get scared. Scared of what?"

Behind us I heard a moan. We turned, and on the other side of the grass patch in the moonlight we saw a privy with its door open. Two bare legs were spread apart half in the privy and half out with a tumble of lady's nightclothes above a pair of bent knees, the two bare feet attached to them legs digging their heels into a black mudhole just outside the door. Her feet lifted out of the muck and into the privy's shadows, then slapped against the inside of the doorframe on both sides, the wood creaking against the weight. Another moan told me this was for sure a girl or a lady in pain, with grunting low and deadened like her teeth were sunk into cloth. A few seconds later she squealed bad as if she was being split in half. The ratter kept his distance, growling and snapping until the lady quit her screaming and settled into another low moan. The terrier whimpered, then turned tail and took off. Heinie and me were right behind him.

The dog found shimmy space under a garden shack, but me and Heinie kept running till we got outside the bungalows, onto the path that went north, next to the foggy Wissaquessing River. The river was all swelled up and noisy as a rainstorm on account of the dam from the lake was open. A covered footbridge wide enough for buckboards and horseless carriages to pass each other took us across the river and emptied us onto the Volkheimer fairgrounds. Five minutes past the fairgrounds, we were on tannery property.

Knock knock. The brown metal door swung inward, its hinges squealing like scattering mice. A face rimmed with a blond beard appeared on the other side of the screen door.

"Goot morning," the Dutchman said. "Chust in time, boys." We stepped a few feet inside the door and dropped our sacks onto a cart. Heinie crinkled his nose from the smell.

"Wer da, Herr Glocker?" came from across the room, the other side of the tannery's gurgling vats. It was Mr. Volkheimer's voice, except Mr. Volkheimer didn't show himself.

"It's Dogshit Johnny," the Dutchman answered, "und his apprentice."

The Dutchman cinched my potato sack shut and raised it off the cart a few inches to check the weight by hand, then did the same with Heinie's.

His eyebrows arched in our direction until a smile sneaked out through the machine grease on his beard.

"Vait here, fellas," he told us, then he pushed the cart over to a water vat the size of a circus trampoline and emptied our sacks into it. When he got back he laid out our earnings on a worktable. Five pennies each, plus two shiny red apples.

"From Herr Volkheimer," the Dutchman said and turned us around by our shoulders so we were facing a washbasin. "Now clean your hands and spoons real goot then raus mit uch. If you hurry, you can make it back to the orphanage in time for your breakfast. Und Herr Volkheimer says stay out of trouble."

Heinie and me skipped down Schuetten Pass Road, kicking up dust and stones while we ate our apples, me poking fun at him. "Shoulda seen your face with that dog shit all over it. I thought you were gonna puke."

"Wish you wouldn't talk about it, Johnny," Heinie said, his mouth full, "else I'll upchuck this here ap—"

"Shhh." I stopped him with a hand on his shoulder and pointed through the line of maples to another covered bridge. "Look." We hurried over to a tree and poked out our heads from behind its trunk.

The fog was gone, and on the wide dirt path worn into the hillside was a lady in nightclothes wobbling past us, on her way down to the bridge. Seen men stumble out of the taproom walking straighter than her, each of them knowing where they wanted to go but the knowing not helping them much. In the crook of her arm was a bundle that looked like a fat cigar but was near as big as a market-day satchel. Her nighttime bedclothes were unbuttoned halfway up, her white legs slimy-wet in the moonlight, her bare feet caked brown with road dirt. It was her heels that were the filthiest, like they'd been dipped in pig flop. No, more like they'd been dipped in—

Yeah. The black mud that collected outside privies.

The bundle squirmed and mewed inside the cocooned blanket as she reached the bridge. She steadied herself by leaning against the bridge tunnel's framing, then disappeared inside.

We waited for her to step out of the tunnel, onto the river's other bank. The sun pushed over the hill, the inky sky now turning blue as a baby blanket, the trees poking out of the smoky-black night with long shadows attached to their trunks, including the one me and Heinie were tucked behind. Heinie whispered, "Where'd she go?"

I shrugged. We poked our heads out to see better, our eyes watching both sides of the bridge. On our end the tunnel was shadowy-dark as a cave, its opening under another faded hex sign. More waiting.

The bridge window over the middle of the river flipped back on squeaky hinges, making us both jump. I squinted, the window now a black square in the bridge's scuffed red wall, nothing moving inside it. Suddenly two arms split the window's darkness and heaved the fat cigar bundle through it like it was bathwater getting tossed off a back porch. The bundle splashed into the choppy river and didn't come back up. The window stayed open.

"Must be kittens, huh, Johnny? Want to fish them out?"

"Nope. River ain't safe when the dam's open."

The river swallowed up the bundle and didn't seem no worse for it, Heinie and me still staring at the water's shiny twinkle-star surface like we'd been hypnotized. Suddenly a loud pop jolted us both, scattering squirrels and scaring the chirping songbirds out of the maples along the bank. A tiny puff of smoke drifted from the open window, and it was then I knew for sure the lady wouldn't be coming out either end of the tunnel. *Go,* I told myself. *Run.*

The bundle the lady tossed into the river bobbed to the surface before I could move. Wasn't more than a second before we heard it crying, then it went under again.

"Johnny, that ain't no cat! It's—"

Whatever Heinie said after that I never heard since my cap and shoes were already off and I'd gone over the side of the bank, into the chop. The river was maybe six feet deep in the middle, but I was only four-ten, so it might as well been a mile. Water was cold and rough yet with all the runoff it was mostly clean, at least near the top. I took a deep breath, closed my mouth, and ducked under the surface.

I wasn't ready for what I was hearing, or thought I was hearing: a crying baby, clear and strong as a hungry newborn in the orphanage nursery, screaming like it was right next to me, like its little arms were waving around, looking to be picked up, but—

I was underwater so the crying shoulda sounded different, shoulda sounded like gurgles and glugs from when you swallowed too much lake water except it didn't and I was getting scared and—

...the river bottom, filthy, not able to see—

...found something, cloth against my hand.

...other babies were down here, I could hear them, they were screaming.

...they needed to stop. All them screaming babies needed to stop—

* * *

On the bank me and Heinie leaned over the bundle. It wasn't making no more noise.

"Pull the blanket off his face, Johnny."

I was shivering too much. Besides, I figured it was dead already. "You do it."

"Okay. One, two..."

Heinie pulled at the blanket but didn't say nothing after that, his voice stuck inside a scream.

I opened the bundle up all the way. "Jesus..."

I felt my stomach jump. Little arm and leg bones stuck through ragged strips of rotted baby skin, the only skin on the baby's skull its mouth, its lips tiny, and thin, like they'd been painted on, its eyes with no lids, scared and begging and real mad, and—

Shit. The lips. They *moved.*

Heinie and me rounded the bend a couple of hundred feet away from the river and weren't neither of us gonna slow down one bit, no way, no sir, no how, unh-unh. I'd kicked the bundle hard for scaring me, kicked it right back into the choppy river, which must not have been a good thing 'cause I swear on the Bible and a nun's crucifix that I could still hear that baby screaming right behind me like it was me who killed it, me who tossed it away, and me who wouldn't let it go to heaven.

1

APRIL 1964, THREE BRIDGES, PA

So I said to the parish's new priest as I helped him take his suitcases upstairs to the second floor of the rectory, his room at the end of the hall, "Father," I said, "when you have some time, I'd like to hear what it was like playing professional baseball."

Father Duncan was in his early forties and my height, which was six feet tall, give or take. Dark brown hair, peppercorn eyes, and a face like that TV Beaver kid, except his nose was real prominent with a major right turn. His arms were thick but not long. His waist was wide, his pointed bony shoulders wider still. Wrists and hands were big, a few of his knuckles like snapped stogies, and every one of them large. Someone might have picked him for a boxer, a profession that's never been kind to a man's face or fingers. Next good guess could only have been what he once was, a baseball catcher.

Now he was a priest. There had to be something special happen to this man to make a change as drastic as that, and I knew a thing or two about drastic changes. For me it was when I met my Viola. Warmest, saintliest woman I've ever known. She studied to become a nun but changed her mind before she took the vows. Still did nun's work afterward, helping at the church and visiting the prison, which was how she met me. We married soon after I got paroled, me the age of twenty-five, she three years younger, on the way to forty good years together. Lived a good chunk of them years in our house just the other side of Our Lady's schoolyard, Viola working as one of the church housekeepers and me eventually as its lead custodian.

The parish buildings included church, convent, rectory and school. Kept us busy even though we were both almost retired. Soon as Father was unpacked I pointed out our house to him, visible from his window. A row home in the middle of the block, built in '29 with the rest of the row homes that ran north as far as the river, after they'd knocked down the tannery's bungalow housing.

"No time like the present, Mr. Hozer," Father said, then moved around the right half of the room in his skivvy shirt. Before he got into the story-telling, I stopped him.

"Needn't call me Mr. Hozer," I told him. "Sounds too much like my father." Adoptive father actually, which I mentioned. The bastard died at age thirty-six in an ice-fishing accident on Lake Erie. This I didn't mention. "You can call me Wump, Father. Been answering to Wump since I was in my teens."

"Then Wump it is," Father said. He unfolded a cassock, eased right into his prior life. "The Phillies drafted me out of high school..."

Three Bridges was north and east of northeast Philadelphia. The man now known as Father Duncan had been a baseball legend in the Philly Catholic high school league. "Connie" Duncan. Star catcher and home-run hitter. Graduated high school, went into the minor leagues, and eventually got called up to the Phillies, late forties I think it was, but he lasted only two years. Couldn't hit a major league curve ball. Was sent back down and never made it up again. Then shortly after he turned thirty, which was ancient for a minor leaguer to still be playing ball, there was this incident he was telling me now. Something that made the Phillies decide it was time for Connie Duncan to quit baseball. "You know about square pegs and round holes, Wump?"

Sure did. First part of my life I told him, when Mr. Hozer was trying to make a farmer out of me in Turtle Creek, Pennsylvania, a small town near Pittsburgh. Farmer's plough horse was more like it. His two boys by birth got sent off regular to school soon as I got there, left me to do all the goddamn work. When I hit my sixteenth birthday, I hitched a freight train back east. A month later, I was at work at the Volkheimer Tannery here in Schuetten, though they weren't calling the town Schuetten anymore. Started calling it Three Bridges sometime after I got adopted. All them Germans wanted to be Americanized, and Schuetten was too German a name for them; means "to shit," or something like it. But I didn't say all this to Father, didn't pick on the Germans or nothing. Hell, I was one of them. Or so I been told. And I didn't use no curse words either. I was in a rectory talking to a priest, for Christ sake.

"Well then, Wump, maybe you can appreciate this." Father said there was something just wasn't right with his life. Wasn't boredom, and had nothing to do with him figuring he wasn't good enough to make it back to the major leagues. Said it was "not unlike a slap in the face, putting me on notice, telling me I had a purpose. And this purpose wasn't knocking down baseball players at home plate." So when they sent him back to the minors he'd started sorting things out, reading the Bible, that sort of thing.

Father said he was a real cut-up when he played ball, with the coaches, the fans and his teammates. Would tell the players jokes, pull pranks on them, do anything for a laugh. "Late one season we were in Albany," he said, pulling his shaving kit out of a bag. Father rubbed his chin like he was deciding if he should shave again this late in the day. He should.

"I was catching a game that didn't matter, our team far back in the standings, and I wanted the road trip to end so I could get back home to see my folks, especially my sick grandmother." He lathered up, began dragging a safety razor around his face while he talked about what proved to be his final game as a professional baseball player. It involved a mouthy runner on third base antsy to steal home, a throw from Father that sailed over the third baseman's head, and something Father had slipped into his catcher's mitt during a timeout moments before: a yellow apple. The runner didn't think twice about whether the overthrow was an apple or a ball so he trotted toward Father at home plate. Father tagged him out, the real ball in his mitt. The ump gave Father an earful for pulling the stunt and tossed him out of the game. There was a bus ticket back to Philadelphia waiting for him when he got out of the shower. His baseball career was over.

Father picked out a light blue short-sleeved pullover for when he was done washing up. "Is there a regular supper time each night, Wump?"

"Six o'clock. So Father, if you don't mind me asking—"

"You want to know what the slap in the face was that made me decide to become a priest. I made the decision that day. I was in my hotel room packing when I got a phone call from my grandmother. Nanny called me all the time while we were on road trips, even after she got sick. I told her I'd be home for good the next day, then I told her why.

"'God has another purpose for you, Connie,' she explained to me. She said I'd figure out what it was soon enough."

"Is she gone now?"

"Yes. That was the last time I spoke with her. But here's the thing." Father pulled out his toiletries and lined them up on the dresser. "I called my folks that night to tell them I was coming home. My mother said they'd tried to reach me earlier in the day but couldn't track me down. I laughed, told them they should always check with Nanny because she'd found me easily that afternoon. 'Not possible,' my mother said. 'Nanny died this morning.'"

Father looked himself over in the dresser mirror, then flashed a slight smile in my direction. "Just one of those things that makes a person think."

I'd heard stories like this before, from people who said it happened to an aunt or a niece or someone they knew at work. Never paid much attention to them. Sounded different coming from a priest. Creepy, quivery different. Almost like proof.

Father took his catcher's mitt out of his bag. "I'll let you in on another secret. Something small that never made it to the sports pages, and I haven't mentioned in years." He handed me the mitt and motioned for me to try it on. "But only if you tell me more about yourself."

I said sure, then I pounded my fist into the mitt's pocket a few times before I handed it back. Father placed it on a closet shelf. "I had a nickname when I played ball," he said. "Not 'Connie.' That one's been with me since I was a kid. The players and coaches called me 'Trick.' Wasn't a stretch, mind you, considering the stunts I used to pull. Like I said, a small secret. So tell me, how did you come by the nickname 'Wump'?"

This made me uncomfortable. The man had me in a corner, and it was like he knew he had me cornered, too, since he'd shared all this personal stuff with me. I liked him, so I decided to trust him with the truth.

"From the sound a crowbar makes when it hits a man's head, Father."

I was twenty-one, I told him, and the man I hit didn't die. He was a taproom owner who lived above his bar. One night my buddies and me were burglarizing the place, and we woke him up. The owner had recognized me, so the cops caught up with us a few days later. "Ain't proud of that, Father, and I paid my debt."

I needed to change the subject. "So tell me, Father, what's your given first name?"

I had it figured as Cornelius, like the great Philadelphia Athletics baseball manager Cornelius "Connie" Mack. I knew of no other Connies.

"My first name is Constantine. Yours?"

"Johannes. But as a kid I answered to Johnny."

Dog shit has a natural chemical in it that helps soften animal skins during the leather-tanning process. I learned this from Sister Irene at the orphanage when I was eight years old, so here I was telling Father about it. The Volkheimer Tannery folks would give me money for it was what she told me, so I collected it in potato sacks and delivered it there each morning till I was twelve, around the time Rolf Volkheimer disappeared and was wrote off as dead. Rolf was the oldest of the three Volkheimer brothers, all partners in the tannery, at least until Rolf left on a trip to the old country— Bavaria, in the southern part of Germany, where it was mostly Catholic— and never came back. Soon afterward the Hozers adopted me. It was them who took me on a train out to their farm near Pittsburgh. Weren't no orphanages where they lived, but lucky for them they had a Bucks County, Pennsylvania, uncle who told them about all the free child labor there was back East.

"Pittsburgh," Father repeated through the doorway of the hall bathroom, one door away from his room.

"Yep. Like I said, Father, after the adoption I lived near there, till I was sixteen."

Father was back in the hallway, clean-shaven, a blue shirt tucked into his pants, smiling and ready for dinner. "Once heard a joke about Pittsburgh," he said. "In it the Devil delivers the punch line to some newly condemned souls. 'Hell's full,' he says. 'Go to Pittsburgh.'"

Haw. Father got that right. Good punch line, I told him. Damn good punch line.

We got to the bottom of the stairs just as Monsignor Fassnacht pushed through the rectory's front door, his wide-brimmed hat in one hand, his brass-knobbed walking stick in the other. He dropped them both on the tufted vestibule ottoman, the walking stick rolling onto the floor. The parish's newest novice, Harriet, slipped in quietly behind him, picked up the walking stick and the hat, put them in the vestibule closet, then returned to the parlor. Viola told me Harriet needed looking after, she was so shy. Hailed from the Appalachians in West Virginia. She sat straight-backed in a parlor chair, white blouse, buttoned-up collar, black skirt below her knees, bright blue eyes that followed the monsignor. The man could have at least thanked her, but he wasn't known for that.

Monsignor smoothed back a full head of straight black hair with his palm, shot a small wink in Harriet's direction that perked her face up, then he was done with her. He gave himself the once-over in the vestibule mirror. "Settled in, Father Duncan?"

My hair is as white as a bleached bedsheet, but Monsignor Fassnacht, same age as me at sixty-five, showed no signs of silver. He kept his suit jacket buttoned and his white priest's collar tight around his hefty jowls. He brushed past me to sidle up next to Father, who told him yes, he was settled in and comfortable. Not sure if Father noticed, but Monsignor and me weren't on speaking terms.

"Welcome, then, to Our Lady of the Innocents," Monsignor said. "I know you'll find the work here rewarding. A lot of second-, third- and fourth-generation Germans in the parish. Hard-working, salt-of-the-earth, God-fearing types. And our grade-school baseball team"—he patted Father's shoulder—"could use the guidance of a former professional base-ball player." Monsignor draped an arm over Father and led him into the dining room. "I am ravenous. Let's see what Mrs. Gobel's cooked up for us tonight, shall we?"

Suppertime for me, too. I dug into my shirt pocket for my pencil stub and notepad, then leaned onto the rectory's reception desk to jot down a list of a few thingamajigs the convent needed. Been little call for any hard-ware the past couple of days, which meant Leo, a certain young helper of mine, hadn't earned any extra spending money, least not from me. Leo was the most ambitious twelve-year-old I'd ever met, his enthusiasm bright as a 100-watt bulb, his smarts considerably dimmer. Liked following me around between convent and rectory, in and out and back and forth, looking to do errands. Best to be ready for when Leo caught up with you, which was why I was making the list. Otherwise he'd ask about every item Muehler's Hardware carried, aisle by aisle. I pulled open the rectory's front door.

What a surprise. "Hello, Leo."

"Hi, Wump!" Leo said, his mouth and nose staying busy with giggles and snorts and what could have passed for a baby cooing. Never seen a kid get so excited about hardware. "Muehler's is open late tonight. They got specials on paint and paint products, bug sprays, and cans of hand soap. I seen the signs in the window."

"Yes, I know, son. Here's my list. And hello to you too, Teddy."

Seeing big Teddy Agarn with him surprised me. Leo usually brought Raymond on errands. Raymond was thirteen and a lot worse off than Leo. Blind since birth and in a wheelchair. He could hear but was a mute. Couldn't walk, couldn't get out of the chair. Couldn't clean up after himself. Sickly, too. Leo got errand money from the nuns at the orphanage for tending to Raymond, but I knew he'd do it for nothing.

"Raymond's sick in bed today, so I asked Teddy."

Teddy was the same age as Leo but a head taller and had already filled out. Lived with his father and grandmother, went to Our Lady's school, had been held back twice. Leo and Raymond, on the other hand, were both orphans. They lived at St. Jerome's Home for Foundlings across town, next to the river. Same orphanage where I'd spent my first twelve years.

Leo labored through the list. "Ceil-ing paint, one gal-lon. Paint roll-er, nine inch. Paint thin-ner, one quart." His mouth stayed open after he was done talking, slobbered some. His sandy hair always looked mussed. "Gonna do some painting, Wump?"

"Good guess, son. Yes." We started down the walk, away from the rectory's front door. Leo had a forward lean near as bad as a ship's bowsprit. He bounced up next to me, asked, "The new Father all unpacked?"

I told him yes. Teddy fell in behind us.

"I helped him with his bags today, Wump," Leo said, beaming. "He needed help from the taxi, so I helped him to the front door of the rectory."

"It's good you were here, Leo. Nice, friendly priest, Father Duncan is. I like him."

"Yep. Me too. And tricky. Right, Wump?"

This stopped me. "Did you say 'tricky'?"

The curb to the rectory's front door was no more than fifty feet. There just wasn't enough time for Father to get into any baseball stories or nicknames with him.

"Yep. He gave me a dime for carrying his bags, but I had to pick which hand. I picked the wrong one but he gave it to me anyway. That Father sure is tricky, huh?"

I nodded. We got to the alleyway behind my house, where I had to turn left and he and Teddy had to go straight. "Be careful crossing Schuetten Avenue, fellas, especially where they're digging out for the new restaurant."

I lingered a moment and watched as the two of them reached the corner. They looked both ways, then crossed the street.

A coincidence was all it was, Leo calling Father Duncan by his baseball nickname. Had to be.

* * *

Viola always kidded me about how my hair was thinning on the crown, around my cowlick. It would be like hers soon, sparse enough on top to see some scalp. Salt and pepper, the two of us were, mine a wavy white, hers black from a weekly rinse at the hairdresser's and kept in a tight bun that covered her thin spot. I used my comb before I opened the front door.

When I first met Viola there were prison bars between us. Aside from the soft, full features of her face, there'd been little other sense that she was even a woman. As a volunteer she dressed the way the prison screws told all the female volunteers to dress, in clothing that did little to reveal a woman's charms. Wasn't like she would have vamped it up anyway, considering how close she came to becoming a nun. Even still, I was lucky to have met her that way, in that environment, surrounded by iron and concrete and low yellow lighting and her all flannelled up, everything during prison visitation hours designed to dull a woman's features. Except in Viola's case there'd been one feature the atmosphere couldn't hide: her beautiful soft-green eyes. Her greatest gifts, those eyes were, so cheerful, so full of calm and compassion, and so able to make me relax on the spot, with just one glance. I learned a great truth the day I met Viola, something some men go entire lifetimes without ever discovering: To sincerely love a woman you must first love her eyes. And if her eyes loved you back, you were truly blessed.

I smelled supper from the door stoop. Baked macaroni and cheese.

How would Viola's eyes be tonight, I wondered. For the forty years of our marriage they'd been full of life, so large and warm and bright. When our son, Harry, got sick last year, they started fading. When he died in February they nearly died with him. I reckoned the past two months my eyes hadn't fared much better, but around her I did my best to keep them bright enough so she saw in their reflection just what she meant to me.

"Hi, sweetie," I called to her. I made my way into the kitchen where she stood in front of the stove, stirring a pot. I planted a big one on the back of her neck, moved in behind her and wrapped my arms around her waist, me looking to stir up a pot of a different kind. I pulled her close, whispered something naughty in her ear. She blushed then reached her cupped hand back to pat my cheek.

"If I'm not too tired," she said, and the smile in her voice tried to find its way to her eyes. I hugged her tightly, told her it was okay either way, and the truth was, it was. Okay if she was too tired, me knowing how the parish housekeeping chores been taking so much out of her lately. Okay otherwise, just in general.

"No corn on the cob today, Johnny," she added. Viola wouldn't call me Wump; had never liked my nickname. "Too dear this time of year. Tonight it's canned. And tomorrow night, too, until the price comes down."

* * *

I was scraping the dinner dishes into the garbage strainer in the sink when the doorbell chimed. Viola left the kitchen to answer it.

"My goodness, Leo, look at you. Johnny, come here."

Leo stood full of mud on the front stoop, some of it caked, some still dripping, brown up to his waist, and he was shaking. I got up close to him. The boy smelled like a sewer.

"Teddy fell in, Wump!" Leo said, panting. "Slid down the side of the hole for the restaurant, right to the bottom. We were on Schuetten Avenue, carrying the paint and he was talking to me, telling me about his dad, the tannery, stuff like that, then all of a sudden there's no more Teddy, and I see he's in the big hole, in water and, ah, yucky stuff, up to his belt. That hole wasn't like that yesterday. I helped get him out, but I couldn't get him to leave with me."

"Get me some blankets and towels," I told Viola.

We wiped Leo down real quick, then draped a blanket around him; he stopped shivering. I told him to get into my truck, a faded red and crusty brown '52 Willys pickup that was still a workhorse even though it looked like the river had burped it up. Before we could pull out, I did a double-take. Out for an after-dinner walk was Father Duncan, his cleric's collar back on under a zipped-up spring jacket. I quick told him what happened and he got into the front seat of the truck beside Leo. Schuetten Avenue was four blocks away.

Teddy was still at the site. Light from the street lamps on the avenue showed us the excavated hole, about sixty by sixty, one half deeper than the other, the drop sharp. The deeper section was like a swimming pool, the back half just puddles. "Yucky stuff," Leo's description of the slop the hole contained, just didn't do it justice. Not by a long shot.

We moved toward Teddy, me as fast as my legs would carry me, Father high-stepping it a lot faster. Teddy was shivering something fierce; when Father got there he draped a fresh blanket around him. Father looked at where Teddy pointed, in what was left of the water.

"Sumpin's under there," Teddy said. "Sumpin' crunchy, on the bottom. I was stepping on it. Then Leo got a board and I climbed out."

We all looked but couldn't see what he was talking about, the muddy water below us in the shallower half still foamy in spots. The place stunk to high hell, like rotten eggs mixed with a hundred years of raw sewage. Then something yellow-white and round and smooth as an overturned bowl poked through the tan foam, to our left. The foam kept dissolving, enough so a second bowl was visible. Then a third, over to the right, and a fourth, and a fifth, except now it was obvious they weren't bowls.

They were skulls. I stopped counting.

My legs weakened, some from a smell bad enough to water a person's eyes, some from seeing all these jumbled-up bones and skulls bunched in spots around the hole's floor. But mostly it was from a childhood memory so gruesome it snatched at my sanity for a moment. I steadied myself, listened hard, and waited for the screams I knew were coming, girded myself for the screams and whimpers I was sure no one else would hear because they weren't there to hear them the first time.

Voices gathered, tinny, squealing voices like tiny birds, chirping and jabbering from inside this hole, on its floor, the chirping starting to swell up. I could feel it, could feel them, here they come...

The noise slammed and held me like a siren, assaulted my eardrums, was more earsplitting than my nightmares. I would have screamed if I'd had the breath.

...no heaven no heaven NO HEAVEN—

I willed myself to breathe, willed myself with eyes squeezed tight to not move, to not turn, to not run because this time, at my age, there could be no running. No way, no sir, no how, unh-unh.

—whywhywhyWHY—

I held my ground. The voices snapped in midscream and were gone.

* * *

When a priest drops a coin into a pay phone and says it's an emergency, things happen. The police were now here and so were some city water-works and sewer maintenance folks. Father talked with a cop, the both of them sidled up to a water company fella who studied a blueprint, other long rolls of blueprints under his arm.

I told Teddy and Leo they needed to call it a night. Leo humored me with an "okay," then did what he wanted anyway and wandered over to where Father made conversation with the fella from the water company. I was left with Teddy.

"God was watching over you today, son. You're one lucky young man."

"Yeah. Right. Lucky," he said. It wasn't a sarcastic answer, just Teddy's way of processing what you told him. He sneezed. "I gotta go. Grammy will be worried. My daddy may be, too."

He was right about his grandmother and her worrying. I knew her; she was a good woman. I knew Teddy's father, too. The man was drunk this time of night.

Father Duncan motioned me over to him. "This fellow is a water department supervisor, Wump. Says he might know what's going on with this hole."

The guy was in light blue coveralls with a hardhat, thirty years old maybe, slight build, big Adam's apple, glasses. "These fucking restaurant people," he said, then caught himself and turned real sheepish toward Father Duncan. "Sorry, Father. These, ah, idiots bought this acre and the one behind it from the city, were told they could sink their hole toward the back of the second lot, to the left. So where did they put it? In the front of the first lot and on the right, which is close to a water main. But it still should have been okay because that's not what they hit."

Hadn't heard nothing about any skulls so far. The guy looked down Schuetten Avenue as its amber streetlamps timed on around the avenue's curve, spring's lengthening days not yet figured into the mix. "I'm waiting on someone from the main office," he said. "He's bringing older maps. This hole looks like it's been dug into what used to be a storm sewer tributary. One that was filled in and rerouted. They did some of this around here, way before my time." He turned to me and looked me over. "But probably not before your time, huh, Pops?"

I boxed in prison, knocked out men in and out of the ring for far less than what this guy just called me. This water department asshole had better watch his mouth.

The city engineers were rigging up lights. At the front of the hole for the restaurant, straight down from street level, was a wall of brick at least thirty courses high and a few courses deep. A chunk of it was missing. Looked like the steam shovel operator stopped just short, probably hadn't even known the wall was there. With most of the dirt on this side of the brick gone, part of the wall had buckled. On the other side I could see some vertical black bars, six inches apart or so. Grating for a large sewer or storm drain. The debris on the floor of this hole had come through those bars. Bones and skulls, and fragments of both. The skeletons of fifty or more bodies was my guess.

I looked up Schuetten Avenue to an intersection, squinted to confirm the name on a signpost for the cross street. I knew what was in this hole, now that I was sure of my bearings.

Baby skeletons, every last one of them.

2

My breath lingered in steamy puffs inside the truck, the heater not fully kicked in while the truck idled curbside next to the restaurant excavation. It was chilly this morning, chillier than normal for early April. The cops and waterworks guys were back down in the hole same as they were last night, all blowing in their hands. I sat in my truck behind a black Caddy station wagon with gold-paint stenciling on its two front doors. The letters spelled out its purpose in a sweeping longhand beautiful as a nun's penmanship: *Coroner.* The stenciling didn't fit the car's purpose, a bit too giddy maybe, like it should have had an exclamation point after it, or like maybe the coroner himself was a fairy or something, which I had no reason to believe, not meaning any disrespect one way or the other. And it wasn't like the writing could have thrown a person off either, like someone wouldn't have guessed its business, its rear windows as black and glossy as the car's paint job, just like a hearse. A few nicknames percolated: crypt buggy, cadaver car, meat wagon.

Maybe not meat wagon, considering.

I'd seen this coroner before, on the TV news. A big-waisted Perry Mason look-alike only shorter and heavier. He was down there with the rest of them, a full story underground, all the water pumped out, the pumps on standby. It was set up like a crime scene now, the cops gathering up the small skeletons and placing them in canvas sacks, stuffing as many bones as they could into each one.

Leo was here, and today he had Raymond with him. Leo had already dug out the cans of paint Teddy Agarn lost when he slipped into the hole last night. Without the paint Leo wouldn't get his errand money, and there wasn't much that could stand in the way of Leo and money, cops and crime scenes included.

Leo slid the paint cans into the covered wire basket under the seat of Raymond's wheelchair. My idea, this basket was, knowing how Leo took Raymond on errands with him. Except Leo kept the basket loaded with rubber swords and baseballs and army guns and other toys for when the two of them were play-acting. Still, whenever I asked him to run an errand, he always managed to find room in there, a lot like a magician with a false-bottom box. Of course, poor blind Raymond didn't do much real playing, mind you. He could hold things and lift his arms a bit, but he was too weak for much else. Leo had a grand old time with him anyway.

Leo wheeled Raymond up to the driver's side of my truck and got eye level with me. "Morning, Wump. You want this hardware stuff left out back of the, ah, don't tell me, lemme guess, out back of, um..."

Leo's face pinched. He could have chosen from five places where he could leave it, the church, the school, the rectory, the convent, or the long shot, my house, where I sometimes did prep work for parish projects. He looked back and forth between Raymond and me, studied me like maybe I would give the answer away. My face stayed blank while I tried to remember if I'd told him what my plans were, that I needed to repaint one of the parish nun's rooms—

"The convent!" he said, beaming, then squealed out a giddy ha-ha. "Can I have my errand money now?"

I'd been playing guessing games like this with him for I didn't know how long. It used to be if there were, say, three choices a person might have, Leo would just as likely pick choice number forty-two million, like maybe home plate at Connie Mack Stadium, or the planet Mars.

"That was a real good guess, son. Here." I handed him a dollar and reminded myself even a blind chicken finds a kernel of corn once in a while. He'd use the buck to get some candy for him and Raymond. "And here's another fifty cents for Teddy. You be sure to give it to him."

"Sure," he said, then jerked an openhanded swipe at his itchy nose. "I went to see Teddy this morning. His dad yelled at me. Wasn't my fault he fell in the hole, was it, Wump?"

"Of course it wasn't, son. It was an accident. Don't pay no attention to him."

It was something I expected from Teddy's father, a discontented bozo if I ever knew one. It reaffirmed my opinion he needed a foot up his ass.

I talked with one water department guy, old-timer to old-timer, who'd brought maps he said had been tucked away in a vault at a regional office in downtown Philly. We were at street level above the excavated lot, the maps opened flat on a piece of plywood laid over two sawhorses, bricks holding the maps down.

"Sixty years on this earth and forty-one of them spent in shit," he confessed. A dingy little guy in tan coveralls under a boxy crewcut, he had an upper denture plate that stuck some when he talked. Wouldn't be long before those choppers were in a drawer. "But I can't say I've seen anything like this before. Won't do any good making this a crime scene now. There can't be much of a trail left on crimes committed over thirty years ago."

"More like sixty years ago," I told him. "It was rougher around here back then. Lots of German immigrants trying to make ends meet. Too many mouths to feed. Desperate times for desperate people."

"Around the turn of the century?" He rubbed his chin. "Sure, why not." The man was humoring me. "All I know is," he said, "whatever crimes we're talking about were committed before the late twenties, which was when the water department rerouted the sewers and storm drains in this area to accommodate new housing."

"If they rerouted them," I said, "then what's that?" I was pointing down, into the hole, at a rectangular concrete tunnel about seven feet high and fifteen feet wide, on the other side of the scattered bricks. The morning sun was low enough to brighten maybe twenty feet of the tunnel's darkness.

"On this side of the wall, where the restaurant will go," he said, "the contractors back then did what they were supposed to do: dug down into the tunnel and filled it in. But under Schuetten Avenue and north," he pointed to the darkness beyond the brick, "they shorted the job. My guess is they walled it off at both ends. Without it being active, over time it dried out. I had a blowtorch in here to cut out all the grating," he said, pointing to where the iron bars were visible last night, "and I sent three men in there about twenty minutes ago to see how far north it goes. One thing's for sure" —his mouth click-clacked once as he lifted a dirty thumb to push up his false teeth—"it's carrying wastewater again."

"Untreated wastewater, right?" I said to him. The smell told me this. Still, I wanted him to say it.

He studied the old map real hard, started tracing some of the sketch lines with his index finger, moved his finger north until it ran out of paper. Just when I figured he hadn't heard me, his white eyebrows wrinkled up and he answered real absent-like, like he was the one who posed the question. "Untreated wastewater. Yeah."

It was then he shot me a sideways glance and his eyes narrowed. "What did you say your name was?"

He and I had spoken on the phone a few times, even met once, and now he was close to remembering. I answered him and his mental tumblers clicked into place; his face changed.

"You again? Get off this site now, you crackpot, before I get someone to throw your ass off. We're done talking."

I'd done my begging the last time we met, so I wasn't about to do it again, but him and me were far from done talking. I summed it up real quick for him, just in case he'd forgotten: industrial sewage dumped into a freshwater tributary, foamy creeks and streams, fouled drinking water, people getting sick. People dying, my son Harry one of them.

A hand dropped onto my shoulder from behind me, but I wasn't finished, damn it. "The evidence is right here, under your nose, in that hole. I'd say it's time for you to be a man instead of some heartless, bureaucratic weasel—"

A town cop had hold of me, his arm around my shoulder, firm but gentle like he knew me, which wasn't a stretch considering most folks around here were churchgoers. He guided me around the police barricades and up the street, told me in a calm tone to let the water department folks do their job and sort this out.

All I knew was that a good portion of my days I spent in pain. A dark, emotional pain that had no chance of letting up unless the right folks got clued in on the unhealthy slop that traveled through the waterways around here.

The cop stayed with me until we reached my truck. It was then we heard raised voices and a flurry of noise coming from the hole's floor, the workers scattering like ants looking for higher ground. Out of the tunnel's mouth came a foamy blast of brown water with a jumble of adult arms and legs as three men in slop-covered uniforms appeared at the crest of a small sewage tidal wave. The gushing stopped, the deeper section of the hole a swimming pool of filthy water again. The poor saps who came out with it were on their butts in the upper elevation, coughing and trying to catch their breath, wiping their faces and eyes with mucky fingers.

"Jarret!" the supervisor with the crew cut yelled. "Don't you know to hold your breath if it looks like you're gonna take a shit-dip?"

"But, boss," his worker said through a coughing fit, "we never saw it coming. We stepped off about eight city blocks, up to where the tunnel stopped at another wall just like the one on this end, except there was a hole in the wall's brick." Someone tossed a folded yellow towel down to him. The man buried his face in it, then looked for a dry spot to finish wiping off his eyes. He addressed his boss again. "Some water was still trickling through it. We chiseled at one of the bricks until we heard a rumbling from the other side. Before we could back ourselves out, the whole friggin' wall exploded, and we were taking a ride on a shithouse roller coaster."

The cop deposited me in my truck, told me I should leave, then he wandered off to get a closer look; I could still hear what was going on. The supervisor looked over the newer storm sewer map while his tunnel scouts climbed out of the hole. He waved them over to him. "See here?" he told them. "This sewer tributary was fed on a straight line at one time. Then it was walled up and a newer one was put in at an angle. After thirty years of water pressure, the north wall might have been weak."

"Weak, but it had some help," another of the scouts said. "I grabbed this from the floor before the wall gave way." He showed his boss a brick. Half a brick, actually. "Looks like it was chiseled out. Some of the others looked the same way."

The water guys thought they were onto something, but much as I'd have liked to have seen what they came up with, I had church folks waiting on me. I checked the truck's rearview mirror before I cranked up the engine.

Christ. Leo and Raymond.

"Wump!" Leo called, and with one push on the handles of Raymond's wheelchair, the two of them were at my side window. "The water smells real bad, don't it, Wump?" He rubbed his nose again like something had tickled it.

"That it does, Leo. Such is the offending nature of sewage. Shouldn't you be on the bus for school, son?"

"Yep. But don't you think it smells funny, too? Not just from the, ah, you know, *poop*? Like maybe rotten eggs?" His head bobbed in agreement with himself.

Leo never cursed, had trouble saying near-curses as well. I told him yes, it had a distinct smell. As bad as a whole farm full of rotten eggs, I told him, me smirking. A simple comment like this most times gave him anywhere from a glimmer of a smile to a major laughing fit. Today I got a stone face, one that seemed bent on waiting me out, like he was expecting me to get just as serious.

"What? What is it, Leo?" He still didn't blink, instead stayed quiet, deadpan as a dress dummy until—

An idea drifted into my head from out of nowhere, and damn if it wasn't simple but good: have Leo get a sample of the sewage. He'd been in the hole once already, to retrieve what he got from the hardware store, and no one paid attention to him while he'd been down there.

"Tell you what, Leo. In the back of my truck, why don't you get a—"

"Canning jar! For a sample! Sure thing, Wump!"

"Yes," I managed, "that's right. One of Viola's canning jars. How'd you...?"

Leo stumbled over the tailgate and into the payload. I squeezed out the truck door and slipped past Raymond in his wheelchair. When I got to the rear of the truck, Leo had already scampered off toward the hole.

I'd been hustled. Couldn't say I knew how he did it, but that's what had happened.

Leo wandered unnoticed down the dirt ramp, stayed on the fringe of the pooled sewer water. He scooped up some of the muck.

Raymond was strapped tight into his chair and leaning to one side, his head against the chair's silver rail, his wavy blond hair parted and plastered flat on top with hair cream. His eyes were open but pointed in different directions and vacant as a cadaver's. He'd be a tall man if he got to grow up, but he had so many medical problems a person might pray for God to take him early. Viola told me last night about his newest diagnosis: leukemia. It was what killed our son.

Viola and me, we've had good cries on a regular basis over Harry. It's a grief we'll carry to our graves. My heart sank for this kid.

Leo was back at street level and closing in. "What a pair you two make," I said out loud.

Raymond's afflictions made it so people didn't expect him to be able to reason much neither, but Leo said different. Said he was smart, and that Raymond gave him advice all the time. Out of the corner of my eye, I saw Raymond's right hand raise a few inches off his lap and give the thumb's-up sign. To me or to Leo, I wasn't really sure, but either way it showed he was paying attention.

Leo chattered at me, getting all tongue-tied until I put a hand on his shoulder to steady him. "Take a deep breath, son, and start over."

"Just smell it, Wump! Open it up and smell it!"

He had the glass jar filled near to the top with diluted slop that looked all light brown and mucky yellow. I unscrewed the lid. Floating on the oily surface were a few thick hairs. I smelled what Leo smelled. "Bleach."

"Yeah, Wump. Smells like bleach. Don't it smell like bleach, Raymond?"

Raymond raised his right thumb again.

Back went the lid, and with my last twist something floating in the muck bumped the inside of the glass, something solid, the size of a rabbit's paw. I raised the jar above my head, turned it around in my hand, then shook it once; still couldn't tell what it was, but it made me uneasy. I shook it harder, brought it in closer to my face so's I could study it, all swirly yellow and brown.

C'mon, I know you're in there, just give me a peek...

One more shake—

Quick as a strike fish, a plump but tiny human hand suddenly snatched at the glass from the inside, its pink palm a half inch from my nose. The jar tumbled from my grip and shattered on the pavement, leaving a brown splat of oily liquid and jagged glass crystals that sparkled in the low-level morning sunlight.

Leo and me leaned over the mess on the sidewalk. Inside the muck were bones and bone fragments laid out in the shape of an infant's tiny palm and fingers, none of them attached, with no flesh left on any of the pieces. After a few deep breaths, my breathing evened out again.

"Leo, why don't you—"

"Get another jar from the truck and get another sample. Be right back, Wump!"

Yeah, Leo. Do that.

* * *

I put my Willys into reverse and backed away from the curb, a new jar sitting next to me on the seat and filled with more sewer gunk and the bony hand parts Leo had fished out. The way I had it figured, the sludge was what made them bones snap up tight to the glass like they did—like the hand was alive—maybe even made the other muck-solids in there look like the bones had meat on them. Yeah, that was it.

I paralleled the construction site in my truck, turned the corner, then double-parked. This gave me a good view of a doozy of an argument between the overweight Philly coroner fresh from climbing out of the hole and the sleek, silver-haired Hugh Volkheimer. Restaurant entrepreneur, businessman, and second-generation owner of the tannery, plus all-around, gen-u-ine prick; this was Hughie Volkheimer. The two men stomped down the sidewalk, closer to where I was double-parked. Hughie's knee-length camel-hair topcoat was soiled by black mud-slop splotches dotting his backside.

"You've collected your evidence," Hughie said to the retreating coroner. "I demand you release this crime scene."

The coroner finally stopped and turned. "Look, Mr. Volkheimer." The heavy guy slid a pack of Pall Malls from a shirt pocket, shook out a smoke then lit up. "We'll be done by the end of the day. Then, and only then, will you get your construction site back. Your demanding anything of me or these police officers or the water department workers will only slow our investigation." With a raised eyebrow, he casually removed the cigarette from his mouth and exhaled away from Hugh's face. He tapped the cigarette to loosen ashes that hadn't formed yet. "Much like your arguing with me is doing right now."

Their discussion was of major interest to the crew working inside the hole, since I could see now they'd suddenly decided to take a group cigarette break, too. I was beginning to like this guy.

"Do we have an understanding, Mr. Volkheimer?"

Hughie noticed the men were now milling around, some smoking, some with their hands in their pockets, none of them doing any work. "Damn it, I've got a construction crew here waiting to start their day!" he said, pointing at the rear of the property while glaring at the coroner. "A work stoppage like this costs me thousands of dollars. You hustle these men up or it's going to cost *you*"—Hughie poked a finger into the man's chest— "your fucking medical license. *Now,* I do believe, we have an understanding."

Wasn't my argument so I stayed out of it, though old Hughie and me had had worse over the years. "'Scuse me, Doctor," I said, calling over. I reached my hand out of the truck window so he could see the canning jar I was holding. That pretty much got his attention, although my guess was he'd have looked for any reason to put some distance between him and old Hughie. The heavy guy waddled up to me.

"Wump Hozer," I told him and reached through my open window to shake his hand. "My young friend back there"—I pointed behind my truck —"came away from your crime scene with what's in this jar as a souvenir. Thought you might need it for your investigation."

He gandered at Leo and Raymond farther down the sidewalk, accepted the jar with the bone specimens floating in sewer muck, and thanked me. I let out the clutch and put the Willys into first, goosed the gas a little, then ground second gear hard on purpose for the attention the noise would get me. The truck backfired, stuttered forward, then eased into second, which was where I kept it as I glided past the quick-striding, pissed-off Hugh Volkheimer. I stared ahead, rested my elbow on the windowsill then turned my hand upright and let Hughie know how one of my fingers felt about him.

* * *

A grudge in the hands of the rich and powerful is a terrible thing. Grudges in the hands of their hired help are no less terrible, but with fewer ways to satisfy them, they for sure have a longer life.

The year was 1935, and a skin rash that started on my right wrist, moved north onto my arm and chest, was what finally made me leave the tannery. This and Viola's second miscarriage, plus one confrontation I'd had with Mr. Fucking-Laughing-Pile-of-Shit-College-Boy Hughie Volkheimer soon afterward, him a freshly minted graduate who his old man had made into a tannery supervisor, and me ten years older, just trying to make a living. Leaving the tannery was the best thing I could have done for myself. Best thing for Hughie, too, otherwise I might have killed him.

"You there," he'd called to me on that last day, his finger tapping the air like a hen pecking a barnyard. "Hozer. Hop on down next to that bin, grab a shovel, and start loading up that truck's payload. We're short back here today."

Me and him were the only two people on the tannery loading dock. I was dumping parts of a cow carcass into an open metal box, which was riling up the flies inside the box pretty good. It was then I seen that more than a day's worth of waste was sitting under them buzzing flies, all mixed in with leaking cans of bleach-based cleaning solvent, plus other used leather tanning chemicals. I wanted no part of what he was asking.

"I'm a tanner, not a clean-up guy," I said, shaking my tilted wheelbarrow. A pesky piece of unidentifiable cow scrap refused to budge; I pushed it off with my hand. More buzzing flies. "Get Otto to do it," I told him. Except

I already knew what an extra day of cow parts sitting in the box meant: today there wasn't no Otto.

Out back of the tannery had been, and I expect still is, a half-buried lagoon of arsenic-based insecticides and tanning chemicals, plus hundreds of barrels of crud-eating machinery detergents and other tannery-process by-products, including lead and chromium. The industrial revolution by way of the Three Bridges local tannery industry was doing its damnedest to revolutionize the few small foothills and one green valley on this back section of the Volkheimer property, a couple of hundred acres or so that weren't more than a football field away from a creek feeding the Wissaquessing River. The creek bank had turned into dead space, starting from the pits where animal hides and hair and other slaughterhouse wastes lay rotting, then fanning out across acres of what had once been scrub pine akin to them barrens in New Jersey. It wasn't like the Jersey Pine Barrens scenery ever actually looked good, even though the earth was alive, but it for sure looked a whole lot better than the singed armpit of a spread hidden in the back of the tannery's property.

"Otto's under the weather today," Hughie said. "I want you to do it."

"Under the weather" the prick called it. Christ, Otto had been wheezing for months, which weren't no surprise considering the chemicals he inhaled. Weren't but a few years earlier another kraut fella who handled the tannery's waste, the one before Otto, showed up dead in the north woods, found first by the local wildlife, then afterward, what was left of him at least, by hunters. Cause of death, a Mauser shot to the temple, self-inflicted according to his note. The real cause of death, or what made him pull the trigger, was tumors all over his lungs. The man was all of thirty-eight years old.

"Like I said, Hughie, it's not my job."

"You'll address me as Mr. Volkheimer, and your job is what I tell you it is, Hozer." Hughie unfolded his arms and gave a gentleman's tug to the bottom of his vest with both hands, liberating his chunky neck from a starched shirt collar. "Start loading that waste and those solvent cans in your wheelbarrow and get moving. You know where it goes."

The owner's son was all Hughie amounted to, but this meant that compared to the rest of us, he shit lavender and roses. Still, I weren't never one for ponying up to authority that hadn't really earned it. "Sorry, *Mister* Volkheimer, but I won't be doing that. I'm heading inside now to get back to work."

I turned my back on him and started off, expecting maybe I'd get a biting comment or two, but what came out of his mouth stopped me cold.

"Do what I say *now*, Hozer, or I'll have you sacked. Then you'll wish for your wife to miscarry every time, since you won't be able to support a family."

Hughie didn't stay upright much long after that, and he was lucky to have come away with only a few fractured ribs and a sore jaw, and the gooey yellow contents of one of them open solvent cans stuffed down the pants of his vested management suit. It took three men to pull me off him that day, with the same three men escorting me out of that fucking tannery, me vowing never to return. I kept the vow for six years, right up to the day Otto's wife asked me to collect her deceased husband's work belongings. Cause of his death: tumors on his lungs.

3

I dropped off my tool belt, ready to call it a day, pulled down a note pinned to the chore board in the church basement. "Wump: Taking the baseball team to the Volkheimer fairgrounds after school today for practice. You're welcome to join us. Father Duncan."

Up till now the kids practiced on blacktop and cement in the school-yard, and a person can't really teach boys the basics of baseball without grass and dirt and open space. After I stopped by Mrs. Volkheimer's place, I'd find Father and the kids.

Three Victorian homes sat on rolling green acreage that fanned out from the other side of the Wissaquessing River. Each lot converged south-westward toward its own sissy-colored bridge. What little foot traffic the bridges still got was deposited onto the backside of Our Lady's church property.

When I was a kid, these three bridges were the only way across the river and into town for the Volkheimer families who lived in these houses. The river was wider up north but narrowed soon after it passed under the train trestle bridge that led to the Three Bridges rail stop, a commercial hotspot at the turn of the century because of all the tanneries the area had back then. The river ran southeast, past the fairgrounds and the Volkheimer Tannery, the only tannery still operating, eventually reaching the larger

Delaware River another half mile south. The middle footbridge was the first to go up, originally an open-air job, built by Rolf Volkheimer, uncle to Hughie. The other two brothers liked what they saw, followed suit by erecting bridges on their own properties. A few years later, all three were put under roof and their walkways walled in. Northernmost was lavender, middle one charcoal blue, southernmost daffodil yellow, each brighter and sissier than their original colors from what I remembered. Problem was, they were all so damn close together they looked ridiculous; couldn't have been more than five hundred feet separating the three of them. And all three had second stories like someone had dropped A-frames on them, their roof peaks high enough for two single-pane windows, one on each end. Scalloped roof trim and the bright paint jobs made it easy to match them up to the main houses they belonged to. Local historical folks took to calling them unique displays of Victorian architecture. I felt they were just plain stupid-looking, and still they decided to name the town after them.

The three-story Volkheimer main houses had long white porches on the first floor and white widow's walks on their roofs, and their fancy trim was now painted in soft colors that reminded a person of Easter. Pinks and yellows, more lavender, some light green, some baby blue. The houses were well maintained, the second one occupied by the original owner, Mrs. Werta Volkheimer, Rolf's widowed wife, now in her eighties and the only survivor of any of the three Volkheimer marriages. Mrs. V had regular hired help, including a cook who was also her housekeeper, and a gardener who was the cook's husband, plus she had me. I fixed things when they broke, soon as I could get to them. Mrs. V paid me real well, too.

"Wait on the porch," the housekeeper said. She was a sour woman in her early fifties who thought her husband ought to be doing all the fix-up work around here. She headed back inside, let the screen door snap shut in my face. I never paid her no mind. One of these ladder-back porch rockers suited me just fine.

Wasn't long before I heard the clip-clop-thump, clip-clop-thump of someone approaching the screen door from the inside. Most of Mrs. V's shoes were too big for her shrinking feet, so when she walked they snapped up against her heels, every other step anchored by her rubber-tipped cane.

The clip-clopping got louder; the screen door opened. "Afternoon, Wump. Come inside."

Age had certainly caught up with parts of Mrs. V's body but it hadn't stolen all of her beauty. Her hair swept up from her neck and swirled to a curlicue, mostly all white but with some wide streaks of dark brown. It reminded me of frozen custard from Atlantic City, the twist kind. Her blue eyes were clear above her smooth, fleshy cheeks, with the skin a natural pinkish color that still blushed on occasion. Lately she'd had a tough time of it physically. Was a taller woman once but now stooped so much that each time I saw her it looked like her cane was growing.

"Make yourself comfortable in here, Wump. I have something to show you."

She pulled me by the elbow into a sitting room, then left through another door. Discounting the nine-foot ceiling, the room looked and felt like the parlor car of an old steam train: paisley-patterned red sofa, highboy armchairs upholstered the same way, all with glossy black enameled armrests and legs, paintings and old family photographs on the walls and along the fireplace mantel. I'd been in here lots of times since I started doing chores for Mrs. V, so I pretty much knew if something was out of place. Today it was the Volkheimer's leather-bound family Bible, open on the short table situated in front of the parlor's middle window. It usually sat on a bookstand in the far corner.

Outside of Bibles owned by some Lutheran friends, I'd never seen one this big, and each time I stepped into Mrs. V's parlor I'd read some of it. The family tree pages in the book's front interested me most, all that big lettering in the same fancy gold writing you see on wedding invitations, except everything was in German. Page after page of family trees, back a few centuries. Never seen another book as beautiful as this. I heard the clip-clop-thump approaching, quick flipped the pages back to where the book was open before.

The clip-clopping sounded a little off. Mrs. V entered the parlor dragging a long, faded blue plank with her free hand, pulling it alongside as she walked. I hustled over to help her, and now I could see through the parlor archway, two full rooms back. Christ, there was a jagged scratch running from the kitchen linoleum across the hardwood dining room floor, doorway to doorway, ending at the archway to the parlor.

"See how the wood on this board is rotted, Wump? I snapped it right off the wall of the bridge yesterday. When do you think you can replace it?"

I took the board out of her hands and laid it on the parlor's Persian rug. "Over the weekend, ma'am. But you could have showed it to me out back instead of taking it through your house." And scratching two rooms of hardwood flooring, for Christ sake.

She looked behind her, saw the damage she'd done, and waved it off. "I hid it in the pantry so Horst wouldn't see it. The man wants to fix everything. You've been good to me over the years, Wump. Repair work's your job around here."

"Thanks, ma'am. Your gardener don't mean no harm, but thanks." Her gardener was younger than me, and he knew a thing or two about plumbing and electrical and other general maintenance. Also knew I was slowing down some, so she was right, lately the guy had become a barracuda.

"Beautiful Bible, isn't it?" she said. So much for pretending I hadn't been in it. "It's out so I can look it over before I give it to my daughter. It's been handed down generation to generation, starting with the 1790s. Before any of the Volkheimers came to America. Here—let me show you something."

She passed me her cane. Her hands fumbled with the back of the huge book, her arms not strong enough to flip the book over, so she turned its pages one withered handful at a time. I caught glimpses of scripture, all German, as she worked her way through. Tucked into pouches in the last few beat-up pages were small strips of dog-eared, brown-edged papers and cards, things I hadn't seen before because I'd never looked in the back. She pulled a few of them out, handed them to me. Catholic Mass cards, obituaries, and other death announcements in different shapes and sizes, some of them made up like bookmarks. She saw how puzzled I looked. "How's your German, son?"

"It's in here somewhere, ma'am," I said, tapping my temple. "Just not always easy finding it."

Mrs. V had no accent left after eighty-five years, more than sixty in this country. She knew my schooling ended with the sixth grade, also knew about those four years I spent on a farm near Pittsburgh, where there weren't a call for using Deutsche at all. I read well enough in English, mind you, long as the words weren't too sophisticated; reading German was a chore.

"When I die," she told me, "I'll be the first person in the family to have two sets of Catholic obituary cards done, one in German, one in English. This way my grandkids will be able to read the damned thing."

I could never talk about death as easy as she could. Took me till I was in my fifties to finally make out a will. "With all due respect, ma'am, being a pioneer in death announcements ain't something I'd take all that much pride in. But I suppose your family will appreciate it at some point." Her heirs included four daughters and twelve nephews and nieces. What was left of them all lived local, and the youngest of the nephews, in his late fifties, was Hugh Volkheimer. If he croaked tomorrow, it wouldn't have been soon enough for me.

"Don't be so tight-assed about dying, son. A person's body gets so worn out, you welcome it. I'm just being practical. Here, take these. Light reading in your native tongue." She grabbed all the old announcements and stuffed them into my shirt pocket. "Bring them back when you're done with them. You'll be by on Saturday, then?"

"Yes, ma'am. I'll replace that plank on your bridge. And on Sunday I'll stop in to buff out the new scratch you just put in your dining room floor."

"Oh, pshaw," she said, waving me toward the front door, then added, "I almost forgot. I met that nice new Father Duncan today. You be sure to help him out with those boys and their new ball field. He's over at the fairgrounds now."

"It's my next stop, ma'am. But, Mrs. Volkheimer, about your bridge…"

We'd been over this before. I brought it up every time I did a repair on it. "You might want to think about knocking down the walls and the roof, maybe even the whole darn thing, then have it rebuilt. Most of them wall planks are like kindling, just like the one you brought in here. Are you sure you don't want me to hire a carpenter and—"

"No. Not in my lifetime. My heirs can replace it when I'm gone." She picked up her cane, left me looking at her hunched back as she made her way down the hall. "Until then, the bridge stays as is."

4

Father Duncan had over two hundred acres of Volkheimer land to choose from, but I had a hunch where he'd be because I knew them fairgrounds pretty good. If you ruled out the hilly sections where the kids sled during winter, and the thirty overgrown acres in the back that wrapped around one corner of the tannery's main building, you could pretty much figure the best place to play ball was on the ten or so flat grassy acres just over the first rise. I dropped the Willys into second gear, made a right turn off the paved road, onto the grass. I kept the truck in second, climbed the crest of the hill. Found them.

It gave a person a good feeling watching boys play baseball like this, on grass, not asphalt, their voices and whistles and laughter floating in the spring afternoon breeze, none of it coming back in the echoes that cement sidewalks and street corners gave you. I pulled the truck up next to a small school bus parked in close to where Father Duncan set up the baseball practice. It was the bus the orphanage used for outings. A few of the kids from the orphanage were on the school team.

Father Duncan tipped his school baseball cap to me, then hit another grounder to Our Lady's little shortstop with the big arm, Sonny Goode, who scooped up the ball and hummed it over to Adam St. Jerome, an orphaned eighth-grader who played first base. Next to Father at home plate was Teddy Agarn, apparently no worse for wear from the restaurant hole incident. It looked like Father had made Teddy his catcher. A good choice, since the oafish Teddy was the biggest kid in the school. Teddy lived across the street from Viola and me; he and Sonny Goode were cousins on their mothers' side.

A voice from behind me gave me a start. "Hi, Wump."

"Jiminy Moses, Leo," I said, collecting myself. "You near gave me a heart attack sneaking up like that." He rolled his wheelchair-bound buddy Raymond up next to my truck window.

Scaring me apparently gave Leo a real charge, his head bobbing up and down with each snicker. "Me and Raymond came over on Sister Dimple's bus. We rode lots of buses today. Went to the zoo in one, came back in one, got off and got on another one, and came here." An exciting day for them, Leo's eyes were telling me.

Sister Dimple was Sister Dymphna, an administrator at St. Jerome's orphanage who also taught fourth grade at Our Lady's. Sister had a room at the convent and a room at the orphanage, spent overnight time in both. She'd chosen her nun's name after St. Dymphna, patron saint of the mentally ill and disabled. Doing for these sick and forgotten kids, who oftentimes had no one else to pick up for them, most likely would become Sister's legacy, except Sister was only forty years old, so talk about legacies wouldn't be needed for some time.

And now she was out in right field hitting fly balls to the boys, her big white headpiece giving her trouble. A signature of the Sisters of St. Joseph, these stovepipe wimples were; something that made nuns look bigger than they really were. "Turns Mighty Joe Young into King Kong" was how one of her students once described the effect. It was a fair physical assessment in Sister's case, because she was tall and bulky. But disposition-wise she was as gentle as a sparrow. Still, Sister was no slouch when it came to baseball. She'd coached these boys all by her lonesome last year.

She swung the bat, sent the ball soaring. Her hand went to her wimple headpiece and straightened it up. She picked up another ball, took another swing, then straightened out her wimple again. Her black-and-white high-top sneakers were her only concession to the game, visible from underneath her habit's skirt each time she stopped a returned ball with her foot.

Something was out of place out here—something I couldn't put my finger on. I looked back and forth a few times between Father and Sister. It still wasn't coming to me.

"Look at all the new stuff they got, Wump."

That was it. Damn if Leo hadn't turned into a little mind reader lately. I twisted the door handle and got out of my truck, shielded my eyes from the late afternoon sun so I could get a better look.

How about that. Real canvas bases and a home plate. New balls, or at least they looked new because they were mostly white. And behind Father Duncan was a small pile of new bats. But the real clincher was every kid on the field had a baseball glove. This parish and its parishioners weren't wealthy, the school baseball team not a priority. So now I wondered, where had the equipment come from?

"The new Father got it for them."

"What? Christmas, Leo, you got to cut that out. You're giving me the heebie-jeebies answering questions I ain't even asked yet."

"Sorry, Wump."

His smile was gone. Viola was right; lately I'd been acting like I needed more bran in my diet. But that still didn't change the fact that Leo had been figuring out things real quick of late, something he wasn't able to do his whole young life. Right around when my son Harry died was when this all changed. Nowadays Leo would sometimes finish my sentences for me, and on occasion even tell me what I was thinking. Could be he'd been doing it before and I just hadn't noticed, me preoccupied with Harry and how sick he was. Or could be maybe I was losing some air like most folks did when they got older, and with it a degree or two of sharpness, made up by small doses of paranoia and confusion.

"I'm sorry, Leo. I forgot my manners. Where did Father get the new equipment? It must have cost a fortune."

"I dunno." Leo looked at his sneakers.

"Leo..." Goodness, how could I have yelled at him? "I didn't mean anything by what I said, son. If you know where the equipment came from, you can tell me. If you don't know, or do know but don't want to tell me, that's okay, too."

He raised his head, perked up again. "Father told Sister Dimple he got the bases and the balls from the Phillies 'cause he once played for them, and he meant the real Philadelphia Phillies, the ones we watch on TV on Sundays. The gloves and the bats came from somebody else."

Father called everyone in, gathered the boys around, told them what a great job they did today, thanked them on behalf of him and Sister Dymphna, then closed the practice with a prayer.

The boys collected their gear while Father and Sister started gabbing. The getting-to-know-you talking was apparently already out of the way. I could see Sister's face and she was serious about something.

"It might help if you did speak with her, Father," Sister said. "Sister Magdalena's not doing much of anything anymore. She stays in her room and prays the rosary. Isn't eating; is 'fasting,' she says. She's been like this for a week now."

Sister Magdalena was from Venezuela. When she first arrived, she was real cheerful and sweet, with brown eyes large as a child's on Christmas morning. That was more than fifteen years ago. Lately those wonderful smiling eyes were looking more like two coal lumps sunk into shadowy pits, all the joy in them gone.

"What does Monsignor say about this?" Father asked.

"He was in to see her a few days ago. The next day her sixth-graders had a new teacher. A permanent one, not another substitute. Then he had the Mother assign Sister's church duties for Easter to someone else. He hasn't said anything to us about what he thinks we should do next."

"I'll speak with Monsignor tonight," Father Duncan said. "Tomorrow I'll stop in to see Sister Magdalena."

The boys began filing onto the bus, chunky Teddy Agarn looking real proud, the team's new army-green canvas bag of baseball equipment strapped over his shoulder. Sonny Goode walked behind him with the three canvas bases piled one atop the other, his baseball glove riding the topmost, the bags resting like folded blankets on his outstretched arms. I heard Teddy's voice above the rest.

"Father says he's getting us shirts with the school name on the front. It won't say 'Three Stooges Parish' on it, will it, Sonny?"

"Better not," Sonny said.

"Don't be ridiculous." This was Adam, one of the few kids at the orphanage with no disabilities, unless you counted a creepy outlook and a sharp tongue. Adam was almost fourteen, nearly two years older than Sonny and Teddy. With a long bony face and cassock-black hair, Adam was a dark, handsome kid and smarter than most at his age, but you couldn't mention Adam without bringing up his sister, Ruthie, also a St. Jerome's resident. What Adam had in the way of extra smarts came at the expense of his sister, a twin but not identical. Ruthie was a mute, although doctors said there weren't no physical reason for it, was also as passive as they came. Plus she was a chronic overeater. Hell, that was being too nice. She was fat and in real need of a growth spurt, which now appeared to be kicking in, finally. This was the first year we'd seen a redistribution of her weight, moving south to north, turning her from a pudgy kid to a young lady. But she still ate the wrong foods and way too much of them. She watched her brother from a bus window, a strawberry-red licorice whip in her mouth.

"It won't make any difference what they put on the shirts," Adam said, resetting his baseball cap. "Three Stooges or Three Bridges. There're still just as many defective people living around here."

"Shut up, Adam." This was Sonny, talking over his shoulder, and it was then I got a feeling about what would happen next, knowing Adam was just warming up. I needed to get between the two of them before it did.

"Just like when they repainted those bridges," Adam said. "They look different, but they're still just as stupid-looking as before, because they're right next to each other. A new baseball shirt won't make any difference on you, Teddy. Once a retard, always a retard."

Too late.

Sonny shed the bases he'd been carrying and knocked Adam off his feet. Little Sonny was now on top of him, his knees pinning Adam's shoulders to the grass, Sonny throwing punch after punch at Adam's face and head, getting little resistance. I leaned down and dropped a hand onto Sonny, lifted him off by the back of his shirt; now he was swinging at air. Adam got to his feet with Father Duncan in front of him but made no attempt to retaliate, actually looked near proud of himself. Also looked like he hadn't been touched. No bloody nose, no fat lip. Odd, since I seen Sonny connect bare knuckles to skull maybe five or six times, all over Adam's face and head, but there wasn't a mark on him. I checked Sonny out and, Jesus, his face looked like he'd kissed a swinging shovel. His nose was bleeding, his right eye puffy and his chin scraped. It didn't make any sense. Adam never raised a hand to him.

Sonny was ready to declare war again through red-tinged spit and slobber. "Take it back, Adam! You take that back!"

"Will not. Teddy's the same as the rest of the retards around here, new baseball shirt or not. Just another one of God's rejects."

"That's enough, Adam," Father Duncan said. "This ends right now." Father put his heavy hands on Adam's shoulders, spun him around, and marched him to the bus steps. Sister Dymphna told Adam to sit in the last seat, then ushered the rest of the kids onboard for their return trip to the schoolyard. Sonny was still steamed, his upper body tense as a wound up jack-in-the-box. I handed him my hanky; when his balled-up energy drained, I let him pull away from my loosened grip. He picked up his baseball glove from the grass. It was then I seen all of what was tucked into my shirt pocket had fallen out, into a little pile. My notepad, my pencil stub, them German death announcements, all of it coming from me bending over to stop the fight. Sonny had something to say to Father Duncan, so I was left picking up my things on my own.

"Teddy's not retarded, Father. He's just been, ah"—Sonny teared up, then got mad at himself for it—"hurt a lot." He pushed his cousin away from the bus door. "Let's go, Teddy. We're walking home. Thank you for the new equipment, Father."

Echoes of "thanks, Father Duncan" came from the bus windows as Sister Dymphna revved the old diesel engine through a coughing spell until it leveled off. Adam was in the last seat facing out the window at Father and me, his arm slung over the ledge, his sister Ruthie next to him and facing away from us. An impish look on Adam's face turned serious. He raised his voice over the noise of the bus's throbbing exhaust to shout one of them questions a person didn't really want an answer to: "God can't be so perfect if he creates retards, huh, Father?"

Sister backed the bus up real slow a few feet closer to Father and me, the distance shortened until we were almost face-to-face with Adam. She crammed the stick shift into first gear, the transmission grinding. Adam's smile returned, stayed with him as he spoke again, this time over the ear-grating noise of metal mating with metal, his eyes flicking between my face and the death announcements in my hand. He spoke directly to me.

"Stirb, und betrachte die vernarbene Gesichtbildung von Gott."

The bus pulled forward and Sister steered it into a wide circle, the bus chugging and bouncing over the uneven grass. As she guided it past us on her turnaround I started translating Adam's German in my head. Sister waved to us, and I kept my hand up to wave to Leo in the seat behind her, Leo's frail friend Raymond in his wheelchair in the aisle. Leo was preoccupied, leaning over the seat back, concentrating hard on Adam in the rear of the bus.

Leo's face had a look I'd never seen on it before, but it was one I recognized. Seen it years ago back when I was boxing, on the faces of determined men in the other corner of the ring just before the bell for the next round, and those men seen it on me too. It was a serious look that said *next time, you SOB, you're going down for good*.

5

Father had accepted my offer of a lift so we were in my truck, a few stop signs from the rectory.

"You speak German, Father?"

He wiped some sweat from his forehead and eyes with a hand towel. The towel settled on his mouth a moment before he returned it to his gym bag, open on the seat between us. "Yes. I learned to speak and write German while I was in the seminary. It's one of the reasons I was assigned to this parish."

"Then I take it you understood what Adam said back there." I shifted the truck from first to second gear. Cruising the shorter side of these city blocks, third gear never got much use. As we neared the next stop sign, I got a peek at Father's face. There was another time and place on it.

"Yes, I understood it," he said, finally. "It sounded like a quote, but I can't say I've ever heard it before." The truck bucked a little and I pushed in the clutch to keep it from stalling, then nursed the brake until we stopped. Father continued. "What he said was, 'Die, and behold God's scarred face.'"

"My translation, too, Father. Never heard it before neither. At least not exactly."

"What do you mean, 'not exactly'? Have you heard something like it?"

I pulled out them tiny old German death announcements from my shirt pocket and handed them to him. "Here. Closest I ever seen to it. It's in there somewhere."

It was in my head now, too, somewhere. Just had to sort through nearly sixty years of crap to get to it, then I'd be able to tell Father what things had been like around here, back when I was a kid. A lesson in parish history. *Concentrate*, I told myself.

Found it.

"It was 1911, Father, late June. The parish monsignor had just died. A lot of parishioners were at the cemetery for the burial, even us kids..."

* * *

...Two wrinkly hands grabbed the doorframe of the carriage from the inside. An old monsignor I never seen before dropped his foot onto the carriage step and pulled himself out. Waiting for him in the mud, with his hand out like a gentleman tending to a lady, was a young priest with an open umbrella.

It was a Thursday, but people was all dressed up like they got for Sunday Mass. I was sidled up next to Sister Irene, me and her huddled under her large black umbrella; no idea where Heinie was. He'd be in a heap of trouble if he skipped the monsignor's funeral.

Heinie finally showed at the far end of the cemetery lawn, traipsed up the hill, and squeezed through the crowd of respectable town folk and parents who all took to pulling their kids in close when he brushed past. He edged in next to me, me still next to Sister Irene under her umbrella. Sister shot Heinie a raised-eyebrow, you-oughta-know-better gander.

The visiting monsignor dragged his cassock through the wet grass on stiff legs that for sure had some old-person's condition the way he was walking. All the sniffling parishioners got out of the way so he could hobble up to the casket. Behind us was the new gravesite dug out for our dead monsignor. Must have been two hundred people here come to pay their respects, except parts of what I heard, from parents who didn't think any kids were listening, told me more than what their tears did: a lot of these folks were here just to make sure he was dead. Sister Irene, I figured, was one of them.

I poked Heinie in the ribs. "You still stink," I whispered. "You was supposed to get washed up from this morning. Them people are all looking at us." This I was sure of, since the gap between us orphans and the parish families got twice as big when Heinie showed up. "Sister'll put a stop to our dog-shit business if you don't get washed up afterward."

"Maybe I didn't wanna come," he whispered back. "Maybe I was a-scared of him."

"Maybe I was a-scared of the monsignor, too, like some of these folks are, but I came anyway. And I don't smell like dog shit."

Two sniffling parish nuns turned and raised their pointer fingers to their frumpy lips to shush us, their faces scrunched up like we was diseased. When they straightened up they were facing Sister Irene, her eyes now narrowed at them, her arm still around Heinie and me. The two nuns retreated under their umbrellas and got back to their crying.

The crippled old monsignor circled the casket, stopped once on each side to sprinkle it with holy water. "Tu es pulver et in pulverem reverteris..."

Back at the head of the casket the monsignor closed his prayer book and handed it to an altar boy, then slapped his hands together like he about had enough for the day. When he opened his hands again he talked to us.

"Monsignor Gunther Krause was a true religious visionary. A shaper of men's souls. A student, yet also a protector, of the New Testament. A bastion against evil, with thirty-eight faithful and steadfast years in the service of the Church, the last sixteen in this growing parish of hard-working, humble, and most importantly..."

Sister Irene's hand squeezed my shoulder.

"...obedient—Catholics."

The monsignor raised his palms to us. "Godspeed to heaven, Monsignor Krause, for you are most certainly in His favor. Live eternally in the warmth and splendor of God's unblemished, perfect face. May you rest in peace."

Sister's grip on me tightened, my shoulder all hunched because she was hurting it a little, except she didn't notice.

"Monsignor Krause," Sister whispered to herself, shaking her head, "was insane."

* * *

Father Duncan stayed focused on the death announcements I just gave him, not saying boo about my story on the old monsignor's funeral. My truck eased to a stop in the church parking lot behind the rectory; I turned off the ignition. Father placed some of the cards and announcements next to each other on his lap, studied them while speaking to me without looking up.

"So what do you think, Wump? Was the monsignor crazy?"

"Can't rightly say, Father, I was only a kid. I can tell you he wasn't a nice person, least not to me and the other kids at the orphanage. He gave one boy a penance that nearly killed him. Told him to pick up all the trash around the train station, the tracks included. The little guy lost an arm under a coal car and nearly died. Eight years old, he was. That don't sound too sane, now I think about it."

Father was taking this all in, shaking his head in agreement the way a person did when they were really thinking about something else. "Have you had a chance to look over these death announcements, Wump?"

"Not yet, Father. Just got them this afternoon from Mrs. Volkheimer. I read a few, that was it."

Father picked out two of the cards, both the bookmark kind. He pushed the others around on his lap until he found a third one that interested him. The rest of them went into a pile on the seat. He laid out the three he liked on his lap again. "These are for Volkheimer children, one each from three different sets of surviving parents. The deaths are a few years apart."

"Mrs. Volkheimer pulled them out of her family Bible," I told him. "The others are probably from the families of her husband's two brothers."

Father nodded. "Do you remember any epidemics or widespread illnesses in this area back then?"

"Only real epidemic I can rightly remember," I told him, "was poverty."

Father took this in with another absentminded *uh-huh*, then handed me each of three cards, one by one. "All three are for infant boys who died the day they were born. One in 1896, one in '98, one in '99. Look at the prayers offered on each of them."

This got my attention, but was more because of the date on the last one.

I was born the same day in 1899 as this boy was, or so the sisters at St. Jerome's had told me, except they also said they weren't really sure it was the exact date. The bother of it was, this kid had been born rich, into comfort and protection—into a life with parents—and he never got to experience it. My life began the same day, and I was healthy enough to get abandoned into a childhood filled with pain and want and anger, and a longing that would never get satisfied: to be loved by a mother and a father. It still hurt.

I shook off the self-pity so I could take a harder look at the passages on them cards like Father had asked. "They're all in German," I told him, which meant I needed a couple of minutes. The translation finally came around.

"They say, 'Some shall die so that all shall live.' The next line says, 'May God cleanse your souls so you can enter Heaven and behold God's beautiful face.'"

"Your German's better than you give yourself credit for, Wump. On all three cards, that's the script. Three infant boys from different families, all dead at childbirth."

"Actually, Father," I said, still looking one of the cards over, "there's no mention of childbirth. They just say they died the day they were born."

Father reread them, start to finish. "You're right. And there's something else. They don't read like the other announcements she gave you." He lifted up the small pile from the seat and started sorting through them. "These three are for prayer offerings, not funerals. None of the funeral announcements mentions anything about 'some shall die,' or about beholding God's face, beautiful or otherwise."

"But, Father, don't that make sense? The ones that say them things are for newborns. Don't they go right to heaven, long as they're baptized? Don't that make them different from adults?"

"Correct again," Father said. "Mind if I keep these cards for a bit?"

I told him sure, long as he gave them back to me by Saturday so I could return them to Mrs. V. He agreed, grabbed his gym bag, and climbed out of the truck. He leaned back inside the window.

"How about you come inside the rectory for some iced tea? Monsignor tells me it's one of Mrs. Gobel's specialties."

"Need to be getting home, Father. I got chores around the house need doing."

"One glass, Wump. Besides, I could use some help sorting out what happened after today's practice."

He wanted to talk about Adam. "Okay. One glass."

* * *

Mrs. Gobel, the rectory cook, was built like a puff pastry with legs. She poured some iced tea for us, then she went back to her radio and turned the music up loud while she finished preparing dinner. A sixth sense, this woman had; knew when people were about to talk about something that was none of her business. Had also probably heard things going on elsewhere in the rectory she'd wanted to know nothing about. Behavior unbecoming a priest came to mind. A loud radio came in handy for this sort of thing. Father Duncan would learn soon enough.

"It was plenty nice what you did for them boys, Father, getting all new equipment for their team. Real nice."

Father stuffed his hand under his cassock and into his jeans pocket. "A few phone calls to some friends I still have in baseball was all it took. Not many folks will turn down a priest, right?" He pulled out a folded piece of paper and handed it to me. "You can also thank this person, if you can figure out who wrote this."

I unfolded the paper. The top of it was perforated; it came from a small notepad with a spiral edge, like the one I carried. The paper had blue lines, and the note was printed in shaky capital letters: *FOR BASEBALL GLOVES*.

"It was in a church offering envelope addressed to 'the new Father' along with fifty single dollar bills. Mrs. Gobel found it under the welcome mat at the rectory's back door this morning. You know anything about it?"

Father beamed while he looked at me, like he was expecting me to fess up to something. I did all my confessing on Saturday afternoons at the confessional so's I could take Communion on Sunday. "Sorry, Father, can't say I do."

"No? I was sure it was from you. Look at the other side."

I turned it over, saw a list: *Screws, Phillips head, three-quarter inch, twenty count. Sandpaper, fine, three sheets.* The list was in my handwriting.

"My guess is it's from Leo, one of the boys who lives at the orphanage. He told me he helped carry your bags from the taxi when you arrived. The boy does errands for me. That's one of my hardware store lists. Only explanation I can give you."

Father breathed a few more *uh-huh*s, folded the paper back up and returned it to the church envelope, the money still inside. He tapped the envelope on the kitchen table. "That's as good an explanation as any. Thing is, I didn't know the boys needed new equipment so badly. This donation is what got me started."

Father shrugged this off, but me, I was still thinking about it. This had been a real nice gesture on Leo's part, giving up his errand money. He'd been full of surprises lately, making me see things I wasn't able to see on my own, had now started in doing the same thing with the father. Strange. Still, Father would have figured out how needy the team was soon enough.

"So tell me, Wump," Father said. "Who's your favorite Beatle?"

"'Scuse me, Father?"

Father smiled, gestured with his head past my shoulder, at Mrs. Gobel. I turned to see her chopping salad fixings, her back to us, her big hips swaying to the racket on her radio. "I'm talking about those four British boys with the long hair who sang on Ed Sullivan a couple of months ago. Which one is your favorite?"

I took in the rectory's kitchen while deciding how to answer. It was about twenty by twenty-five, with polished birch cabinets hung on its swirled plaster walls. The cabinets were stained dark and made the kitchen seem somber on days when it was cloudy, but not today, the early evening sun showing through the double windows onto the long birch table where we sat, also stained dark.

"Sorry, Wump," Father finally said. "That wasn't a fair question. You're probably a swing band person who's got no time for this rock 'n' roll music making such a fuss nowadays."

On the other side of the kitchen was a second set of double windows that mirrored the first set. Showing through them like a postcard of side-by-side seashore cabanas were the town's three footbridges.

"Ringo," I told him. "Ringo Starr. A name like that, you don't forget. He was our son's favorite."

Father's look said I surprised him. A moment passed then he asked, "So how many children do you have?"

"Only the one, Father. Our son, Harry. He passed away this past February. He was twenty."

"Oh. I'm so sorry, Wump," he said, and I could see he was about to press me on it, was probably doing the arithmetic in his head about how old me and Viola were when we became parents. I wasn't sure how much I was gonna say about Harry.

Father waited me out. Hell. Maybe it was time I talked some about it.

"Harry wasn't healthy when he came to the orphanage, but Viola still fell in love with him. It was the last year she worked there, before she took the housekeeping job for the church. Age of forty-one, she was, and me at forty-four, and there we were, deciding to adopt a sick two-year-old boy. Sounded a little crazy, even to us, but..."

I caught myself running my finger around the rim of my empty glass on the table. Father poured me more iced tea; he was going to let me babble. "But Viola, she always wanted to be a mother. God knows how we tried. How *she* tried..."

Shit. This was hard.

"Five miscarriages, Father. And after each one it took us a while—years, now that I look back—for her to conceive again, but it never worked out. What this woman went through trying to become a natural mother. Weren't right a person had to suffer like that. Just ain't right."

I was drifting back to times I wasn't comfortable with, and it was making me angry. It took one of them Beatle singers shouting on the radio to finally bring me out of it. The boy said he wanted to hold his girlfriend's hand.

Father asked, "Harry died so young. What happened?"

"Nothing happened; that was the problem. He got the kids' cancer and never got well."

"'Kids' cancer'?"

"Acute lymphocytic leukemia. I won't never forget them words; heard them enough over the years. He didn't have leukemia when we adopted him, just a weak heart. Harry got the leukemia when he was a teenager."

There was no more in me that I could tell him at this point without getting all broke up, and risking that Viola would pick up on it when I got home. "Let's talk about Adam, Father. I got to be shoving off."

Adam was a weird kid, I told him, but it may have been because he was so smart. He knew a lot about a lot, and he often sounded much older than he was. But he had a mean streak that up till now had kept him at the orphanage, the way I understood it. And this mean streak had a lot to do with religion.

"He gives Sister Dymphna fits sometimes. Heard him argue with her about God the Father, and about sickness, and wars, and how could they happen if God was so good?"

Father had his chair pushed back, slouching some in it, his buggered-up fingers folded in his lap. One hand went to his chin to rub his stubble; maybe also to help him size up what was being said. Finally he said to me, "So, Adam knows his German fairly well?"

"Sure sounded like it. Not unusual for this area. Sister Dymphna speaks it also." Time for me to wrap things up. "One other thing worth mentioning, then I got to be going. A family's interested in adopting him. His sister Ruthie's part of the deal, too. Close to a miracle in my mind, her being mute and all, and the two of them nearly fourteen, no less. Wonders never cease, I suppose."

I thanked Father and Mrs. Gobel for their hospitality and headed for the back door.

"Certainly sounds like good news for them," Father said. "When are the adoptions final?"

"A few weeks maybe. Sometime after Easter." Viola heard these things, often told me about them. "Just has to be approved by Monsignor Fassnacht and the other members of St. Jerome's Board. Why you asking?"

"No special reason. We'll need to recruit another ballplayer for the parish team."

No big loss, I thought. The boy's head was too big for his baseball cap anyway, and most of his teammates and kids at school didn't like him much. As for me, fresh from the incident at the ball field, Adam gave me the creeps.

6

Without being able to explain the geometry of it, the town of Three Bridges took up an area close to two square miles of real estate, except it was packed into a big triangle, kind of like the shape of one of them alpine ski houses with a steeply pointed roof. Along the bottom of the house's first floor was Schuetten Avenue's two east-west travel lanes, its four lanes carrying buses and trackless trolleys and cars. Fewer trolleys and more buses nowadays, and I could say for sure I wouldn't know near as much about Barry Goldwater and what he stood for if it weren't for this reason. Billboards on wheels was what they were. Chalk this up to progress in the sixties, which also brought us the new restaurant that had caused all the commotion, or at least the hole they'd dug for it had. Word was the restaurant would sell twelve-cent hamburgers and ten-cent orders of French fries from a counter you walk up to. The teenagers in the neighborhood were already talking about it. Cheap food, and fast, but no place to sit. As far as this alpine house went, put the hole for this restaurant where it belonged: in the house's cellar, below Schuetten Avenue.

My red suspenders weren't in any of my drawers. "Viola, where's my red suspenders?" I raised my voice. "Viola? Honey?"

The bottom floor of this alpine house was maybe eight city blocks' worth of storefronts. Next level up began layer after layer of brick row homes built where the bungalows and shanties had been when I was a kid. On the left side of our alpine house, running north on a slant like a roof, were the Reading Railroad train tracks. Elevated in the south, where Schuetten Avenue ran under them, they outlined the western side of the roof right up to the Three Bridges railway station about a mile north, at the roof's peak.

Right side of the town was the most interesting part. The Wissaquessing River came down from the northwest, ran southeast under the train bridge to form the right roofline. Near its tip were the Volkheimer fairgrounds, fed by the one bridge in the area that carried cars across the river, a silver two-laner. The Volkheimer Tannery was behind the fairgrounds in the distance, its two smokestacks making like it was an underway ocean liner full-steaming its way past the low rise Wissaquessing Mountain Ridge skyline. The tannery's stacks were a red brick, except their south sides were badly spoiled by long tan and white stains that reminded a person of overflowed oatmeal, the staining a byproduct of the tanning process. Southeast of the stacks were the three Volkheimer houses. Across the river from these properties and inside the town limits were the orphanage and Our Lady's church and school, and next to the schoolyard was the block of row houses where Viola and me lived.

No red suspenders anywhere I could see around this bedroom. I held my jeans up with my hand, smelled burnt toast on my way down the stairs. "Ain't walking around like this all day," I mumbled, "and I ain't wearing a belt neither. *Viola.*"

We kept a small portable TV in the kitchen that gave snowy reception through a busted antenna. Viola had a chair pulled up right in front of it. She twisted a dishcloth around her fingers, still not hearing me. "Viola, don't you smell the toast?"

"Oh, dear God. My goodness. Look at this, Johnny, on the television. We're in the news."

I popped up the toaster and joined her in front of the portable. Hugh Downs was showing pictures of a train wreck on *The Today Show*. The footage was mostly from overhead and real shaky; they'd put a TV camera in a helicopter.

Mr. Downs was busy telling us what had happened "in this small Pennsylvania town known as Three Bridges north and east of Philadelphia. There's a report of one person dead..."

* * *

I wasn't able to get real close to the train wreck—police and fire departments had everything blocked off—so I pulled my truck onto the grass a hundred yards or so before the train bridge that spanned the river, then I craned my neck and squinted. The railroad crossing poles were lowered on both sides of the track, their red lights and signal bells flashing.

A Reading Railroad coal train had jackknifed. Not one of them long freighters that take a half hour to pass and always seemed to show up when you were in a hurry. This one was only fifteen cars or so, mostly all black except for a brown locomotive and a burnt orange caboose. The locomotive was still on the tracks a few car lengths past the other side of the bridge. The actual wreck started on the bridge itself. Seven cars had derailed, were unattached and zigzagged across both sides of the tracks, two of the cars on the bridge. The coal the two had been carrying fell twenty feet down, into the Wissaquessing River.

Before I left the house I'd heard the train's engineer explain the wreck to the news folks on national TV: "I checked my watch; it was around six a.m. I saw someone in the haze up ahead, walking on the tracks, their back to my train. I had the throttle down, going slower on account of the crossing signal and the station on the other side of the bridge. I blasted the whistle to high Hades, but the person kept right on walking. As we rolled closer, I saw it was actually three people." The engineer puffed on a smoke, took a long drag. "I'm only carrying coal, no passengers. Just me and my three crewmen. I don't wanna kill nobody, so if someone's on the tracks, we're stopping the train. The brakeman engaged the brakes"—the guy shook his head, had about had it with the newsman and his microphone. "It was a woman; she had hold of two kids..."

Authorities at the scene wouldn't tell the news folks who the victim was, but they did say she'd been identified from some belongings in a packed blue suitcase found nearby. There was a search underway for the children.

The Philly coroner probably never had occasion to visit Three Bridges prior to a few days ago, and now he had a second incident needing his attention here. I watched him pull away in his official station wagon, the woman's body in there with him.

"Half a body and body parts, Wump," a middle-aged town cop with a drinker's nose said when I asked him about it. He knew me from church but his name wasn't coming to me. "That's what the coroner's got. Didn't see the body myself, but those two officers over there, they got sick scraping up pieces of her from the tracks and the wheels of the train. Not a fair match, a freight engine against flesh and blood. Top half of her was laying on the bridge, bottom half was churned into hamburger and crammed into the engine's undercarriage."

"Sounds horrible. Any witnesses?"

"Only the engineer and his crew. The engineer swears there were two kids walking with her. If he's right, they vanished." He looked right then left. "Look, do me a favor, Wump, and move it on along. If I fraternize with the citizens too long it looks bad, know what I mean?"

* * *

Soon as I got to the school custodian's office, I picked up my projects for the day. First one was to pick open the lock to Sister Magdalena's room at the convent. She'd been in it for two straight days and hadn't said a word to no one.

Sister Dymphna, Father Duncan's baseball assistant, was a sturdy midforties woman with flat feet, her sturdiness and fallen arches both coming from her weight, with said flat feet requiring her to wear orthopedic footwear most of the time. Sister raised her hammy fist, knocked on Sister Magdalena's door, called to her. Neither got a response. Sister moved out of the way. I got down on a creaky knee in front of the door handle, its old-fashioned lock complete with a keyhole. I could have picked it, but all it really needed was a rap on a screwdriver stuck between the strike plate on the doorjamb and a thingy-piece coming out of the lock.

Pop. The door swung back.

The room was the size of the other bedrooms at the convent, a twelve-foot square give or take, with two windows. It was a mess, and there was no

Sister Magdalena. Next thing I noticed was the drippy candle wax. It had formed a little river of orange and green and blue on the surface of her mahogany nightstand. Smelled nice in here because of them candles; near as fragrant as a flower shop. On the wall above the nightstand was a painting, the Blessed Virgin, her palms open, looking down at someone who wasn't in the picture. On the floor in front of the painting was a bed pillow, the indentations from two kneeling knees still visible. The bed wasn't made, and all the drawers of her mahogany dresser and her bureau were open, some wider than others. Closet door was open, too. If I hadn't known Sister's recent state of mind I might have considered the room ransacked. Her desk was scattered with papers that looked like kids' tests. "From Sister's sixth-grade class," Sister Dymphna volunteered.

It didn't take Sister long to inventory what was and wasn't in the room. She checked the closet, saw Sister Magdalena's three nun's habits. This was one too many.

"And her blue suitcase is missing. Oh, Wump, I have a sinking feeling..."

* * *

A crowd of people had gathered in the convent's parlor when Sister Dymphna and me got downstairs: two police officers, the same Philly coroner, and a woman in plainclothes, plus the convent mother, and the rest of the sisterhood. Sister Dymphna's legs buckled when she realized who these people were; I propped her up quick.

Standing upright on the floor next to the plainclothes woman was the dented suitcase from the train wreck this morning. I helped Sister over to a couch, sat her next to Harriet, the convent's novice nun, the youngest person in the room. Harriet was blank-faced, handling the news better than the rest of them.

Weren't any words I knew of to calm the mourning sisterhood. I felt the pain, too; death left such an emptiness. In this case, it left a heap of guilt as well, something most everyone in the room felt some of. Sister Magdalena walking on them tracks just wasn't something a happy person would have done, and what with Sister having been on the edge in recent weeks... someone should have done something.

When Monsignor Fassnacht and Father Duncan arrived, the coroner pulled them aside. This left two cops and the woman in plainclothes, a social worker, I figure, to chat with the sisters.

"I need someone to identify the body," the coroner said in a low tone to Monsignor.

Sister Magdalena had no relatives in the States that I knew of.

"And you shall have someone," Monsignor said. He scanned the parlor full of sobbing sisters for a candidate, eventually made eye contact with the only one not crying, young Harriet. "How about—"

This wasn't right. Couldn't be having a woman—a novice nun, for Christ sake—do what a man should do. "I'll go with the coroner to make the identification," I said, interrupting the monsignor without apologizing. "Just let me find my wife to tell her where I'll be."

Father Duncan noticed my disgusted look. "I'll come with you," he volunteered.

Viola was usually at the rectory this time of morning. I slipped out the convent's kitchen door onto the back stoop. First step after I raised my head, I nearly knocked Leo over.

"Jiminy Crackers, Leo. You're like a bolt of lightning anymore, son." One look past Leo's shoulder showed me blond-haired Raymond in his wheelchair at the bottom of the steps, a pair of loose-fitting blue jeans pulled high above his waist by snap suspenders. His white shirt was buttoned up to his neck and not ironed but clean, which was more than I could say about Leo's shirt. A red soda stain had traveled down half its polo stripes. "Today's not a good day for errands, fellas. Maybe tomorrow."

Leo had questions. "The police here about Sister? They come to say it was Sister Magdalena run over by the train?" His hair was more mussed than usual, and Raymond's eye sockets were near as black as checkers. Looked like neither of them had had much sleep.

"That's what they're saying, son." He'd need to talk to someone who could help him handle this. "How about I drive you back home real quick so's you and one of the sisters can talk?"

When I reached the bottom of the cement steps I turned to talk to him face-to-face, but he was still on the top of the stoop. "Leo? You coming?"

Leo danced from leg to leg like he was about to wet his pants. "But...

but..." He scooted to the edge of the stoop, looked back and forth between me and Sister Magdalena's second-floor bedroom window. "Raymond and me are wondering why she didn't tell no one, Wump. Why didn't she say nothing about doing what she did? Maybe she left a note or something..."

The convent had a second stairway in the back that went from the kitchen to the second floor. Leo's cue had me back upstairs, in Sister's bedroom. The boy could have been right; maybe we'd missed something.

Only papers I saw in her room were the tests Sister had been grading. Page after page of true-false questions in purplish-blue mimeograph ink. A Religion quiz. Sister had put a small red *c* after each correct answer and a small red *x* next to the wrong ones. It took me till I got to the last few tests to realize there was one question every kid had gotten wrong: *Christ died. Christ rose from the dead. Christ will come again. True or false?*

Easy test question. All twenty-some kids answered *true,* but Sister's *x* on every paper said it wasn't the right answer. On the last test in the pile, Sister had put a red circle around *Christ will come again.* In a shaky longhand, in the same marking-pencil-red under the *x,* she wrote, *Not if someone else arrives first. Forgive me, heavenly Father. He is mine.*

I folded up this last test and stuck it in my jeans pocket then took another look around her room, all dull and dark and brown, the sunlight held out by two shades pulled down in front of the closed windows. The place needed some air. The window shade snapped up when I reached for it, startling me. I was left looking one floor down at Leo, who stood on the grass behind Raymond in his wheelchair, Leo's head on an upward tilt, like he'd been waiting for me to come to the window the whole time. The little wiseacre deserved a nod for sending me back in here, except his expectant stare froze me for a moment. When I finally broke the trance and nodded, he nodded eagerly back. He carefully spun Raymond's wheelchair around, guided it onto the sidewalk. Then the two of them were off, crossing the church parking lot.

7

I once saw a body cut in half by shrapnel from an artillery shell that exploded not fifteen yards from me. Saw a sleeping man at the end of my trench lose his legs and his manhood when a hand grenade landed in his lap. Saw so much carnage at the age of nineteen during World War I, in the Argonne in France, that to me every living human body I seen for a long time afterward seemed nothing more than a flimsy container of flesh ready to burst open with the next loud bang. I prayed that what the coroner wanted to show me was more than just pieces of a person.

Father and me hitched a ride in the coroner's station wagon. The coroner's name was Kermit Frink, MD. When I addressed him as "Doctor," he shushed me, said to call him Kerm, so I told him to call me Wump. Kerm drove us to Nazarene Hospital, just inside the Philly city limits; we followed Kerm into the morgue.

I'd never been in a morgue before. Cold like I expected, with two walls of stainless steel facing each other, two rows of small doors on each wall. The doors all opened to reveal rollout slabs, enough for twenty-five, maybe thirty bodies. The drains in the tile floor were stainless, too, but the luster on them was gone, probably from whatever solvents they used to remove the blood. The room had a full ceiling of fluorescent lights that all came on with one switch. Kerm tugged on a handle to unlatch one of the stainless-

steel doors, then pulled on a horizontal handhold. Out slid a slab with a
zippered silvery bag laying on it. The top half of the bag was the right size
and shape, like a person's head and chest were in there; the bag's bottom
half was almost flat. If there were legs and feet in there, they weren't much
more than shepherd's pie.

Jesus. Poor Sister Magdalena.

Across the bag from me, Kerm looked out from under bushy peppery
eyebrows, studied me, and said, "No need to see much more than her face, I
hope."

"No need."

Kerm pulled the zipper down. Sister's brown eyes were open but with
nothing behind them. Her hair was cropped, still black, with mousy nubs
above her ears. Her cheeks were taut, stretched over bony cheekbones; her
lips were parted. She was barely recognizable to me, but not because of the
accident. In fact her face wasn't bruised much at all. It was more because of
Sister refusing to take food, plus whatever state of confusion she'd been in
these last few weeks, a time I hadn't seen much of her. It didn't make no
never-mind, though. This was Sister Magdalena, and I told Kerm as much.
He zippered the bag back up.

Such a cheerful young woman, Sister was, when first we met. Pudgy
cheeks, bright, brown eyes, some straggling black hair escaping her headpiece and framing her light and sweet brownish face. A warm glow
surrounded her. What made her leave? Why was she on those tracks?

The door to the morgue swung open. A young man in a white lab coat
came over to Kerm and whispered in his ear, except me and Father could
hear most of what he said because he was out of breath. Two words made
me perk up: baby skeletons.

* * *

Kerm led Father and me down a hallway from the morgue, the hall's cinder
block walls painted white above black-and-white checker-boarded
linoleum flooring. It was wide enough for the three of us to walk side by
side with room left over for a gurney to roll past us, a covered body on it.

The entire hallway stretch was spotless. Kerm spoke to me. "So you've lived in Three Bridges your whole life?"

"Most all of it," I told him. No need to mention Pittsburgh or prison. "Much obliged you're letting us see this."

"You did a good thing volunteering to come down here. That monsignor of yours is a piece of work," he said, stopping in front of a windowless metal door. He unlocked it and peeked inside. "And you didn't get sick on me back there either, so I decided to return the favor, if you can call it that. Come in."

We entered a well-lit room, about double the size of a hospital chapel. On the smooth cement floor were thin, overlapping canvases, forest green in color. What was laid out on them showed up real well. Tiny skeletons, all lined up, eight in each row, nine rows in total. More nightmare material.

There was room to walk between the rows, and this was what the young fella who fetched Kerm was doing, a pair of light green hospital booties pulled over his shoes. Two more young people in the room were dressed the same way, standing at attention against the wall. The three of them, two men and a woman, beamed like they were waiting for Kerm to put blue ribbons on their masterpieces. I could still smell some of the sewage. Kerm lifted his hand to direct us down an uncluttered path against the wall. He spoke to his assistants.

"Nice work, kids. I'll be with you in a sec. Just wanted to show these men where we are in this case." Kerm talked to Father and me as we walked past each row. "They've finished matching up what they could, bone to bone, on these infants. Over seventy skulls, with bones enough for sixty-four complete bodies. We didn't try to match each bone to the correct body."

He pointed to a row in the back, away from the others, in the far right corner. In it were bones and fragments of bones, all the pieces laid out separate. "The extra bones back there tell us the body count exceeds the sixty-four we have here."

I walked farther toward the back of the room and approached a counter. On it sat two bone piles, the bones about the same in size as the bones in each of the assembled skeletons. "So do you know how they died?" Father asked.

"My opinion," Kerm said, "based some on forensics but mostly on common sense, is they all drowned. We found no head traumas, no indications of strangulation in the neck area, nothing of this nature. Any bone breaks are consistent with those caused by brittleness due to decay." Kerm raised his voice. "Ah, Wump, I'd appreciate it if you would step back from there, please."

I stopped short of the counter but close enough to see what was on it. Two more babies, but these were real bodies, not skeletons. Two small piles of shredded cloth also sat on the counter, outside a row of surgical instruments laid out next to the exposed bodies. A lot of the material was soiled so bad it was black, except for a few places where you could see some blue.

Blue receiving blankets. For baby boys.

Kerm and Father filled in beside me. "Here's where the logic kicks in," Kerm said, with all three of us focused on the counter. "The victims behind us on the floor died sometime before the city rerouted the sewers and storm drains. That makes it at least thirty years."

More than double that, Kerm.

"I was able to do autopsies on the two newer ones. Their cause of death was drowning. Two baby boys with no indications of illness."

"How many boys, how many girls?" Father said.

"The structure of the pelvis would give that away, but only at an older age. Aside from the two newer ones, because there was no flesh on the bones of the other babies, there's no way to tell the sex."

"What about what they were found floating in?" I asked. "The sewage, I mean. Anybody looking at that as a cause?"

By now, Kerm wanted us out of here, directed Father and me to retrace our steps toward the door. "We've got chemists looking at its composition. The fact they were found in sewage had nothing to do with their deaths, in my opinion. The skeletons were probably in that walled-in, unused section of storm sewer and got swept away with new sewage when the walls collapsed. We let the sewer department people replace the brick wall at the north end, to keep it dry in there while someone checked for any more bones. We found little else worthwhile as evidence. But one thing's for sure," he said, pulling the door shut behind us. "Someone put a chisel to that wall to weaken it."

So we heard, Kerm.

Kerm locked the door behind him and pointed to a stairwell he wanted us to take up to the first floor. For me, something felt very wrong. I caught myself staring at the locked metal door. "But, Kerm—"

"If you're thinking something doesn't add up," Kerm said, reading my face, "you're right. Those two babies drowned in the active part of the sewer, not in the closed-off and dry tributary the skeletons were in. The two bodies must have come in with the seeping sewage when the hole in the north wall got large enough."

We exited the stairwell onto the first floor of the hospital. A flight of stairs didn't take much out of me, and it didn't seem to bother Father neither, but Kerm was all out of breath and coughing from the climb. "Damn cigarettes," he said with his first full breath then waddled out ahead, toward the brightness of an outside exit. Being a hundred pounds overweight didn't much help you neither, Kerm.

The exit door opened and the three of us squinted at the late-morning sun. The air still had a cool bite to it, typical for April. Kerm pulled out his pack of Pall Malls. Father and me declined; Kerm lit one up. "If you're wondering why I let you fellas see all this," he said, "it's because I already reported my findings to my superiors, and released a statement to the news people."

"What did you tell them?" Father asked. I was all ears.

"Official cause of death for two of the babies was drowning," Kerm said, "but as far as the remaining seventy-two infants were concerned, they all died a long time ago, and a definitive cause of death can't be determined. No doubt there was foul play involved, but I can't be forensically sure with any of them."

Kerm patted my shoulder. It was the kind of pat that said *Thanks for everything, we're done talking.* "Much obliged you came down here to ID the sister, Wump. I'll have someone call a cab to take you and Father Duncan back. I'm sure the sisters are wondering."

The convent needed to be told about Sister Magdalena, but we could do that with a phone call. The doc just wasn't seeing the whole picture. I may have been a kid through it all, but I'd seen a lot of what went on. This was about as long as I could go staying quiet.

"Kerm, you got somewhere inside the hospital we can talk? There's some things I need to tell you. About what it was like growing up around here."

Kerm stamped out his smoke, said okay, and ushered us back inside. I started telling him while we walked. "In the winter of 1910, I think it was, one morning me and an orphan friend of mine waited for our breakfast..."

* * *

..."You smell like flowers, Johnny."

Heinie and me leaned our backs against the wall as the orphanage dining room filled up with kids all hungry and as sleepy-eyed as we were. I had on a pair of gray wool pants with white pinstripes and a pants seat a lot fatter than me, the legs so wide I could fit a whole shelf of candy in them on my next trip to the general store. I slid down the wall to the hardwood floor, then curled my legs around in front of me, flapped them a couple of times. Heinie slid down the wall just like me, his shorter legs tenting upward until he saw how I had mine and sat with his the same way. The nuns hustled between the kitchen and the dining room setting up breakfast for us kids, thirty-six of us we were now. When we were all settled in we'd take up the table space in both rooms. Our hands were clean; washing up after our trip to the tannery had been easy today since most of the dog stuff we'd picked up was frozen hard as marbles.

I had my nose against my knee. "It's these pants that smell like flowers. Used to be Mr. Pigholtzer's."

"Pine Box Pigholtzer? From the funeral parlor? But he's taller than you. He's a *man*, Johnny."

"He ain't taller than me no more. Ain't taller than nobody no more." I felt the fabric again. "These pants are made of wool. They're better'n what most boys with parents get. Real warm, too." I checked the doorway for what should have been the last of the sisters' oatmeal trips from the kitchen.

Sister Irene entered the dining room carrying a steaming pot of cereal. A long, brown-handled knife was tucked through the front of her habit's waistband, sticking up like a sword on some Arabian guard. She set the oatmeal pot at the edge of the table, bowls and glasses clattering, then left in a hurry through a different doorway. I leaned over to watch her. She stomped through two rooms till she got to the orphanage's front door, where she wrapped a scarf around her neck and put on a heavy overcoat. She pulled some papers out of a desk drawer and stuffed them into her coat pocket, the other coat pocket getting the kitchen knife. Last thing she grabbed was a thick walking stick from an umbrella stand. She opened the front door and slammed it behind her.

"Where she going, Johnny?"

"I told her about the kid we seen this morning."

"Oh."

Me and Heinie shoveled down our oatmeal then asked to be excused. I grabbed a pair of coats and hats from the cloakroom. The two of us headed out the front door.

Chimney smoke rose above the gravy-brown, blanched bungalows of the tannery workers as Sister Irene approached their border, not looking mindful of us tailing her. She threaded her way through a bunch of men and boys all wearing dull work clothes and old turned-up overcoats beneath hand-me-down derbies, porkpies, and other make-do clothing used for headgear. The men were gathered near one of the grassy areas.

Sister reached a split rail fence and followed it a few hundred feet to the edge of the settlement to where she found the boy me and Heinie seen this morning, the kid still sitting on the frozen dirt, wearing a light jacket and pants too short to cover his legs. The kid was lashed with rope to the fence post at the edge of the grass, his skinny calves black with machine grease, his bare hands folded in his lap. Sister placed her hand real gentle-like beneath his chin and lifted his droopy blond head, could now see what we seen, his white lips cracked and caked, his ears too red to touch, his eyes swollen and dazed. The kid was older than me, looked maybe thirteen. She unsheathed the knife and quickly sliced through the ropes. When the boy was freed, she took off her coat and wrapped it around his shoulders.

"Where are this boy's parents?" she shouted at the nearby crowd. "He'll die in weather as cold as this. What's wrong with you people? *Where is his father?*"

The men resettled their kerchief sacks and canvas lunch bags under their arms, the fathers in the crowd turning the shoulders of their gawking sons away from Sister and the boy, aiming them in the direction of the tannery. One arm rose from the center of the crowd, its fingers pointing past all the bobbing hats to somewhere behind Sister. "He's a Zerhoffer," said a voice, "und here the father comes."

Sister rose to see a man with a forward lean that said he weren't planning on slowing up any. She bent down again to hover over the boy then raised her head toward the shacks that surrounded the fenced-in grass area, where me and Heinie were both hiding.

Jesus. She was looking right at me.

"Johnny!" Sister Irene called. "Don't think I don't see you two boys back there. Get over here and wrap your scarf around this boy's head, then rub each of his fingers to get the circulation going. Heinie, you go tell the sisters to bring a doctor back to the orphanage. Quickly, the both of you!"

We did as Sister said. The kid was nearly blue, his fingers stiff as tongue depressors. I put my gloves on him 'cause rubbing his fingers wasn't doing enough.

Sister clenched her walking stick in its middle and high-stepped her way into Mr. Zerhoffer's path. Pushing the walking stick across his chest, she forced him to stop. "How dare you do this to a boy—"

"Got nothing to say to you," the boy's father said. "He don't want to work. We're just teaching him a lesson. His momma will be out here to fetch him soon und clean him up, then she'll drag him over to the tannery." He leaned in the direction of me and his frozen son and snarled, "Where he better get back to scrubbing down the machinery und doing all his normal work, you hear me, boy!" Then, facing Sister Irene again: "You mind your own business, Sister."

"So if the boy doesn't want to work, you tie him up outside to freeze to death? You crossed the line, Mr. Zerhoffer. This is cruelty, plain and simple."

"He is *my* boy. *Mine*," Zerhoffer said, pounding his chest once. "I can treat my children any damn way I want, und you can't do nothing about it. Get out of the way. I am late for work. Und *you*..."

Zerhoffer leaned over to me. "You worthless little shit-monger, you get your filthy fingers off my son."

He lifted me by the front of my coat collar, raised me close to his face with one hand. "What were you doing, picking his pockets?" Zerhoffer slammed me down hard against the frozen ground. "I know what you need, boy."

He slipped off his belt, folded it, and slapped it against the palm of his bare hand. Sister bolted forward, her hand fumbling in a pocket in her nun's habit.

"That's enough. Stop this! *Now!*" Sister approached Zerhoffer from behind, drew her hand out of her pocket. This gave me the opening I needed. I crabbed my way out of the man's reach.

Sister Irene raised her fist in front of Zerhoffer's face, a long piece of writing paper trailing from it. "You are dead wrong, Mr. Zerhoffer! I can do a lot about it. This is the last time you or any of your godforsaken friends will harm another child like this, unless you want to pay a fine. Or go to jail."

"Go to jail? You are crazy, Sister. Go to jail for what?"

"I filed a complaint with the town. I know what's going on around here. These children"—her tight fist jammed Zerhoffer's shoulder—"are living, breathing creatures of God, all of whom deserve protection. They are not to be beaten senseless and left out in the cold if they can't or won't go to work. This is abuse," she snarled, shaking her papers, "and this ordinance says the town agrees with me. I'm reporting you to the police."

Zerhoffer threw the belt down, grabbed the paper from her and started mouthing the words on it. Soon a big grin crossed his face. "*Ha.* I see what it says, Sister. This is a goddamn joke. It don't say nothing about no children. Says right here, 'This ordinance,'" his voice boomed like a preacher from a pulpit, "'is hereby invoked to make it unlawful to be cruel to *canines, felines, and other animals.*' This ain't nothing more than a cruelty-to-animals law, Sister. My kids are my property. I can scold them any damn way I want." He leaned in, his face close to pressing against hers. "Long as I don't hurt no dogs in the process."

She leaned in even closer. "Read the rest of it."

A putt-putting horseless carriage appeared at the southern corner of the shanties and made a sharp left off the main road. It bounced shaky-like as its tires dipped into and out of the nooks in the frozen earth, crunching their way toward us in the open space between the rows of houses. I got to my feet, took up a position on the other side of this Zerhoffer bastard who'd been looking to give me a strapping.

The Zerhoffer boy stirred. "C-can't f-f-feel my hands, Pa..."

"The Church," Sister announced, "had a judge make an addendum. It's at the bottom."

She squatted to take the Zerhoffer boy's hands into her own, then she began reciting. "'The rights of animals are hereby imparted to include the rights of human beings—'"

Zerhoffer threw the paper onto his son's chest. "I saw what it says, Sister. I saw it real good." The horseless carriage bounced to a stop behind them.

"No, you don't see it, Mr. Zerhoffer." Sister cradled the boy to her shivering chest, tried to get him to his feet. "We built the orphanage to give the poor an option, and more will be built if they're needed. The Church can care for these children, can place these children, if people will let it. No more starving them or beating them if they can't or won't do a man's job. And no more throwing unwanted babies into the rivers, or stuffing them into sewers and storm drains. I know what's happening around here, and it must stop."

"I need them wages, Sister," Zerhoffer said, "und my son will do the job the Volkheimers tell him to do to earn them." He searched the ground for his missing belt, turned left then right then left again, real clumsy-like on both feet. He leaned his puzzled head closer to the dirt to get a better look.

The perfect height for me.

Snap. I whipped the belt's buckle across his eyes and screamed at him. "That'll teach *you* to think you can strap *me,* you stupid fuck-face!"

"Johnny!" Sister screamed. "Stop it. *Johnny!*"

Zerhoffer covered his eyes with one arm while the other groped at me, but I circled away from him and to his left, still whipping blow after blow of belt leather and buckle iron against his head and face.

"Owww, you little orphan bastard! *Owww*..."

"Got more coming to you, you grubby nasty sack of—"

Suddenly my arm stopped in midair, gripped from behind. A smiling man in a black leather overcoat worked the belt out of my hand.

"So much anger," said the man from the horseless carriage, "und from so young a man."

"Mr. Volkheimer!" Sister said. "My goodness. Thank you for stopping him." Sister gripped the back of my shirt collar and pulled me to her side. Her grip turned into a firm hold on my shoulder. "Johnny's not, ah, so much a bad boy as he is spirited. And he was defending himself against...against..."

"Against Herr Zerhoffer, one of our tannery workers," the man said, "who has apparently left in a hurry, not concerned about keeping his pants up." He held out the belt and eyed the turned-tail SOB who was making his way back toward his bungalow. Mr. Volkheimer, tall and bulky as two stacked beer barrels, tossed the belt into the back seat of his carriage. "I witnessed the exchange, Sister. You needn't explain the boy's actions."

Mr. Volkheimer's gaze lingered a moment on me. I turned up my coat collar, closed it with one hand and hunched my shoulders over to cover my neck; I was cold from sweating. He crouched down eye level to me, thick wavy lines appearing on his forehead. "You must learn to control your temper, son," he said. "You must fight those violent urges. The ones that sometime turn men into demons. This is very important. Do you understand?"

I nodded. His stare held onto me a moment longer, like he wanted what he'd said to sink in. He raised his hand; I flinched. His hand settled on my shoulder then patted my upper arm instead, his small grin disappearing with a slight nod of his head.

He stood and retied the waist of his leather coat around his huge belly, turned to Sister. "Und now we shall get the stricken Zerhoffer boy home."

"No. He's going back to the orphanage with me. I'll have a doctor examine him. Please, Mr. Volkheimer..." Sister unwrapped the scarf from around the boy's head and ears, then recovered them with the black waistband of her habit. She returned my scarf to me. "You must put a stop to the use of child labor in your tannery. It is deplorable."

"You have heard my feelings on this matter before, Sister." Rolf Volkheimer was a full German, but his accent wasn't too bad. "I am trying to change things but my brothers do not agree. As they are my partners, I have, for the time being, been overruled. But I have petitioned the courts about it, und I assure you, I will fight this mistreatment. Here, let me carry the boy to my automobile. I can take all of you back to St. Jerome's."

Mr. Volkheimer lifted the stiff boy into his arms and placed him gently in the back seat of his carriage, then gave the sister his leather coat, which she wasn't wanting to take, but then she did. Sister pulled herself onto the carriage's running board, then settled into the front seat. Her hands, raw from the cold as mine were, went into Mr. Volkheimer's coat pockets. One hand came out with a silver box in the shape of a treasure chest, but small enough to fit in her palm.

"That's a snuff box," I told her, looking over her shoulder. "Seen people at the hotel with them."

"Yes, Johnny, I know. Using snuff tobacco is a nasty, nasty habit."

Mr. Volkheimer gripped the carriage's crank in both hands and gave it one rotation; the engine backfired. With the second and third turns the engine settled into a low, rat-a-tat-tatting purr. He climbed aboard behind the steering wheel. Sister handed him his snuffbox.

"Well, thank you, Sister, but it could have stayed in the pocket. Nevertheless..." He opened the tiny hinged box and pinched out a dark, sifted powder, brought it to his nose and sniffed until the snuff tobacco was gone. He returned the box to a pants pocket. Sister looked the other way.

"I will investigate more suitable use of these boys at the tannery, Sister," Mr. Volkheimer said, "und for this boy in particular. My brothers have them crawling into the machinery where most men can't fit, scrubbing down the parts with solvent. I give you my word that I will see what I can do to change this."

I balanced myself on the running board outside where Sister sat. Mr. Volkheimer looked past Sister's shoulder and spoke to me above the noise of the puttering engine. "Now be sure to hold on tight, boy."

8

Coroner Kermit Frink was settled behind a small desk that didn't give him much room between it and a window with Venetian blinds, the blinds pulled halfway up and open, sunlight striping his head and shoulders. Took him a few tries before he got the desk chair rotated to where he wanted it. Now it was tilted back and he was in a full slouch, his arm on the desk, a hand around a can of soda. Near the end of me telling him about Zerhoffer and the dead babies and the sewers, he got full upright in the chair, started tugging at his cigarette pack, then said with a few deliberate nods soon as I was done, "Finally. About time you spoke up."

"Really, now," I said, surprised. "How's that?"

"When I saw you and those boys at the restaurant excavation," he said, his hammy fingers working the cellophane off his soft pack of smokes, "I felt you knew something. At least more than the rest of us did. Then you showed up at the train wreck." Kerm took a filtered cigarette out of the pack, put it in his mouth, and sucked on air. He pulled it away from his lips. "So I wasn't all that surprised to run into you again at the convent. I went with my instincts when I let you and Father see the skeletons."

The office we were in was no bigger than a prison cell and a half and was stuffed with a desk and desk chair, the two side chairs Father and me occupied, and a trash can. No name on the door, just the word *office*. Space was tight at the hospital; Kerm may have been a squatter. "So what you're saying is the German immigrants were just throwing their babies away?"

"Tossing them into the river, or stuffing them down the storm sewers at night like they were table scraps. Who knows where else they were putting them; too many mouths, not enough wages."

"You saw people doing this?"

"Yeah. Once." I shuddered and took a tight-lipped swallow. "But other kids seen people do it, too. We spent a lot of time on the streets when I was at the orphanage. The sisters did what they could to control us kids, but we managed to sneak out enough."

Kerm rubbed his temple like he had a headache. "I can see the headlines," he said. "'Turn-of-the-Century Mass Genocide in Three Bridges, Pennsylvania.' Look, it'll be in your town's best interest for you to stay mum about this."

The town had a lot to be ashamed of, but it still came down to the state of things back then, I told him, with poor immigrant husbands and wives doing what all husbands and wives did together, then ending up with more mouths to feed because of it.

And to think how Viola and me had tried for years to have kids. Knowing all them people were having babies and just throwing them away, I wondered how God was able to square that. And I wondered how come I hadn't ended up on the floor with the rest of them skeletons, and how come I'd been left at the orphanage gate, and—

"Wump?" Father squeezed my shoulder. "You okay?"

"I'm fine."

Kerm spoke again. "Since I can't determine forensically when the deaths occurred, my report will say they could have been spread out over the past sixty or seventy years, citing the age of these sewers."

"But what about—"

"The two decomposing bodies? I checked with the sewage treatment plants in the area, and yes, I'm sorry to say they report finding baby bodies jamming up the pumping equipment every once in a while, mixed in with discarded pets, careless raccoons, and other small animals. They could have been tossed into the river or crammed into those openings in the sewer drains between curb and street. By the time a body gets to the treatment plant, if it makes it that far, it's pretty much unidentifiable. Shameful, but that's the way it is. So, there you have it, gentlemen. My take on the situation."

* * *

Kerm called a cab to give Father and me a lift back to Our Lady's, the city of Philadelphia picking up the fare. Father didn't say nothing the first four blocks. Me, I didn't feel like talking either. Seeing death at work like this pushed me into thinking about my son, Harry. Most kids at age twenty think they're invincible. Harry was forced to face reality early, got philosophical about it, a calm and rational voice above the pain. *"Pop, I just get to find out what is or isn't next, sooner than you,"* he'd told me near the end, *"with less of a chance of screwing things up before I get there."*

Amen to that, son.

About a block from the rectory, Father's voice startled me. "That boy didn't have a mark on him."

"What boy, Father?"

"Adam. At baseball practice yesterday."

Little Sonny had nailed Adam with some good hard punches to the face and head, and Adam hadn't retaliated. Yet Sonny "looked like he'd been in the ring with Cassius Clay. I'm having trouble with that, and something else, too. I find it odd there weren't two more bodies at the train wreck this morning."

The hack leaned his Checker cab into a corner as we approached Our Lady's rectory from the rear. It was the end of morning recess and the schoolyard was packed with kids, so he slowed down; the cab's tires squealed around the corner anyway. We came out of the turn with Father still talking. "Why weren't the other two dragged under the train with her? The train engineer said Sister Magdalena had a grip on their wrists right up till impact."

"The engineer could have been wrong. Maybe she let go in time."

"Right. So, the question is, what made her let go?" Father leaned forward and grabbed the top of the front seat. He spoke into the hack's ear. "Turn the cab around."

* * *

The stainless-steel door opened, and Kerm the coroner pulled out the slab. He unzipped Sister Magdalena's body bag halfway, close to where it dipped down and leveled off. "What is it you want to see, Father?"

"Her hands."

Kerm reached in, pulled on each arm by the wrist, and sat her hands outside the bag. Everything was attached: arms, hands, all ten fingers. Kerm turned her left hand up, said, "Well, I'll be damned..."

"Open it up," Father said.

Sister's olive-colored hand was grimy from rubbing against the creosote-dipped railroad ties and the dusty cinders around them. Her fingernails were jagged and short, but this made sense because she'd been chewing them pretty regular for some time, ever since she'd gotten anxious. Kerm was having a devil of a time uncurling her fingers. "I had to do this once already. Can't say I've ever seen a dead person's hand reclose itself, especially after rigor mortis has set in."

It was like whatever she'd been holding needed to still be in it, with her determined not to let go, even in death. Except she had let go, and her palms and curled fingers showed why.

"The skin's mostly burned off. That's bone in there," Kerm said, pointing through the parted black flesh of her palm at things that looked like tan sticks inside melting Fudgsicles. "Something hot came in contact with her palm and fingers. My guess is it was the train engine's wheels. They'll retain heat with all that friction, iron wheel against iron rail, even after they stop turning. It's already in my report, fellas. And in case I didn't mention this before, I'm calling this an accident, not a suicide."

Sister's other hand was the same way, all curled up but revealing charred flesh in its palm and the underside of its fingers.

It didn't matter how Kerm wrote it up. I might have bought that one hand got burned by the iron wheels, but not both. The train dragged the lower part of her body, but the upper half of it with both arms and hands had been left behind on the side of the tracks. Her hands and those big wheels might not have even come in contact with each other. What she'd been holding had gotten hot as hell after she'd started holding it.

Something happened here that wasn't normal. Something no coroner's language could do justice to.

* * *

The Checker cab dropped Father Duncan and me curbside out front of the convent. It was early afternoon, a little past one.

"Got a question for you, Father. Yesterday after baseball practice, you said being able to speak German was one of the reasons they assigned you to this parish, right?"

Both of us were on the sidewalk ready to part ways, Father to spend some time with the mourning sisterhood, me to head home to see if Viola was still there eating her lunch so's I could fill her in on all the hubbub. The convent, the church, and the rectory loomed over Father's shoulder in that order, like thunderheads gathering offshore, all three buildings a darker colored granite than I'd ever noticed before.

"That's right. I speak German fairly well." Father checked the front of his cassock with his hand, touched each of its buttons on his chest to make sure they were closed as far north as his collar. An absentminded gesture; one maybe to keep me from bothering him with more questions.

"'*One* of the reasons' is what you said, right?" I repeated for him. "So, give me another."

This parish never had more than one priest for a few generations, and all of a sudden, the archdiocese decided to put another one out here. I'd found this real strange the first time I heard he was coming. For sure it weren't no less strange now.

"Ah. I see." Father looked up the street then down, a one-way three-laner that traveled northwest as it passed the parish buildings. Traffic moved too fast along this block most of the time, like it was doing today. But on Sundays, before each of the parish's two Masses, it funneled into two lanes and slowed to a respectable crawl so as not to hit people crossing the street in the middle of the block. Drivers were at least smart enough to know that hitting a grandmother on her way to church on a Sunday would pretty much tip the Judgment Day scales in the wrong direction.

"I suppose," Father said, "I could argue it's because the parish has been growing, with a lot of ex-GIs from Philadelphia settling here and starting families." Father's tired black-brown eyes were focused real good now, staring at me. "But I think you know the real reason why."

"Come again, Father?"

"I'll spell it out. There have been some alleged..." he searched for the right word, "improprieties reported to the archdiocese. Anonymously, of course." Father's stare drilled me, but I didn't flinch. "They involve the monsignor."

Improprieties, *hell*. Monsignor Fassnacht was shaming the priesthood and the Catholic Church. He'd been bringing women back to the rectory at night and banging them, right there in his room for Christ sake. Been doing this for years, and nobody said nothing about it. Some of them been street women, some not. It was the ones that weren't prostitutes that worried me. I saw the way he looked at all them young nuns, like they were meat. Saw and heard him around them, too. A man in his position of authority, with the sisterhood always taught to obey their Catholic elders...He was a disgrace, taking advantage like that. Someone had to do something.

"Really doesn't matter who contacted the archdiocese," Father said. "The Cardinal put me here to investigate the allegations and report back to him. Except—"

Father had a stumped look. His eyes settled on Our Lady's front doors a moment. When he raised them to the round stained-glass window, I followed them. The window was wider than the church's double-door entrance, and the glass showed two large angels on bent knees as they witnessed the Virgin Mary's ascent into heaven.

"Except what, Father?"

"Except..." Father's expression changed, and I got a glimpse of how he must have looked guarding home plate in a tight ball game. "Except there may be other forces at work here."

His jaw muscles clenched, and his lips pressed together. "Why don't you and I meet at the orphanage after school today? We'll have a talk with Adam."

* * *

I headed home on foot past the schoolyard, hoping to catch Viola for a few minutes.

Click-a-clack, click-a-clack. A sister stood in the doorway to the school's back entrance, her tin cricket between her thumb and forefinger. The signal pierced the din of a chattering schoolyard; lunch period was over. Girls in blue uniforms with white blouses and spring jackets assembled behind each other in rows according to grade. Boys in white shirts with clip-on blue ties pushed and elbowed each other within their own lines. I was halfway past the schoolyard on the sidewalk, outside the fence, as the late arrivals straggled through the gate and fell in behind their classmates. The laughing, giggling, jostling, and tugging at one another stopped, replaced by covered-mouth whispering, and a few nervous coughs. *Click-a-clack, click-a-clack.* The children began filing inside.

I got to the corner of the schoolyard. The sister closed the glass door behind the last kid entering the school, sealing the exit like it was a bulkhead on a submarine. Now the yard was empty. No, that wasn't right. The cyclone fence was blurring my vision. In the far corner were two figures. I got closer to the fencing and looked through the crisscrossed links.

One of the figures was unmistakable: Raymond, strapped into his wheelchair, his head tilted left, his neck muscles not strong enough to carry it erect. A red Phillies baseball cap sat on top his long sandy hair. In his right hand was a toy sword with a short silver blade made of hard rubber above a plastic T-shaped gold handle. He was holding the sword weakly upright, its handle bottom balanced on his knee. The other figure was Leo, facing Raymond's wheelchair with a sword just like his friend's. Leo raised it skyward then slowly lowered it level with the blacktop. He pointed it at Raymond and spoke. "Ready?"

Raymond's sword wiggled.

Leo thrust at Raymond's midsection; Raymond tilted his play sword to meet the plunge, rubber blade to rubber blade, except what I heard was the sound of metal on metal. This made me look closely at their weapons. Toys, I told myself; I was sure.

Leo thrust again like a gladiator in one of them Roman movies, the thrust quicker this time. Raymond's sword again matched him, and Leo again pulled back, the only other noise Leo's heavy breathing. Leo got back to it, thrust a third time and retreated, a fourth, a fifth, each plunge a little quicker than the one before it, all of them met by flicks of Raymond's wrist, no hint of metal striking metal. Leo then raised his sword with both hands on the handle and attacked from overhead, slicing down toward Raymond's shoulders and neck and upper torso, but none of his blows connected, all of them greeted by his sparring partner's weak-armed yet swift sword.

Leo circled left for an opening; the wheelchair followed. Leo moved right; Raymond mirrored him. Movements that were at first cautious and unhurried became furious and whirling, these two young warriors in mock mortal combat. I got dizzy following them until suddenly their play stopped, Leo stutter-stepping then sprawling at the foot of the wheelchair, his head angled against Raymond's bent legs. He'd been tripped up by an untied shoelace. The tip of Raymond's sword moved in close to his fallen partner's neck and stayed there. Raymond finally pulled it back.

Since I known him, Leo had never been so full of himself that he couldn't laugh at his mistakes, but this time there weren't no laughter. He double-knotted both sneakers in silence, picked up his sword, stood, and faced Raymond again. "I'm ready," he said.

I checked my watch. If I didn't leave now, I'd miss Viola at the house.

I didn't make much out of what I'd just seen, or what I'd thought I'd just seen. Toys or not, boys playing with weapons of any kind, ancient or modern, was something I never got used to seeing since my days in the trenches in France, and it didn't take much to bring them war nightmares back. So yeah, I'd get a little confused sometimes, seeing and hearing things that weren't really there. Two young boys playing with toy rubber swords was all it was. Not gallant warriors swinging steel blade against steel blade, their ringing blows echoing throughout the schoolyard, which was what I thought I heard a second time, just as I closed the front door of my house.

One thing was for sure. Raymond was blind, but his other senses did a hell of a job of making up the difference.

9

A date was chiseled into the granite block in front of where I stood, near eye high. 1899. The year St. Jerome's Home for Foundlings was rededicated. Same year I was born.

I put my fingertips inside the etched numbers. They were polished and smooth to the touch, so smooth the feel reminded me of the porcelain cherubs standing witness over Our Lady's baptismal font.

One-eight-nine-nine.

Sixty-five years it had been. Young for things made of granite. Old for a man.

It was late afternoon and I was on the orphanage's front stoop, waiting for Father Duncan. The original, one-story version of St. Jerome's went up in 1896, its exterior sided with used clapboard not much better than tinder, and near as bad as the shacks the tannery workers lived in. Two years later the German Catholic parishes of Philadelphia put the city's masons to work, adding two more stories and replacing the orphanage's wood siding with block granite from the same local quarry that supplied the stone for Our Lady's church and school. The masons worked through a harsh, snowy winter, and when construction fell behind, donations from Rolf Volkheimer put enough manpower in place to finish the home's new exterior in time for a first-day-of-spring dedication.

This time of day, the exterior was a few shades lighter than the parish buildings, the sun angled low enough to catch the pink and white flecks in the rough facing of each block, giving the place a fuzzy, speckled glow. Sister Irene once said more orphanages would be built if the need arose. It must have worked out they weren't needed; to this day, St. Jerome's was the only one in the county. Seemed the orphan population in these parts declined not long after I got adopted and moved near Pittsburgh.

"Hell's full. Go to Pittsburgh." The punch line to Father's joke. About summed up my experience with the area, far as I could recollect it.

So, when I ran away from them bastard parents of mine to go back east in 1915 at the age of sixteen, St. Jerome's had some beds open, and the sisters let me stay till I got my legs under me and found a place of my own. Heinie was gone, adopted not long after me, but his adoption had ended a lot worse. His new parents found him face down in a pile of manure in the family's stables, kicked in the head by a horse. Killed instantly, one of the sisters had told me. Broke my heart hearing that.

I'd also overheard the sisters talking about how the folks in Three Bridges had by then apparently quit throwing their newborns away. Sounded odd at the time, from what I remembered. The German Catholics in the area, and in the bungalows especially, were just as poor as when I'd left, so it made no sense why the killing had stopped.

Father Duncan was now on his way up the walk, his cassock replaced by a black spring jacket over a navy-blue turtleneck. I pushed St. Jerome's bell.

A breathless Sister Dymphna, her face red and flustered, opened the door. Now that she was in her forties, her weight was finally catching up with her. "Come in," she said. She led us out of the large vestibule, her head tilted forward, her wimple looking like the pillbox hat on that little bellhop Phillip Morris used to sell its cigarettes.

Counting the sisters and the home's administrators, and all the orphans who passed through here, I was the oldest person I knew of who'd been a regular visitor at St. Jerome's over the years. Most of my visits were to work on a project of some sort, like plastering interior walls, replacing the wooden porches with masonry, and digging the tunnel ditching when the orphanage went from well and septic to city and sewer water back in the twenties. For me it had always been anything for the money, glad for the extra work tossed my way after I'd started with the church. Never got anything extra while I was at the tannery. The two younger Volkheimer brothers had kept me on as an adult, for no reason other than I was a bull of a worker. They weren't near as nice to me as their older brother Rolf was, back when I was a kid picking up dog shit for pennies. After Rolf's disappearance a lot changed, both in the way the tannery was run and—coincidentally—for me personally, with me getting sent off to live in Pittsburgh. I'd concluded, right or wrong, that Rolf's two brothers had something to do with it. "It" being Rolf's disappearance. But hell, that was over fifty years ago and both brothers had long since cashed in. Any wrongdoing they'd done, God would have made them pay for it and righted it by now.

Christ, I was rambling. That's what this place did to me soon as I walked through them front doors. Pieces of memories all hitting me at once, gunking up my brain, not letting me complete one thought before I started going on about the next. Made me forget sometimes how much love and caring there'd been inside these walls. A real refuge for kids like Heinie and me. Still, no one ever heard me say it made up for not having real parents. Never, because it never did.

Sister Dymphna walked Father and me into the hallway. Each time the doors to the kitchen swung open there was a clear view back to the oak threshold that was the rear exit of the orphanage. A few children buzzed by on their way to the dining room.

Sister reacted. "No running, Robert. *Vincent!* Fingers out of your nose, child! You're serving dinner tonight!"

She stopped us next to a pair of wooden pocket doors pulled shut. On the other side of the doors was the orphanage's library. Her fingers went to the handles; before she pulled them apart, she turned to Father Duncan.

"We need to have an understanding," she said, her jaw a little tight. "Adam's been under a lot of stress lately and he's doing some acting out because of it. The adoptions are nearly final, and his new parents are very eager. I think it best if I stayed with him for your discussion. If he gets upset and wants to stop talking, you'll have to leave."

Father nodded, said, "I'm here only because I'm concerned about what happened to Sister Magdalena."

"Yes. I know what's got you concerned, Father."

I'd seen this air about her before, her face all scrunched, her lips straight and thin like some character in the funny papers. A special breed, these nuns were, always ready to circle the wagons when it came to St. Jerome's kids. A lot like Sister Irene had been with Heinie and me.

"The staff here and the parish's sisterhood are grieving deeply because of the train accident," Sister said. "And we are watching keenly for any changes that Sister's death may cause in the children's behavior. We had one small fistfight after we got back from Good Friday practice, but that's normal for a school day afternoon. And it didn't involve Adam."

Good Friday practice. Sister had planned to get the children involved in Our Lady's Stations of the Cross service next week. I was supposed to help her get things organized. Rats.

"We missed you, Wump," she said, seeing right through me. "But we found things to make do."

The props. I was supposed to find props for them to use. A cloth for Jesus to wipe his face on, some toy spears for the Roman centurions. And something light and small enough for a grade-school kid to carry as Christ's cross. "I'm sorry, Sister. Forgot all about it. I'll get those things together early part of next week."

Sister nodded then pulled the library doors apart. "I'll look for Adam upstairs. Wait in here, please." Her dimpled chin disappeared into bulging jowls as she started down the hallway, speaking over her shoulder as she walked. "We're arranging our archives for the anniversary. Anything in the library you look at, please return it to the same general vicinity." She hustled into the kitchen through the swinging door.

The library was also an arts and crafts room with glue bottles and wax crayons and colored construction paper and pairs of scissors in two of the corners. What had everything all cluttered up in here was a number of water-stained, misshapen cardboard boxes with their flaps open and a stale-smelling steamer trunk with its top raised. The anniversary the sisters would be celebrating was Sister Irene's one hundredth birthday. She'd only made it to her late forties, but the sisterhood had celebrated her birthday every year since. Founding St. Jerome's, and looking after the likes of little trouble-making pugs like me...no better person than Sister Irene I had ever known, although my Viola could give most anyone a good run.

The library had changed a bit over the years. Furniture came and went, the walls and wood trim defaced with either pencil or pen or penknife so often they'd needed repainting and staining more times than I could count. Current coloring was a cream yellow on the plaster, and a light oak stain on the woodwork. The room looked cheerful, but with all this musty old stuff opened up and sitting out, the place smelled a lot like boys' Phys Ed.

Father worked his way up the right side of the library, and I followed in his wake, both of us sidestepping flaps of interfering cardboard and leaning stacks of plaques and black-and-white photographs and some old paintings, the floor and all the furniture cluttered.

"What was St. Jerome's like when you were young, Wump?"

"For starters, there's been some structural changes," I told him. "The babies originally slept in the same room with us older kids. Walls were eventually put up to make separate bedrooms and a nursery. Now the kids sleep two and three to a room. A few of the older ones get singles."

"Not much privacy, then," Father said. "I mean back when you lived here." He was examining trinkets as he walked, fingering through plaques, framed pictures, books. I was doing the same, both of us headed toward the large trunk in the back, near the wall.

"Little privacy is right. And there wasn't much of anything a kid could call his own, not even what we wore. There were long closets on each floor where clothes were kept. Shirts, pants, extra shoes, and dresses and petticoats for the girls. But them sisters were good about selecting clothes for us each day. Most times the stuff they pulled out of the closets actually fit."

The coming anniversary was about to turn the entire orphanage into a shrine to Sister Irene. So many plaques and framed letters, some from Philadelphia Bishops, and Cardinals, and three from a succession of Popes, Leo XIII through Pope Benedict XV.

"Can you tell me who these people are, Wump?"

Father neared the back of the room, stopped to pick up a beat-up black enamel picture frame. As I got closer to him, I saw it was a photograph under glass with a small brass plate below it, the plate screwed into the frame. It had been taken in front of the orphanage, with all the people posed. The engraved brass plate read *St. Jerome's Rededication—April 2, 1899.*

"The person seated in the center is Sister Irene," I told him, looking over his shoulder. "She was in her thirties back then. Bless that wonderful woman's soul. I, ah..."

Father gently patted me on the back then put the picture in my hands so I could get as close to it as I needed to. I choked back some tears. The woman was as near to a mother as I'd ever known.

"And this one over here, Father, is Monsignor Krause, the parish's pastor and only priest, and a crazy one at that, if you listened to Sister Irene. She and him didn't get along."

"How about these two men here?"

"Judging from the top hat, I'd say the one standing on Sister's left is a political dignitary of some sort. The mayor of Philadelphia is my guess. Or maybe he was called Sheriff back then. I don't recognize him; he was before my time. The second top-hatted fella, the heavy one with the full-length leather coat, is Rolf Volkheimer. And to his left, seated with her hands folded across her stomach, is his wife. Looking real pregnant, I might add."

It wasn't a good picture of Mrs. Volkheimer. Her eyes were focused on her hands, like she wasn't thrilled to be there. I lingered on her image. It was then Father offered an insight that jolted me.

"Those Volkheimer prayer offering cards you showed me: based on their dates, and the date of this photograph," he said, pausing, "I think her baby died."

10

Father was right. Her first child was born late April of that year. Jesus. How horrible.

Father Duncan didn't wait for me to return the picture, instead began working his way into the second half of the library. I hadn't been able to take another step, still reeling from Father's insight on St. Jerome's rededication. I rallied, returned the photograph to the table, picked up another one.

"Hey, Father, look at this picture here. Remember Honus Wagner? He played shortstop for Pittsburgh in the early 1900s. Here he is visiting the kids at St. Jerome's. Wow."

Wagner was in uniform and there were other baseball players with him. "You gotta see this, Father. It's a real gem. Father?"

Father Duncan didn't hear me. He'd circled back, was now focused on the innards of the opened trunk, his face all pasty white. He made the sign of the cross on himself then reached into the trunk with both hands.

Out came something that looked like one of them stagecoach strong-boxes you see in cowboy movies only smaller, a handle on each side, its lid flat and covered in a light brown leather. I pushed some of the clutter on the sideboard out of the way so he could put it down. Father straightened himself up, not taking his eyes off it. Now I could see what was on the box's lid: a large cartoon-like drawing etched into the leather, in color, of a smiling devil baby.

Father wasn't saying nothing, just stared at it. The devil's eyes were like large black buttons floating in larger white circles, one eye lazy, but both of them real loony-looking, like how a sideshow swami hypnotist gets when he puts a whammy on a volunteer from his audience. Inside the devil's wild grin was a full set of pointy uppers. His arms were raised and groping, like he was looking to be picked up. There was a swaddled white cloth over his groin area with no other clothing, the rest of the body the color of charcoal-smeared salmon. Three fingers and a thumb were on each hand, four toes on each foot, and claws on all of them, red as spurting arteries. And sticking out of his forehead, horns. Same color red as the claws, and as tall as the demon's face was long. Father passed his open hand slowly over the box, made another sign of the cross, tighter this time. He opened the lid.

I got a sudden whiff of what had to be the sickest shit-heap in Creation. A rush of spit drenched the insides of my cheeks and churned my stomach. After a few gags, the smell was gone. Father looked like he hadn't flinched.

"*Codex Gigas,*" he said real sober-like, most to himself, and the book that was in the box was now on the table. Bulky as a toolbox and warped, its wavy brown pages were bound by three leather strips twice as thick as the cowhide shoelaces on my work boots. Father's fingers started working their way through the swollen pages.

"Repeat that for me in English, Father."

"'The Giant Book' is the translation. But it's also known by another name."

"'The Devil's Bible,'" Sister Dymphna said from under the archway between the library and the hall. Still no Adam, and Sister was looking real cranky. "That should go back in the box, Father. Let's concentrate on why you're here. Adam should be along shortly."

Father stopped paging through the book but left it open. "You know the history of *Codex Gigas*, Sister?"

"Of this one, yes. As you can see," she said, joining him, "it's in German. I believe the oldest one found was written in pre-Vulgate Latin in the thirteenth century by a Benedictine monk, a penance for some breach of monastic discipline."

"Legend has it," Father said, "*Codex Gigas* was written in a single night with the help of the Devil, whom the monk had summoned to his Bohemian monastery." The book had to be over a thousand pages thick. Father was turning them again. "The one you're speaking of, the oldest version of the manuscript, is in the Royal Library in Sweden, taken as spoils from one European conflict or another."

"A manuscript written on vellum," Sister chimed in. "Prepared from the skins of a hundred and sixty asses. Or so goes the legend."

"Yes. So goes the legend, Sister."

They were like Pete and Repeat, speaking each other's language like I wasn't even in the room. This evil book with a cartoon demon on its container was written in pig latin on a bunch of donkey hides, and now the orphanage had some German version of it. Why did either of them know this crap?

"Sister Irene inherited it," Sister Dymphna said to Father. "From Rolf Volkheimer, one of the orphanage's benefactors."

"I see. Ever looked through it, Sister?"

"Certainly not, Father; it's sacrilegious. It's here only because Monsignor said the archdiocese felt it should stay where it was bequeathed. What good can come from a book with so blasphemous a history?"

"Not much, I suppose," said Father, his hands working the pages again, carefully gathering and turning them, bunches at a time. "Unless you count as a good thing learning about the evils out there. It's why the Church has had its scholars study other versions of it over the years."

While the two of them went on about evil Bible stories, I instead stayed quiet and worked my way around the library. Plenty of interesting antiques and paintings and other trinkets to look at, some of them from before I was born. On the other side of the room was a gold-colored Victorian couch in great condition. And there were even some kitchen utensils I remembered using as a kid, like a wood-handled iron contraption that looked like a fly swatter with a small cage at one end. It held big bars of soap that you swished around in sink water to make suds for washing dishes. And there was an old-fashioned bread slicer, and—

"Jeez. Hello, Adam. You startled me sneaking up like that."

Adam stood in the middle of the library archway, taking the three of us in. The boy was cursed with two cowlicks near the front of his head that swept the black hair away from his tan forehead. Cowlicks are cute as candy corn on smaller kids; boys nearing their fourteenth birthday had to despise them. Still, it was tough to tell with Adam. He pretty much despised everything. "You wanted to see me, Father?" he said.

Father closed the devil book, and he and Sister quickly returned it to the box. Father moved over to the gold Victorian couch, made room on it by lifting a stack of papers and placing them on the floor. "Have a seat, Adam."

There was some nervous foot rearranging on Adam's part that reminded me of a first-grader trying to protect his flank from the teacher's yardstick. Father sat, then Adam sat, then Father asked, "Would you mind talking a few minutes about what happened to Sister Magdalena this morning?"

Adam's hands were in his lap, fingertip to fingertip, revealing fidgety thumbs. "Does Sister Dymphna have to listen?"

I leaned through the archway for a quick look down the hallway, about to pull the library's pocket doors together. Two small boys came storming through the kitchen's swinging doors into the dining room, then into the hall. They quick-stepped past me to the base of the stairway, their right hands moving behind their backs, each sneaking a glance at the other. The little buggers were guilty of something for sure, but what? Taking food from the kitchen?

No. Guilty of breaking St. Jerome's no-candy-before-dinner rule. They hopped onto the first step of the stairway, their small hands not able to hide the long licorice whips pressed into their palms, the pieces of the red rope candy sticking out of their white fists at both ends. I cracked a smile at them. I been there, fellas. Your secret was safe with me. Except—

It was then I sensed it, a presence at the end of the hallway, someone watching. I swiveled my head, slowly, to look down the hall. No one was there, in either the hall or the dining room. But beyond the dining room—

I craned my neck to watch as the kitchen doors continued swinging past each other following the boys' rushed exit through them, back and forth, back and forth, *th-thump th-THUMP, th-thump th-THUMP*—

As the door swings shortened, I got reduced glimpses into the kitchen.

Standing in front of the butcher block was Adam's sister, Ruthie, unchanged from her blue school uniform and snow-white blouse, her plump hand attached to a licorice whip in her mouth. The twisted licorice piece grew smaller with each pass of the kitchen doors, Ruthie not paying me no attention until, with the doors near at rest, she gave me one midchew, open-mouth glance, her teeth all drippy red from strawberry-licorice spit. Her glance became a childish smile, her chewing and smiling reminding me how this neighborhood had more than its fair share of dull kids. I pulled my head back inside the library as Father answered Adam's question.

"Sister Dymphna's concerned about you, son, so yes, I think she should be here."

This decided, I pulled at the pocket doors, but instead of the clack-snap of wood against wood, there was a dry thud when the doors suddenly stopped a few inches from closing, cushioned by a plump fist filled with red licorice whips. The doors opened wider. Ruthie entered, stepped quietly over to stand next to me. She raised a floppy licorice twist in my direction; I declined with a headshake. She returned my smile, more licorice dribble sneaking out the corner of her mouth, her tongue recapturing it.

"But I don't want Sister getting upset with, you know, stuff I say," Adam said, "because that's what happens sometimes. People get upset when I say stuff."

Sister Dymphna moved to Ruthie's side. I expected Sister to march Ruthie back out through the library doors, but this didn't happen. Instead the nun wagged the fingers of her upturned hand at Ruthie, wanting her to ante up the candy, which she did, but with Ruthie quick to gobble up the last few bites of the piece she was working on. How the girl had money enough to keep herself and half the orphanage in penny licorice the way she did, I didn't know. I pulled the library doors closed.

Adam was right about his smart mouth. There'd been some real gems come out of it at times. Like last Christmas, when donations to the orphanage were coming up short. The little wiseass told the younger kids there weren't as many toys because some of Santa's elves came down with penguin clap.

"How about you, Adam?" Father said. "Does it upset you when you say things that bother people?"

Adam looked away from Father, dropped his gaze to his busy thumbs. "Yeah."

"So, sometimes you can't help it? It just comes out?"

"Yeah. I don't even know what some of it means."

"I see. Fine. So, let's talk about Sister Magdalena. There were two children with her this morning on the tracks, just before the accident. Do you know who they were?"

"I...she..." Adam said, squirming. "It was me and Ruthie! *We* were with her. But it wasn't our fault. Sister started pulling at us, hard. She thought we could make it across the bridge, but I knew we couldn't. When I broke loose, Sister slipped backward and, ah, you think the police—"

"Whoa, slow down, son," Father said. "The police will want to talk with you, but they've already decided it was an accident. Just tell me what happened."

Adam started with how he'd slipped out at sunrise to go fishing, something he did a few mornings each week before breakfast, the railroad bridge his favorite place because he could get out over the middle of the river, where the water was deeper. "Ruthie was with me because that's what she does sometimes, gets up with me when I get up. Most mornings there's trains, some of them faster than others, but even the faster ones slow down because the station stop is just across the bridge. The slow-movers are the diesel freighters carrying coal. You have to pay attention because if you don't give yourself enough time to get off the bridge..."

He explained how a woman wearing a dark overcoat with a white scarf tied under her chin appeared in the middle of the tracks off the west end of the bridge. She was carrying a suitcase.

"At first she was just looking at us, and I didn't know it was Sister Magdalena. When she started across the bridge, I went back to fishing, but I knew something was stupid about her, because nobody crosses the bridge to get to the train station. There's no room to walk except between the tracks."

Sister Dymphna glided over toward the open end of the couch and sat next to Adam, Father on his other side, leaving Ruthie and me to stand.

"She started walking faster as she got closer. The wind got under her scarf and blew it off her head and, and, it was then I could see her hair was cut real short, and..." his eyes moistened, "I, ah, could tell. I could tell for sure."

"You could tell for sure what, Adam?" said Father.

Adam's lower lip quivered. "That what some of the sisters say but think I don't hear *is true*! That she was my mother! My *mother*! I never saw her hair before, but when I did—" His mouth snapped shut and his breathing labored, coming only through his nose. He touched his hairline just above the forehead and said, sneering. "I saw she had two cowlicks in the front, just like mine!"

Hadn't thought about it in a while, but damn if I hadn't had the same opinion years ago. Weren't because of them cowlicks though, because I'd never seen Sister Magdalena without her wimple headpiece. It was because the neighborhood was full up with Germans. A hundred percent Anglo for all I knew, all except for our Sister Magdalena, a Venezuelan, and a darker one at that. So along came this orphaned baby boy and girl, with beautiful deep, dark olive skin just like Sister's own. Twins, no less. Them babies were the only other persons in the parish with that kind of coloring. But I'd shaken the whole thing off. Sister Magdalena was a nun, for Christ sake.

Adam had more to say. Sister Dymphna was looking real stern but stayed calm, even with the news. She still eyed Adam real close.

"Sister Magdalena told me our new parents were creeps, and our adoption was off because she was taking us on the train away from here, to some other place. A *nice* place, and to other nice places, too, she said. Places where moms took good care of their kids."

Sister Dymphna rested her arm on the couch, behind Adam's head; her eyes were welling up. Father stayed even-tempered. "Go on," he said.

"There's trees. Big trees on both sides of the bend, and the tracks run through them before they get to the river. She kept talking, telling me she was sorry she gave us up, that she was our mother, and she loved us, and, and, I got mixed up, and scared, and I didn't hear the train."

Adam's long, skinny face started twisting up in anger. "She grabbed my wrist, then pulled and kept right on pulling at me and Ruthie, and the whistle was blowing and, and...but by then it was already too late. The train was on the bridge."

Adam's upper lip raised. Suddenly his breathing picked up and his canines showed. "It was all her fault! She...she was a nun! My m-m-mother was a fucking nun!"

"Adam!" Sister Dymphna's hand went for his collar, but he got to his feet ahead of her fingers.

"I...We pulled away from her, then we jumped between the girders, into the water. That's what happened"—his chest puffed up—"and I don't give a crap if you or anyone else believes me or not."

He was facing Father and Sister, his back to me and Ruthie. Adam slowed his breathing, the two of them looking at him shocked enough they weren't doing any talking. Adam broke the silence. "Can I go now?"

The language hadn't caught me off guard like it had Sister and Father, so while they regrouped, I figured to get my two cents in. "Must have been awful for you, son. Big train like that with tons of coal comes out of nowhere, chugging right at the two of you and the sister. Scary, huh?"

"Yeah," he said, turning to face me. "Scary."

"And all that coal got dumped into the water when the cars derailed, right after the brakeman stopped the train. Lucky for you the carload of coal missed the both of you, huh?"

Adam studied me. It was then I decided to do what I'd been wanting to do ever since he walked into the library. Ever since I'd seen Sister Magdalena's charred palms. Or maybe it was since I witnessed little Sonny Goode's injuries from his spat on the ball field with him. I nudged Ruthie out of the way, reached up and put my hand on Adam's bony shoulder, and squeezed.

"Yeah," he said, looking deep into my eyes, deeper than most folks did. "Lucky."

Nothing happened. I felt no heat, no fire, no pain of any kind. Nothing like what happened before to Sister Magdalena or little Sonny when they touched him, which gave me no reason to remove my hand other than maybe because the moment was over, so I did. Except now I smelled something.

"You can go now, Adam," Sister said firmly. "We'll talk later about your use of profanity, young man. Take your sister so the two of you can get washed up for dinner. Father, if it's all right with you, I'd like to hold off until after the children have eaten before we call the police."

I couldn't stick around to hear the rest of Sister's suggestion. I needed air, fast. The shit-heap smell was back, so disgusting it was making my head spin, had to get out the front door, before I fainted—

The circus is in town with high trapeze artists under buzzing stars and a full moon and a spinning carousel with kaleidoscope lights keeping time with an organ and Sousa's whipped us up a dandy down in the sawdust but it ain't all sawdust there's elephants and horses and straw and a bad awful smell and oh Jesus there's Heinie and ohnonoNO there he is he's DEAD oh Christ ohno Heinie's DEAD and all bloody and DEAD in the red sawdust on the floor.

"Wump—wake up, Wump."

Why, it's Father Duncan who's took me to the circus, and he's got a peppermint-flavored snow cone for me.

"Lift your head and drink more of this, Wump. Here."

Don't count me out, Ref, show me your fingers put 'em closer to my face

*see I'm getting up getting up right now at the count of eight
but wait, holy fucking Christ you ain't no ref
you're a priest! Oh Lord I'm dying—*

"Stay down, Wump. Just lie here on the grass a little longer. Sister's getting a cold towel."

I closed my eyes until things stopped spinning. "How long I been out, Father?"

"A minute maybe. You've got a hard head, my friend. You knocked out a loose brick on this stoop on your way down."

"Father, I—the last thing I remember…"

Father lifted my head again and gave me another sip. Jesus, was that hot going down. No wonder. Peppermint schnapps. Good as smelling salts. I touched the back of my head. Sure enough there was a doozy of a lump back there.

"You were complaining about a smell, Wump."

"Yeah. A smell. And—"

An image hit me. A sickening shot of a boy's face on a dirty floor, his, ah, his head split open, his whole forehead smashed in and open and…oh mymymy.

"I saw my kid friend Heinie on a sawdust floor, dead from a horse-kick to the forehead. It was like I was there, watching from overhead. But what I smelled was dog crap. His face and head were covered in it. Dog crap never made me gag before, ever."

"Tell me what you had to eat today," Father asked.

I heard the front door to the orphanage close. Sister Dymphna clopped down the steps with dripping dishtowels and some ice in a washcloth. She lifted my head and put a cool towel behind my neck, put the icy washcloth on my lumpy crown and placed my hand on it to hold it in place, then put the other cold towel on my forehead. That felt much better.

"I had half a piece of burnt toast for breakfast. I missed Viola at the house, so I didn't take lunch."

"That's it? A piece of burned toast?" Father said, shaking his head. "No wonder you fainted, stressful as today was. Three squares a day ought to be a staple for you, Wump. A man your size. Really."

Sister removed the towel from my forehead, and I could see a slight, caring smile push up her chubby cheeks. I never knew how these sisters managed to stay as up as they did in the face of the suffering they saw, dealing with all these sick and troubled children.

"So, when can I expect you to come by to repair this damage to our stoop, you big troublemaker, you?" she said, her smile still there. "See? Now there's more than one brick loose."

We'd all been pushed to the limit today. I hadn't had much to eat, and God was asking me to digest all this crap about a deflowered sister cut in half by a train, her bastard kids there to witness it. Hell, if Sister Dymphna was able to make light of circumstances like this, I could, too.

"How about I take care of that stoop right now, Sister? What, you think I can't? Got the tools right there in the back of my truck. Just give me a minute and I'll have all them bricks chiseled out for you and cleaned up, ready for the quick cement."

Sister and me shared a small belly laugh. I lifted myself off the grass onto one elbow and she helped me to another sip of the schnapps. Father chuckled too, but it seemed he was only humoring us because his mouth kept its smile and stayed open, even after he stopped laughing. He was eyeing my truck parked out front, and the puzzled look he was giving its low-riding, tool-filled rear end made me think something or other had just dawned on him. Either that or he wanted to head home pronto. I tossed him my keys.

"Here, Father, my head still hurts. Hope you can drive a stick."

11

Physically, I'm not like a lot of your other sixty-five-year-old males. First off, I'm in really good physical condition. My doctor told me I would beat the male lifespan averages by a decent margin. Second, I could still knock the living butt-squirts out of men half my age. Working at the tannery into my thirties and pushing around them heavy carts piled with cow and pig carcasses had bulked me up pretty good. God gave me big wrists and hands, prison boxing gave me the tools for using them and the confidence in knowing I could take a heavy blow to the head and still keep my legs and my wits. Most of the time, at least.

So, when Father Duncan said he wanted to drive me to the hospital, I told him if he did, I wouldn't get out of the truck when we got there. Sure, it was a concussion. So what? Boxers got a hundred of them each time they stepped into the ring, and I sure wasn't an exception.

"Just take me home," I told him. "Viola can care for me. She's done it before."

So here we were, Father grinding through the gears of my Willys, coming up on the church rectory where we'd need to make a right at the traffic light and then another right at the stop sign to my house in the middle of the block.

"Here, Father, I wanted to show you this." I pulled out a folded paper from my jeans pocket. "I found it in Sister Magdalena's room this morning." Father Duncan downshifted as we approached the traffic light, his footwork on the clutch better this time, the truck easing to a stop. I unfolded the test paper Sister Magdalena had graded. I put it between us, on the seat. "Tell me what you make of it."

The light changed to green and Father's hands and feet got busy shifting and foot-clutching and turning the steering wheel. One glance at the paper was all he needed. "It's a catechism test."

"Right. But look at what Sister wrote in red at the bottom after the last true-false question. It says, 'Forgive me, he is mine.'"

We needed to be at a full stop for him to do as I'd asked, and since we had only one more turn to make before we got to my street, Father held off looking at the paper. It was coming up on six p.m. Still some sunlight left, dusk not yet surrendered to dark.

It was past my suppertime but apparently not Father's, since I was hearing noise as we cruised by the side entry for Our Lady's rectory. Tinny, blaring music coming from the open kitchen window, near as loud as the school's PA system. Mrs. Gobel's radio. Which meant that, among other things, the rectory supper hadn't been served yet.

The side door to the rectory opened and out came Our Lady's young novice Harriet looking a bit flushed, a small laundry bag held tight to her bosom with both hands. Harriet was a dutiful young girl given to Mona Lisa smiles and few words. Wasn't really a novice yet but rather a postulant, or pre-novice, which meant that among other things she still had all her hair, a wispy auburn under a black veil, both veil and hair off her waify face because she was walking fast.

"Evening, Harriet," I called to her from the truck, trying to better Mrs. Gobel's radio.

I saw Harriet's lips move, but I didn't hear her because of the music. When she passed in front of the rectory's kitchen window, the wild rock 'n' roll piano playing stopped. Harriet flinched, her voice lowering so as not to be shouting.

"Pickin' up Monsignor's warsh," she repeated for me then raised the gathered white bag she was carrying by its drawstring so I couldn't miss it. I nodded to her just before she entered the back of the convent, managed a smile to go with it. The truck rolled to the stop sign.

"Monsignor's 'warsh,'" I repeated for Father, the hillbilly accent intentional. "Seems the monsignor don't let his dirty laundry pile up for very long, seeing how often he has her collect it for him."

For sure I wasn't as dumb as that comment made me sound, but Father's poker face said he wasn't taking the bait. After a few seconds I lost my patience.

"Look, in case you haven't picked up on it, there's a real problem here, Father. I don't know what the monsignor's selling, to Harriet or to anyone else, but he's for sure selling it through false promises, outright lies, and bullying, and taking advantage of his position just so he can get some jangle for his dangle, know what I mean? This girl comes from a poor West Virginia family. She's someone's daughter who's gone off to a place her folks probably won't never get to visit, to serve the Church and to obey God. She's as pure as they come, and she's fallen prey to this, this crazy, sonovabitchin' monster. Sorry for the language, Father, but you need to understand. The monsignor is ruining lives."

Father guided the truck onto my block, and now I saw Viola poking her head out from behind our silver aluminum storm door, looking anxious.

"Whatever stories he's feeding people," Father said as he pulled the truck curbside, "I don't think he sees them as lies. So maybe you're right. Maybe he is unbalanced. It happens to clerics as well as laypeople. You'll have to trust me when I say I'm working on it."

Before I could respond, Father added, "Remember, it's innocent until proven guilty. Works the same way with the Church. But the Church is going to send him a message I think he'll understand, and soon."

Viola came down our front stoop as fast as her arthritic joints could take her, calling to me every other step. "Johnny! Oh, Johnny! Sister Dymphna called about what happened. Are you all right?" Father handed me my truck keys.

"I'm fine, sweetie," I called back to her. "Another dose of aspirin and some supper is all I need."

Father was out of the truck a few seconds after me. "Sister Magdalena's note on this test paper," he said in a low voice before Viola got to the bottom of the steps, "tells me she may have fallen victim to Monsignor as well. With predictable consequences."

He tucked the paper into his jacket pocket. Sister's funeral Mass was scheduled for Wednesday of next week, and a number of Church dignitaries were expected to attend. Maybe Father and the Cardinal were going to do some talking beforehand, to work on this "message" for Monsignor that Father had just mentioned. His face turned pleasant as Viola clamped her hand onto my wrist. She gave me a hug.

"Told you I'd get him to stop by, honey. Viola, this is Father Connie Duncan, all growed up and filled out, come back to us here in Three Bridges as Our Lady's new parish priest."

Viola gave him a hug and they talked, but I wasn't paying attention. Father's last comment about Sister Magdalena and the monsignor had my mind all tied up.

"Predictable consequences."

Sure enough, her pregnancy was a real possibility. But trying to kill her own children?

What could bring a person to do that?

12

"Johnny, you have a visitor," Viola said, calling to me from the cellar.

Much as I never liked going back on promises, I'd called Mrs. Volkheimer to tell her I wouldn't be by her place to replace them boards on her bridge because I was still a bit hungover from the run-in with the orphanage's brick stoop. I figured to relax a bit and let Viola fuss over me. So here I was, lying on my living room couch at one o'clock in the afternoon on a Saturday with the television on, checking out what Gene Mauch's Phillies looked like this year.

I heard the squeak-squeak-squeak of my visitor coming up the wooden cellar steps, but when the squeaking stopped, I heard nothing else. After a few seconds I saw the side of a head with uncombed sandy hair inching its way around the corner of the dining room wall, then one eye, then a nose, then a mouth with its tongue showing, like it was about to take a swipe at a snotty upper lip, which it did.

"No need to pussyfoot around me, Leo." This drew him into the open. "A knock on the noggin was all it was. Come on in. You can watch the Phillies with me."

His face lit up at the mention of baseball. He gave me an *okay* but then caught himself.

"Er, maybe later, Wump. See, Mrs. Gobel told me the rectory's kitchen sink has got a rusted-out pipe that's leaking, so I got this pipe piece for it. Cost me a dollar seventeen." He pulled a two-foot-long S-shaped drain trap out of a brown grocery bag. Some screw fittings flew out with the pipe and scattered across the dining room's hardwood floor. "Oops..."

So much for a quiet Saturday. I popped two more aspirins and reminded Viola how bad it would be if she couldn't use her kitchen sink, then Leo and me hoofed it over to the rectory. No Raymond today, Leo said, because he was too sick to be outside. I reimbursed Leo his buck seventeen. He stuffed the money in his pants pocket then took to skipping next to me on the sidewalk. The boy was likely to hurt himself waving around a piece of pipe that big, so I relieved him of the bag.

Words and music by young Leo St. Jerome, catching his breath between skips:

"We'll watch the Phillies when we're done, Bunning, Short, and Callison.
"Watch the Phillies when we're done, Bunning, Short, and Callison.
"Bunning-Short, Bunning-Short..."

* * *

I was on my back in the rectory's kitchen, my head and shoulders and arms a tight fit inside the cabinetry under the sink, my butt on the linoleum floor. Not a good place to be for overhearing conversations from the dining room, which was fine with me, but with Monsignor shouting into the phone, I could hear most of what he was saying anyway.

"I am revered by my parishioners, Cardinal! They worship me. Yes, worship! And not in the way the bishop has those altar boys worship him. I know all about the bishop!"

Leo was here handing me tools, but he didn't need to be hearing this. "Son, get me the large pipe wrench from the tool box on the back of my truck. The one with the red handle. Now, please."

"Okeydokey."

Monsignor shouted again. "Cardinal, your administration is a disgrace. I will not forget this. I've been passed over—and pushed around—for the last time! You have crossed the line with your accusations. You don't know schuetten from Shinola when it comes to leading a flock. This is *my* parish, and Sister Magdalena was one of *my* parishioners. *I* should be the bishop's acolyte for her funeral Mass, not Father Duncan! I demand to know my accuser!"

Message delivered. Nice work, Father.

13

Sister Magdalena's funeral Mass was scheduled for ten o'clock on Wednesday morning.

It took until I saw Father Duncan in his vestments saying today's nine o'clock Sunday Mass for it to sink in. It must have been a struggle for this man through the first part of his adult life, a minor league baseball player waiting on a call to return to the majors who got a call from God instead.

As he raised his hands above the altar, his thumbs and forefingers together, his eyes closed in prayer, he readied himself to receive the body and blood of Jesus Christ, the Son of God. It was then I realized how we'd been deprived all these years, having to listen to Monsignor Fassnacht mumble through his Latin so fast the altar boys couldn't keep up, and us watching him make love to his wine-filled chalice like a wino does to a bottle. If there was a Catholic priest out there more devout to his calling than Father Duncan was, I'd never known one. And as I looked at the folks in the pews around me, I felt they sensed the same thing.

Today was Palm Sunday, the start of the holiest week on the church calendar. The Stations of the Cross would be on Good Friday, the Resurrection on Easter Sunday. It couldn't have been a more fitting week than the one in front of us for exposing a religious phony the likes of Monsignor Fassnacht.

Father Duncan addressed the congregation from the pulpit, asking for prayers for the parish sick. When he ended his list by naming Monsignor Fassnacht among them, there was a gasp. A hundred or more rosary-beaded hands went from lap to forehead almost on cue, all signing the cross. "Please," he told us, raising his palms to a church full of muttering parishioners, "it's nothing serious. Monsignor is just a little under the weather and will not be saying any of Our Lady's Masses today."

Physically, Father should have said. Nothing seriously wrong with him *physically*.

* * *

After a good Sunday breakfast of scrambled eggs, creamed chipped beef on toast, and a bran muffin for the plumbing, I dropped the news on Viola that I was headed out to replace those rotted boards on Mrs. Volkheimer's footbridge.

Mrs. V kept a stash of wood planking in a shed on the back of her property. The new planks stored there looked near as old as the originals, but the difference was they'd never been exposed to the elements or the wear and tear, although her bridge never got much wear and tear anyway. Only real traffic had been years ago, coming from her and her husband and their hired help. Over time this became just her and the help, then just the help, all of them using it to cross the river to either traipse off to church or into town, or to maybe deliver food donations to the orphanage. Of course, there'd been other traffic a long time ago, back when some of us kids would sneak across to get onto her property. Mrs. Volkheimer had dogs, and dogs meant lawn biscuits, and lawn biscuits meant money.

"How many need replacing, Wump?"

Mrs. V spoke to me from her back porch, sitting in a wicker chair with a blanket across her lap. She sipped hot tea from a glass cup, the tea with a hint of orange from the Tang mixed with it. I pulled the wood out of the shed, the planks near as washed out as the shed's weathered siding. Couldn't hardly notice her in that chair it was so tall, its fan-shaped back sprouting up and away from her, the chair made more for the likes of Cleopatra than for the hunched-over speck of a person Mrs. V had become.

Her sweet, dentured smile accepted another sip from the cup and saucer she held close to her mouth.

"Four boards," I told her. "Two on the walls, two on the floor. But we ought to do something about them overhead planks. The ceiling's sagging in spots."

"For my kids to worry about," she reminded me, smacking her lips together then patting her chin with a napkin, to clean up after some dribble. "The ceiling planks, the roof, and the storage space up there in between. The whole godforsaken bridge. They'll deal with it when they inherit this place. For now, let's just keep to the first floor so nobody falls into the drink when they cross the bridge."

I loaded the wood into the truck, put the truck into second gear and let it coast down the grass toward the river, a hundred or so yards from the back of her house. The path the truck took was the path a person would use on foot, since the rest of the back of her property was laid out like a garden, with sculpted evergreens and flowering dogwoods and manicured bushes, and every blade of grass in between as thick as a green wool blanket. I stopped the truck at the bottom of the incline, in front of the covered bridge's shadowed interior, at an angle that let me see the entire backyard garden from its southernmost point, plus the bridge downstream. Different color, the bridge downstream was, as was the one upstream, the other two in better shape, or at least their second floors were.

Mrs. V's gardener did a good job on her property, especially the back lawn. Fifty years ago, this incline had a few medium-size maples at its bottom, the garden covering only the area close up to the house. After she had the maples felled and their stumps removed, the incline looked near as good as them botanical gardens south of Philly that Viola and me used to visit once a year. This was the beginning of the growing season, so the tulips were up but not popped yet. When the flowers started filling in around the sculpted angels and crosses and Roman pillars, it could get just plain heavenly back here. I stayed in the truck a few minutes to take it all in, do some reflecting.

All the traditions of the Catholic Church, the sacraments, obeying the Holy Father, not eating meat on Fridays, I stayed with them mostly because they meant so much to Viola. Far as my adult life went, I'd been living on simpler terms. Won't never be able to explain it any better than the way I'd heard Abe Lincoln once put it: "When I do good, I feel good. When I do bad, I feel bad. That's my religion."

* * *

Creeeak. "C'mon, you splintery bastard, you should be loose by now."

There was no leverage, me leaning out the window with a claw hammer, trying to get under the old nails that held in the wood siding. I needed to try a different angle.

"Umph...Goddamn it—" *Creak-creak-creak. POP.* "Got you, you sonovabitch."

The second plank loosened up and came off same as the first, in one long piece, each the size of a small seesaw.

My elbows rested on the bridge's windowsill; I took a moment to appreciate the scenery upstream. The window was hardly ever open, the panes painted over in a barn red, same color as the walls. Hikers and tourists were the reason; mostly the reason, I should say. They'd sneak onto the footbridge, paying no never-mind to the *No Trespassing* sign, then snap pictures of the river and its scenic banks from its windows. The rumored second reason: Mrs. V once seen a floating baby body from this window.

What a nice view. Upstream the river bent a little right and gave way to the northernmost bridge, same two-story shape and size as this one but in a soft lavender. Farther up from that the river turned a hard left. The maples set back on the orphanage side were budding this time of year, and for this moment at least, the breeze pushing the hair off my forehead smelled clean as springtime in the mountains.

The river was a bit choppy, running fast, noisy; Lake Walapaken dam was open. They opened it different times of the year but more so in the spring, to handle the runoff from the winter thaw. If you put a canoe in the water when it was like this, you'd be out of sight around the bend in twenty seconds without paddling. Other times the water was as dead calm as a cup of cold coffee, and almost as black. It smelled better outside the bridge than inside, so I closed my lids and took a few more deep breaths.

"Hal-lo, Wump!"

I shielded my eyes. The call came from upstream, on the left bank.

It was Leo, in jeans and sneakers and a pullover hooded sweatshirt, a pile of tree branches next to him. He winged a branch into the river, slapped his knee in amusement. His mouth slacked open, and out came a hearty laugh that took near all his breath before it was done. One of his favorite pastimes, watching twigs float. He cupped his hands around his mouth. "Hal-ohhh, Wump! Here I come!"

Now the whole pile of branches was in the river, all of them tossed in together, and he was screaming with convulsive laughter as he ran and skipped along the bank, hurdling tree stumps and roots and dips in the grass until he got to the footbridge entrance. Inside the bridge tunnel and out of breath, he pushed between me and the open window and leaned his head outside. "Look—the branches! They're all going under the bridge. Ha-*ha*! Be right back, Wump!"

Leo scampered out the way he came in, and I could still hear him making a ruckus about them damn sticks as they came floating out from under the bridge. In less than a minute he was back inside, calmed down and looking over my shoulder.

"Fixin' the walls, Wump?"

"Yes, I am, son. And a few floorboards. Want to help?"

While Leo handed me tools, I learned that his best buddy Raymond was feeling more poorly than usual from the leukemia. Raymond would have some good days in between a lot of bad days, I told Leo. Just like my son.

"Raymond's just resting up," Leo said as he handed me some nails. "He wants to be strong for the end of the week. Sister Dimple's got us helping with the Easter pageant and other stuff." His lower lip quivered a bit. "He's been sick, so he just, like, you know, needs to rest up."

Oh my. Leo's eyes were misting; I patted him on the shoulder. "It'll be all right, son. Raymond's a fighter, I'm sure."

"Yep. A really good fighter, Wump. He just needs some rest is all."

We got to work and nailed the new wall planks in so they'd be ready for a paint job on some other Sunday after the weather warmed up. Time for the two floorboards. "Leo, there's a long pry bar in the back of my truck. Think you can bring it in here for us to pull up some of the flooring?"

"You bet!"

The pry bar was a bit heavy for him, his clenched teeth showing the strain while he dragged it inside the bridge. "Where you want it, Wump?"

"Hold on to it a second, son. I need to measure how much to saw off the new planks. Be careful."

I heard an *oomph*, and Leo now had the bar leaning against his shoulder like a pole-vaulter ready for his run. He grunted again, hoisting the bar off his shoulder and up, above his head and near the ceiling, getting ready to work the flattened pry tip in between one of the two floorboards to be replaced.

"No, son. Wait. I'll do that. Don't—"

Suddenly a puff of dust and wood shavings floated onto us from overhead, with the top end of the bar still rubbing against one of the sagging ceiling planks. He moved the pry bar away from the sagging plank but knocked it against a crossbeam. The beam loosened up some, then—*SNAP!* —one end of it swiveled a full foot away from the attic space, settling at an angle. More dust and dirt sprinkled our head and shoulders.

"Oops. Sorry, Wump."

The beam was still attached at the other end but had splintered and was looking real unstable. I pulled Leo back by his shoulders then—shit— two rotting beams parallel to the first one showed new cracks in them. "Stay back, Leo, those pieces are coming down—"

The ceiling beams groaned like a car door with ungreased hinges. Nails pulled free, then—

CRACK! CRACK-CRACK-CRACK!

A section of attic suddenly separated and crashed to the floor in a large rectangle. I had Leo by the collar, and we were out of the way, except...

Holy Mother of God.

"Who's that?"

"I—I don't know, Leo."

Time just sat still a moment, like in them dreams where you tried to move but couldn't. At the far end of the rectangle was a wooden kitchen chair that stood upright on all four legs, facing away from us, and by God there was someone sitting in it, fully clothed. Someone who all of a sudden was without a head as we watched it bounce and roll away from us until it ran out of floor at the bridge entrance, stopping upright on the grass outside. We coughed through the puffs of stirred-up sawdust now settling around us. This person had been dead a long time; what was staring back at us was a skull.

"I'm gettin' Sister Dimple!" Leo said and sprinted past the seated person and the skull, not looking back at either one.

Debris crunched underfoot as I stepped closer to get a better look. It was a man dressed for winter in a leather overcoat. The only parts of his body exposed were his hands, and there was no flesh on them. Something in his lap caught a glint off the angled sunlight. Something silver, something else gold. The gold was from the extended barrel of a spyglass, the silver from a small box no bigger than...no bigger than a...

Snuff box, because that's what it was. My God.

14

I'd been fooling myself all these years. A leopard can't change his spots except maybe for prison stripes. Fate had finally caught up to me, was about to make me pay for all the bad things I did when I was younger.

"Wump?" Sister Dymphna leaned over me, her voice cutting through the cobwebs. "Leo told me what happened. Are you all right?" Leo was behind her, talking to himself. Car doors squeaked open then thudded closed.

I was sitting on my duff next to a maple tree on the orphanage side of the river, picking blades of grass, lifting my head every few seconds to get another look. The fully clothed skeleton of Rolf Volkheimer, Mrs. V's husband, was just inside the overhang of the footbridge, seated upright on the bottom floor after having dropped a full flight from the bridge's attic storage. His skull was ten feet from his body, on the lip of the grass. There was a hole in the skull where a hole shouldn't have been, between his lower teeth and chin. He'd been sitting there in front of the window with a spyglass, his snuffbox in his lap, when the bullet hit him. I hadn't touched a thing.

Two bullets, the plainclothes cop said from a stepladder, correcting himself. They'd entered the side planking from ground level and to the left of the window, or so it appeared, the way he had a pencil angled through one of the holes. It knocked out a large divot of wood as it passed through.

Two bullets shot from a gun powerful enough to penetrate the wood, and from a fairly close range.

Two shots, he said. One missed, one didn't.

I remembered them shots. They came from a rifle.

* * *

...I leaned back against a tree beside the footbridge, away from the bridge entrance, watched the sun creep up over the ridge behind Rolf Volkheimer's house. I crammed my hands into my coat pockets; jeepers, was it cold. Only good thing about days cold as this was what they did to the dog shit, which was freeze it up so solid it made it easier to handle, except for when we had to use our penknives to separate it from the hardened turf.

My tater sack was on the ground in front of me, the top twisted shut. Heinie's haul wasn't near as good today, so he took off to scavenge the lower part of the Volkheimer property just across the bridge, the other side of the river.

Voices from the path behind me made me stiffen up. Men's voices, low and laughing, coughing, spitting, complaining in German about the cold. I nudged my sack out of sight, pulled it flush with me against the tree trunk, took small breaths. Too deep a breath in frigid air like this would give me away. The men were headed into the woods outside of town, to hunt for deer, rabbit, squirrel, any meat that could be used for a meal, or stock for a soup. I took tiny, sneaky steps around the tree trunk, keeping the tree between me and the voices; I didn't need to make no false moves around men with guns. The hunters stayed on the path. Their voices faded.

Whew; that was better.

"Got you, you filthy little bastard."

A large hand closed on my chest and pulled me away from the tree trunk, snapping me to my toes. It drew me up to the straggler's pockmarked cheeks, into his foggy breath.

"*Agghh*! Herr Zerhoffer!"

His face had welts, around the eyes and forehead, from the day I belt-whaled him, the same day his frostbit son nearly died. He sprayed me with spit as he talked. "Thought you could strap a man und get away with it, did you? I got news for you, boy."

"Owww. Lemme go."

"Now you'll pay for what you did to my face, und for what that meddling nun of yours is trying to do to my family."

Zerhoffer slung his rifle off his shoulder, lowered it behind him. With his free hand, he slid the belt away from his long wool overcoat and bunched the leather up so the metal of its large square buckle was at its tip.

"The Church," Zerhoffer said through gritted teeth, "took my first son, God rest his infant soul. They won't never catch me being so obedient again." He gave my chest another hard shake. "I don't much care for your Sister Irene throwing her weight around neither. Und her horseshit animal cruelty laws won't never make me give up my second boy, just so he can end up with the likes of you."

I caught my breath with a shift in his weight and quick got to swinging and kicking, my boots connecting hard against his shin. He winced, then the hand on my chest retightened and lifted, and I was helpless again, digging my nails into Zerhoffer's thick, factory-scarred knuckles. He slapped his belt once against his thigh, narrowed his eyes, then brought the leather back, readying for the first strike.

"Time for the strapping of your life, you little motherless sonova—"

Whap!

Zerhoffer's hand left my throat and went to the side of his head to stem the sudden pain. He spun around, groaning through a string of curses.

Whap! went Heinie's shit-filled tater sack again, hitting Zerhoffer flush in the face, the frozen dog turds whacking his nose bone with the force of a gunstock. A second later Zerhoffer's mouth and chin and neutral overcoat were a scarlet red, the blood gushing from his nostrils. He stumbled back, away from us, and Heinie readied the sack for a third blow. He got a running start, followed Zerhoffer around the corner of the bridge toward the tunnel entrance. I turned the corner. Zerhoffer was holding one hand up to his own nose and the other around Heinie's neck. Heinie's sack was spilled over, his hands both pulling at Zerhoffer's fingers as they tightened around his throat.

"Let him go!" I yelled but it didn't make no difference. Zerhoffer stepped toward me, dragging Heinie with him, Heinie's eyes now rolling to the top of his head. The prick bastard was squeezing the life out of my best friend... I had to do something—

Zerhoffer suddenly stopped short. Heinie's eyes were closing, but Zerhoffer's were now open real wide.

I steadied the man's hunting rifle, trained it on his chest. "Let him go. Now."

Zerhoffer released his grip. Heinie dropped to his knees in a coughing fit.

"Put the gun down, boy," Zerhoffer said, pleading into a hand-cupped mouthful of blood. "You don't want to shoot me—"

Oh, but I did.

"How's it feel to be really scared, you prick of a father, you?" I lifted the heavy gun to my shoulder, pulled the barrel up so it was eye level to him. "Put your hands up. Now!" His arms went up, the blood from his nose now dripping from his chin. I leaned my head in close to the rifle, Zerhoffer still bitching in between curses. I squinted into the rifle's sight.

"How 'bout I just shoot off some of your fingers? Then you'll know what it'll be like for your boy because of the frostbite he got. How 'bout I do that?"

Zerhoffer backed up closer to the bridge's tunnel entrance. I lifted the rifle barrel up higher, at his raised hand, tightened my finger around the trigger.

"No. Stop! Have mercy, boy—"

Crack! I fired the rifle and the bullet zipped past him, into the wood of the bridge. I steadied the gun again, making sure my second shot was raised high enough.

Crack! The shot clipped his pinky finger, and he slapped one hand inside the other, blood flowing from his knuckle like it was an open tap on a beer keg. He squealed then lunged at us. We stumbled out of his reach, scattered into the tunnel and across the bridge, one after the other. On the other side of the river I flung the rifle out onto the middle of the ice. The gun skittered and slid until it slipped through a hole near a rock, disappearing into the river.

* * *

"Both bullets had nowhere to go other than into the second story of this bridge," I told the police officer. "1911 was the year. Same year Rolf Volkheimer went missing. And he went missing because a careless kid shot him. That careless kid was me."

Poor Mrs. V. What would she think of me? What would they all think of me now?

Hearing everyone talking about this, the police, Sister Dymphna and all, this was going to make the papers for sure. Finding the skeleton of a man people thought had been kidnapped—on his own property—as wealthy as Rolf Volkheimer was back then, this would definitely be a news story. Poor Viola. And poor, poor Mrs. Volkheimer.

* * *

Kerm the Coroner waddled out of the bridge entrance, headed in my direction. He waved a police officer away. "I think we're about done here, Wump," he said. "You can leave now."

"What? You're letting me go?"

"Yes. Go home. Get some rest. You've been through enough today."

"But I killed Mr. Volkheimer. Weren't no kidnappers like they thought. It was me. Aren't you going to arrest me or something?"

"Listen to me," Kerm said, raising his eyebrows. A quick flick of his lighter and he was inhaling another cigarette. Now his other hand was on my shoulder and he was leading me away from the group, back to the maple tree, the one I hid behind the day I shot this man.

"They did find a slug sitting loose under the victim's coat collar. They'll check it out against what they can research on firearms from back then. And there do appear to be two bullet holes in the wood siding to the left of the window, both of them painted over. So yes, a slug from the rifle you shot could have put the hole in this man's skull. But what I'm hearing you describe here was an accident, and you were what, eleven or twelve years old? The DA won't be pressing charges. Not against an old-timer for an accidental death he may or may not have caused when he was a juvenile."

He pointed his cigarette hand at me, then at my truck on the other side of the river. "Look at it this way. You and your young friend here closed out what was probably the oldest unsolved crime on record in Three Bridges. Relax, get in your truck, and go."

Relax, hell. The more I learned about myself, the more I understood why the first part of my life was so hard. It was the anger. It kept me alive as a kid, and it made me a survivor, but I expect it guaranteed I stayed an orphan for as long as I had, too. Angry at being an orphan, and an orphan because I was angry. A sad waste of a childhood.

One last comment from Kerm after he flicked his cigarette butt into the river: "I almost forgot. About the wastewater from the cave-in of that sewer wall. You wanted to know what was in it."

"Sure do," I said. "Loaded up with harmful chemicals, right, Doc?"

"Well, yes, some chemicals were found. Sulfuric acid was one."

Damn straight. Rotted out iron pipes faster than road salt rusted car fenders.

"TCE, and PERC..."

I knew them abbreviations. They're short for hazardous solvents some factories used to dissolve grease and oil caked on heavy machinery.

"...and a copper sulfate called Blue Vitriol."

Another out-and-out, skull-and-crossbones poison. No industry upstream other than the Volkheimer tannery, and I used all them acids to clean the machinery when I worked there back in my twenties. So I knew. I fucking *knew*.

Wait. "What do you mean 'some,' Kerm?"

"Traces, is what they said. Not enough parts per million to get the authorities riled up. They're not looking into it any further."

"Jesus, Kerm, c'mon. You were at the restaurant site, just like I was." I felt my face flush. "You saw what the water looked like. That shit is making people sick. Kids. Adults. Unborn children, for Christ sake. What you saw came from the sewers, but it's in the well water, too."

Kerm gave me a sympathy shrug and shook his head. "Sorry, Wump. I have to go by what the authorities said."

That irresponsible, disease-causing, motherfucker Hughie Volkheimer. The bastard paid somebody off.

A commotion came from inside the covered bridge, a repeated ranting in Leo's excited, high-pitched voice. He hurdled the dust-covered jumble of snapped ceiling planks at the bridge's entrance, galloped outside and down the river bank, screaming and pointing into the center of the surging water, then skipping and screaming and pointing some more. Something bobbed to the dark water's rippled surface then went under again. Kerm and the cops who came with him started quickly toward the bank, tracing Leo's footsteps.

Relax, fellas. More floating sticks was all it was.

No. Wait.

"Look!" Leo shouted, pointing nervously at something that had just gone underwater twenty feet out. "Out there. I saw sumpin' float under the bridge. Look! There it is!"

A cop stripped off his jacket and holster and entered a river still rowdy from the extra flow of dam water. He waded up to his waist before the current slowed him down. When he was in as far as his shoulders he took a bead on what Leo spotted. The cop's head dropped below the surface. Another cop waded in. Fifteen to twenty seconds later the first one resurfaced. He raised a twig-snagged bundle of blanket eye level, above the water.

The first cop cleared his mouth. "It's a baby," he shouted, his shoulder leaning into the current. The second cop pushed ahead, rushed out to take the bundle then pushed his way back to the bank with it, handing it out of the water to a third cop. With each step closer to Kerm, the cop peeled more of the blanket out of the way.

I got a crush of terror so sudden it made my legs weak.

A skull, inside the blanket bundle. It was going to be bones and a tiny skull with moving lips, same as what me and Heinie fished out of the river more than fifty years ago, and in damn near the same spot. The fucking nightmares I had. Screaming, decomposing babies, soulless eyes, all hovering, groping, pleading. I'd be having them all over again. Please, God, no...

The cop handed the baby to Kerm. Kerm unraveled the rest of the blanket.

"His face and body, Doc," the cop pleaded, "they're already blue. He got a chance?"

The officer first into the river lifted his waterlogged legs onto the grassy bank. He doubled over at the waist, hands on his knees, coughing, spitting, then looked hopefully over at Kerm in time to see Kerm answer the other cop's question with a shake of his head no.

I let out a grateful sigh and hoped no one noticed, ashamed my prayer had been answered.

15

Kerm the coroner pronounced the baby dead on the riverbank, said the death would be investigated. The whole thing left me sick to my stomach, watching the police put the small body bag in a container in the rear of Kerm's station wagon, right there next to a longer bag with Rolf Volkheimer's fully clothed skeleton in it.

As disgusted as I felt already, I couldn't go home yet. Something else needed handling, and I needed to handle it now.

My truck chugged up the grassy incline and I circled it to the front of Mrs. V's house, the tires crunching the stones in her half-moon driveway. I turned off the key with the truck in neutral. It drifted to a stop in front of her porch.

It didn't make a difference if the authorities officially accused me of killing her husband or not, or that it had been an accident. Probably no way to prove it, but I knew it was me who'd done it. Back when I was a kid, when I heard about his supposed kidnapping, it choked me up pretty good. The man had been real kind to me, and accident or not, I took his life, so now I had to tell his widow.

Her oak front door was already open, the springs on the outer screen so old and forgiving, they didn't make any real noise when I stepped through. "Hello? Mrs. Volkheimer?"

Her sweet old voice answered me. "In the parlor."

She was seated in a tufted red chair next to a sofa, a photo album on her lap. Her head lifted to acknowledge me; she put the album on a table. She had a smile, somber but warm, and the tilt of her face said she was glad to see me. With some effort she pushed against the chair's padded arms to raise herself, then she started across the parlor without her cane, taking tiny steps. I should have met her halfway, but my feet weren't cooperating.

"Ma'am, I need to talk with you."

She arrived and reached up with both arms, her fingers wagging for me to lean down, and for one brief, timeless moment, I got the most comforting hug I'd ever had. I dug my hanky out of a trouser pocket, dabbed my eyes.

"I know you do, Wump," she said, squeezing my arm. "I've been watching from the back porch. How about we have some hot tea and Tang, hmm?"

Her kitchen door swung open two rooms away, and as her cook came through it with a tray, the smell of sauerkraut and pork was pulled in with her. Sunday dinner, Mrs. V told me, her daughters and their families expected at four. The place would be overrun with her children, and the children of her children, and their children, too. "And won't my family have a lot to talk about," she said, pointing me to a parlor chair.

She waited for her cook to leave. "Wump, before you say anything, you need to understand something."

"Mrs. Volkheimer," I started, knowing the only thing needing understanding was what I had to say, "I'm so sorry about what happened to your husband. That's why I'm here. See, one day when I was a kid—"

"I remember the day well, Wump."

She surprised me with this statement, but then again of course she'd remember it. It was the day her husband went missing. The same day the town heard how an orphan kid shot off part of a man's finger with the man's own rifle. But there wasn't nearly as much tongue wagging going on about me and Zerhoffer, considering its competition. And also considering that later on, Sister Irene had offered Zerhoffer a deal: I didn't get sent upstate to a home for incorrigible boys, and in return Sister dropped her complaint against him for abusing his son. And his boy made out, too. Her complaint put enough of the fear of God into the boy's father to set the man straight. That, and Sister's frequent unannounced visits to their place for some time after.

"Years later your incident with the man's gun came back to me," she said. Her damp eyes told me this memory was painful. "Why is it, might you think, I've wanted repairs to my bridge kept to the first floor? Hmm?"

After a few seconds thinking about her question, I got the chills. "You telling me you knew he was up there?"

She sipped her tea. "Rolf left on one of his infrequent trips to Deutschland, this one to help with the dispersal of a dead relative's estate. He was to take a train then board an ocean liner. *The Liberty Belle of the Atlantic*, out of Philadelphia." A far-off look crossed her face. "It wasn't like he was expecting any sort of monetary settlement from the will. Just planning to tie up loose ends on the other side for him and his brothers, Rolf being the oldest. And the most trustworthy."

Bet my wrinkled ass he was. The only trustworthy one. Hugh Volkheimer was the son of one of them other brothers. A businessman with no conscience.

"One of our wait staff boarded his baggage on the train so Rolf could attend Mass before his trip. The train was less than a mile down the track when it was stopped by men on horseback. Bandits. We had some of that going on back then, even around here."

"A train robbery?"

"So it appeared," she said, flattening out her cloth napkin on her lap. "They made everyone empty their purses and pockets, and went about asking all the male passengers for their names. Then they made four of the men, all Germans, get off the train. They also had a railroad employee find Rolf's steamer trunk in the baggage car."

I remembered this now. The men they pulled off the train had children. A few of them ended up at the orphanage.

"A note appeared in my postbox the next day. It said to put ten thousand dollars in gold coins in the last pew of the church, or they'd kill my husband."

"But he wasn't on the train, so how, I mean, why—"

"But his baggage was. The bandits had to think he was one of the men they'd taken, maybe figured Rolf wouldn't admit to who he was, given the stakes.

"I took the money to the church myself. Rolf was to be released the next day. The waiting was horrible. Every day I expected him to walk through the front door. Every day, for weeks. Oh, how I loved that man.

"A month or so later the police found three bodies inside Rolf's trunk in a cave in the northern woods, none of them Rolf. The fourth man abducted was never found. I turned on them. Turned on the police, the politicians, Rolf's brothers, even the Church. And I sued the railroad. Lost of course, but I didn't care. I caused everyone so much trouble, bitter as I was, the town wanted no part of me for years. The bandits were never found. A few summers after Rolf was declared dead, I went looking for things to donate to the orphanage. That's when I found his body.

"Funny thing is, no one smelled anything. A rotting corpse stinks to high heaven, but the weather had been heavy snows on and off, well into March. It's something I remember, the weather that winter. Had me wondering if Rolf could have been out there in it, a frozen body on a frozen countryside. Instead he was a frozen body in a cold attic. When the thaw hit in the spring, the stink of all the tanneries was there to disguise the smell. I went back into the attic space only once afterward, to paint over the windows."

Jesus. Fifty years he'd been up there. How could she have stayed quiet for so long? And for Christ sake, why?

"I don't understand, ma'am. Why not take his body down when you found him, if for nothing else, to give him a decent burial?"

Her eyes were still so clear for her age. I'd known this woman my whole life, and them blue eyes were studying me like a referee about to count out a jumble-headed boxer who didn't know enough to fall down.

"You were in your early twenties around when I found him, correct?"

That would have been right. Adding twelve or thirteen years to when I shot off Zerhoffer's finger would have made me around twenty-four. Fresh out of prison, and not too long after Viola and me were married. Mrs. V had just gotten me the job at the tannery. Life was starting to turn around for me.

Oh.

"I was already fond of you and your young wife, Wump."

"You left him up there because of me? You knew it was me who shot him?"

"As I recollected, Rolf went missing the same day you'd taken potshots at that fool Zerhoffer near the bridge, so I pieced it together. You had become a good and decent young man, Wump; I couldn't take the chance. They would have torn apart the bridge looking for evidence of foul play, might have sent you back to prison even though Rolf's death had been an accident. So I said goodbye to him, apologized for what I was about to do, padlocked the attic's trap door, and removed the ladder."

I was speechless. I swallowed hard, struggled to find my voice. "Pardon me, Mrs. Volkheimer, but"—out came my hanky again—"I'm so sorry about your husband. And I don't know what else to say other than thank you, so very, very much, for your kindness."

"Oh, hush. It was the right thing to do. As far as Rolf's burial goes"—she looked out the back window at the beauty of her manicured lawn and the three bridges—"before, now, later, it didn't much matter how it worked out, in my opinion. My will says to rebuild the whole bridge within a year of my death, so he would have gotten his Catholic burial soon after I had mine. It would have been romantic, don't you agree?"

What I was thinking was, unlike poor Rolf, I maybe dodged one of the biggest bullets in my life right there. I nodded.

Wait. There was something else.

"Here," I said, reaching into my jacket pocket. "I almost forgot." I extended my hand to her, Rolf's silver snuffbox in my palm. "This was how I knew it was your husband."

I saw her crinkled lips part slightly, heard the breath she took suddenly cut itself in half like a butcher had cleaved it. She looked at the snuffbox in my hand then raised her troubled eyes to greet mine. There was a fright in them so overpowering it made me think she was about to die right here and now.

"Mrs. Volkheimer. Are you all right? What's wrong?"

She turned her head in the direction of the parlor's overburdened fireplace mantle. Above it were hanged family pictures, many of Rolf. Grainy photographs of him as a mature man plus two painted portraits of the same. One showed him sitting in this parlor, holding the snuffbox on his knee. The mantle was cluttered with trinkets that ran its entire length, all except for a foot or so of empty space directly beneath his portrait, where something was missing.

"I left his body up there, entombed, in the bridge attic," she said, her lips trembling, "but I took his snuff box with me."

16

I had no natural explanation for this, other than maybe someone was playing tricks. She accepted my story, something she didn't ask for but I gave her anyway, that I had nothing to do with any snuffbox moving from her mantle to the footbridge to be reunited with its owner's remains. Mrs. V's gardener Horst and his wife, now they were possibilities. I knew she'd question them about it, but I could tell she was already ruling them out, too. No sensible motive, far as she could figure, and I agreed with her.

That left us to think about Rolf's spyglass. Mrs. V and me couldn't make head or tails about that neither, Rolf up in the footbridge's half-story attic space, looking out the window with a sea captain's telescope before leaving on his trip to Germany. It weren't anything of significance to her, the spyglass was, so with no fond memories attached to it—no memories of it at all, she said—she'd left it behind with the body.

I had so much stuff in my head from the past couple of days it was a wonder I could find my way home, but home was where I was headed, to do some catching up with Viola, and to eat my supper if I could stomach it. Dead babies and an old Bible that Father Duncan said was written by the Devil himself. Then there was our crazy, lecherous Monsignor. Make it two crazy monsignors, if you counted the one who ran the parish back when I was a kid. And a tannery that was poisoning the town but hadn't been found out yet. Finding Rolf Volkheimer's skeleton, and learning his beloved snuff box had joined back up with him postmortem by a full fifty years, this hadn't made things any smoother. Been a bumpy ride lately. Near as bumpy a ride as my truck was giving me right now. Had to be the clutch. One more block and I'd be home.

Rolf's view from the bridge's window back then would have been the tannery shanties to his left at say, ten o'clock, all since turned under and replaced by row homes; the fronts of Our Lady's church and school buildings straight ahead; and the orphanage property on the right from about one to two o'clock. Farther right of the orphanage had been, and still were, some vegetable gardens sharing space with tree swings for the kids, same as when I lived there, except now there were swing sets and metal sliding boards and see-saws, and a few stacks of them bone-jarring iron monkey bars. The side of the footbridge was where me and Zerhoffer first got into it, then he stumbled around the bridge's squared corner, me following him with the man's rifle, the two of us ending up where Rolf could have seen us for only a moment or two before I pulled the trigger.

Viola had a real nice Sunday supper waiting for me that I could smell as soon as I stepped through the front door. Corned beef and cabbage. One little problem with it, though: I gave up corned beef and cabbage for Lent. Hell, she must not have remembered so I wasn't gonna remember for her. I was hungry, and there weren't much that could stand in the way of me and corned beef and cabbage, least of all some made-up Lenten obedience vow.

Wait.

Wait just a goddamn minute.

Obedience.

Them babies got tossed away not because of town poverty; it had been a religious directive. Zerhoffer as much as said it the day I shot off his finger, talked about how the Church took the life of his first son. "Won't catch me being so obedient again," were his words.

I always had the Catholic Church pegged as a New Testament, Jesus-and-Mary-loving bunch of pleasant folks, but now I wasn't so sure. It must have been pure thou-shalt-not-disobey-else-you're-gonna-feel-the-wrath-of-the-Old-Testament bullshit that had made them people do what they did to their newborns. A test of their faith, maybe. Hell, what did I know? It still didn't make enough sense. Something was missing. The Church's "why." But one thing I did decide on. The Church told them parents they had to make this sacrifice. Christ, how could anyone have been so cruel?

I gave Viola a peck on the cheek, then a hug. "Honey, I need to call Father Duncan after we eat."

"But Johnny, you've been gone all day. Why on earth—?"

"I'll tell you about it over supper, sweetie."

Also figured to remind her of my abstinence vow for Lent, but not till we were done eating.

* * *

"Father's out at the cemetery, ja," Mrs. Gobel told me over the phone, me at home, her speaking above the racket the rectory's kitchen radio was making. She danke-schoened me for fixing the sink drain pipe yesterday. I danke-schoened her back for saying she'd leave Father a message, the message being I wanted to talk with him after Sister Magdalena's funeral on Wednesday. I also asked her if Monsignor Fassnacht was still feeling under the weather.

"Monsignor has been in his room since Saturday afternoon, ja. He has had visits from some frauleins. The ladies, they make him feel better, ja?"

Ja. They were making him feel much better even right now, the loud music told me.

* * *

It was after dinner and Viola was all up to speed on Rolf Volkheimer and how I shot him. It upset her some, knowing I took a man's life and there weren't a war involved. Still, she'd come to grips years ago with how violent my childhood was, and how I became a jailbird and all, so I got some leeway. She said to me, "You were only a child, Johnny. Mourn his death, but not your part in it." Now the TV was on; she had me watching Ed Sullivan, figuring it would calm me down. Which made it not such a good time for me to tell her some of my reasoning behind the infant deaths. She'd get upset about me picking on the Catholic Church.

I also didn't tell her how old I been feeling lately neither, and about how maybe I was slowing down some. Would never say that to her.

And for sure I didn't tell her how pissed I was at the city for ignoring what Hugh Volkheimer's tannery was doing, else she'd have seen clear through it and confronted me with some now-you-listen-to-*me* finger-raising, with her guessing I might be planning on doing something about it, and her being right.

Sullivan had the Italian mouse-puppet Topo Gigio on tonight. This would have me sawing wood on the couch for sure. And when the Sullivan show was over Viola would kiss me on the forehead then go off to bed, and I'd wake up in the middle of a loud snore like I usually did, sometime after ten o'clock was my guess.

Then I planned to go out.

* * *

The chisel felt like an icicle in my hand, chilly as it was down here.

CLINK-a-chip-chip.

There was once a part of me willing to do the right thing. Willing to blow the whistle and let the authorities handle the punishment. When we first learned Harry had the leukemia, I called the mayor's office and told someone on his staff that the water around here tasted funny. "My boy's real sick, and the water in this town is causing it," I'd said. I was told they'd heard it before, and "you ought to get yourself a water purifier, old man." No water purifier I knew of could purify this water.

CLINK-a-chip-chip.

"Don't the home's pipes rot out a lot?" young Leo said to me last month. Him and me were replacing a sink pipe in the orphanage kitchen, just like what I did yesterday in the rectory. His question got me to thinking: *well water.* The orphanage hadn't switched over to city water until a few years ago. My Viola worked as an orphanage housekeeper and housemother for more than fifteen years, left that job for the church housekeeping job, when she was in her thirties. She'd washed dishes in that water; bathed kids in that water. Drank it, too.

Five miscarriages she had during those fifteen years. *Five.*

CLINK-a-chip-chip.

There was a section of tannery property nothing grew on, maybe twenty acres, just above Lake Walapaken. Looked like a forest fire destroyed it, except if it had been a fire, some of the evergreens would have come back by now. Been a long time, thirty years or more, that it looked this way. Ever since Mrs. V's nephew Hugh got involved in the business. Yep, far back as when the bastard was just a tannery supervisor, deciding that dumping solvents and waste into trenches on the tannery's property was easier and cheaper than having it hauled away. Back then, it was legal because they didn't know any better. But it isn't legal now.

CLINK-CLINK.

CLOINK.

"Ouch."

Felt that one, iron mallet to iron chisel, all the way up to my elbow. Stronger than the bricks, this mortar was, no matter how old the wall.

I heard water running on the other side. Correction: cancer-causing, baby-killing, chemical-carrying sewage was what it was, on its way to the Delaware River. All it needed was a few more whacks and the wall would be weak enough, then I could go home to bed. Had to be getting close to one a.m.

CLINK-a-chip-chip, CLINK-a-chip-chip, CLINK-a-chip—

Crunch.

What was that? It came from behind me, around the bend. Crushed glass maybe, or gravel, under someone's foot. I turned and squared myself, my grip tightening on the mallet.

"Anybody there?" I strained to listen above the low rumble of water surging against brick as the sewage runoff slapped into the high wall to my back, me listening hard at the dark, underground silence that lead away from me. Hundreds of feet of empty cement tunnel darkness, so far with no indications. Then I heard something. Another crunch, followed by another, and another, and then—

Squealing.

I concentrated. Is it squealing, or screaming?

Squeaking rats came running at me, didn't know how many, a dozen maybe, and I dropped my mallet to pick up my nine-volt flashlight. They scattered back in the other direction. This storm tunnel was closed off on both ends, hadn't carried water for thirty years but hell, they were rats, and rats always figured a way in. Creepy little bastards. I picked up the mallet again.

CLINK-a-chip-chip, CLINK-a chip—

Crunch.

Shit, not again. "Look, you little fuckers, take a god-damn hike—"

"Wump." A distorted voice reached me from behind, nearly made my breathing quit. The voice echoed a second time. "You need to stop. Right now. Not one more blow to that wall. Stop. Please."

I turned to face a flashlight that blinded me. I nudged my work lantern with my foot, to direct it at the voice.

"Father Duncan."

I was a little less excited seeing it was the father and not them damn rats. "Guess I should say how nice it is to see you, Father, but I won't."

Father walked out of the tunnel's darkness, was in street clothes and an old baseball jacket. Right about then I figured he had a good idea of what I done to the brick wall in the other tunnel that led to the restaurant excavation site.

"Wump, please don't do this. Let the authorities—"

"Let the authorities do *what,* Father?"

"Go after whoever's dumping poisons into the sewers. Let someone else sort it out. You're an ex-con. There are bigger issues..."

"The authorities already know." *CLINK-a-chip-chip.* "It's in the groundwater, too, Father. But Kerm our coroner friend told me today they're not investigating nothing." *CLINK-a-chip.* "Hugh Volkheimer buries some of his tannery waste, pours the rest of it into the sewers. Pays someone to look the other way. Saves money because he doesn't haul it away and get it treated. Makes him rich. Makes all them SOBs rich. Makes innocent people—"

CLINK.

"...innocent young people like my son, Harry, suffer and die. And mark my words, Father. This is the reason there's been so many children born in Three Bridges who are either dimwits, deformed, or sickly. Or never got born at all." *CLINK!*

My blood pressure was up, my heart was in my throat. "That'll do it."

Six course of brick chiseled out, four bricks deep. The water pressure would take care of the rest.

"I suggest we get back above ground. So tell me, Father, what made you come looking for me, and why look here?"

No answer. Father looked at the chiseled mortar and broken bricks strewn on the tunnel floor. "Wump, you've done a bad thing. We'll call the water department to let them know. Maybe they can repair the wall before—"

"I ain't calling nobody. Forgive me, Father, but don't give me any of this two-wrongs horseshit either. I'm sixty-five years old. I'll be six feet under by the time the folks around here figure out how much damage has been done to their water. I gave them bastards a chance. This'll be payback and a message. *My* message."

"But I could help with this message, Wump. I could get the Church involved. The Church has a powerful voice..."

"You keep the Church out of this. You keep those crazy fuckers out of this!"

CLINK!

"Wump—"

"Tell me something, Father. You see anything else down here? No? How about more baby skeletons? They're here damn it, all bunched up at the other end of this cold, damp, unholy tunnel, against another brick wall. And there's more of them, in other tunnels, too. I worked on these sewers, back in the twenties when they were being rerouted. The construction company paid us not to say nothing. 'We're walling them off at both ends instead of filling them in. No one will know. Those skeletons are ancient history. Can't do nothing about them babies now,' is what they said.

"Goddamn the Church! They told these poor people to throw their infants away. Why would they do that, Father? Tell me! WHY, DAMN IT?"

"Wump, no more hammering—"

CLOINNNK!

"Oh no—"

A brick shot past my ear. I turned, and a gush of filthy brown water hit me flush in the chest. "Go, Father! *GO!*"

Loose bricks and mortar shot past our heads from behind us like red and white chiclets, their fragments bouncing off the cement floor until a tide of sewage collected them in a sudsy filth underfoot. We legged it around the tunnel's slight bend, the wastewater already near knee-deep and pushing us, my legs getting heavy as I swished through it. Father reached the ladder first but leaned back to drop a hand on my shirt collar. He pulled me in front of him, pushed me onto the first rung. I began the climb, Father on the rungs beneath me, and each time I slipped, he jammed his shoulder against my butt, propping me up and holding me steady until I regained my footing. Now the entire tunnel was a rising river, alive with waves of sewage and dead things and the stink of flooded cesspools. Near the top of the ladder I slapped a hand onto the sidewalk cement, ready to pull myself out. It was then I felt a rumble, growing quickly, the ladder shaking from a vibrating thunder hard as a subway platform just before a train appeared. I dropped down a step as my ears pricked up, and I froze. I knew what was coming at us from the other direction.

"C'mon, Wump, move!"

"Grab the ladder, Father, tight, and hold on!"

He did as I said then cocked his flashlight to the left, and for a second we were able to stare into the empty darkness at the other end of the tunnel, one side wall illuminated but not far, ten feet maybe, the light reflecting off the smoky wall's cement, the shiny brown river still gushing beneath us.

No. Please, no...

I heard them, could hear their tiny, innocent voices echoing at the other end of the tunnel, heard them screaming, heard them bleating like frightened, helpless sheep all crying out, all lost, and all forgotten, and—

They were moving, coming toward us, getting closer.

—and all unprotected and unloved and unsaved and—

The rush of screaming baby voices stopped, leaving us with a roar loud as a busy sewer in a thunderstorm. I lifted a soggy boot onto the next rung, about to climb again. It was then I felt a hot breath near my temple, no more than an inch away. I sensed a pair of lips as they moved to within a kiss of my ear, two suckling desperate lips whispering crazy baby-talk what wasn't really crazy, least not to me, no-sir no-how unh-unh, their message boring into me like a drill bit into plywood—

—unbaptized

—we're all unbaptized

—why, why, WHY—

We were slammed by a frothy tidal wave of backwash from the south, catching us between two wastewater surges with undertow that collided like surf crashing onto a beach. I held the ladder rails tight, felt Father still beneath me, his head jammed into the back of my legs, his arms wrapped around me and the rails together. My eyes and mouth were closed tight, trying to blank out the things nudging up against me in the water, bumping into my arms and legs, swirling around my head. When I felt a slight drop in water pressure I reached my arm through the open manhole a second time and pulled myself up and out of the tunnel, onto the sidewalk, the black, starlit sky overhead. I dropped a hand onto Father's shoulder and pulled at him as he fought his way up the ladder. At street level and out of danger, the two of us doubled over, hacking and coughing and erping our stomach contents onto the sidewalk like we each had bad cases of the taproom twirlies.

"Father," I said, still clearing my throat. "I won't never be able to thank you enough for your help down there."

"Forget it, Wump. Glad I was here." He shivered once, took off his red satin jacket now stained a mucky black and brown, tossed it toward the payload of my truck. "So where does this tunnel lead?"

Father mustn't have heard down there what I heard down there, else he'd have brought it up right about now. Then again I didn't suppose Father had nightmares about tiny skeletons of babies who weren't quite dead, their suckling lips speaking crazy messages to an old man who'd maybe gotten crazy enough to think they were real.

I was getting a chill like Father was. I motioned to the back of the truck, where there were clean towels and rags.

"Well, Wump?" Father said, pulling his shirttail out of his pants and shaking it. "How about it? Where does this tunnel go?"

"This one travels south maybe three blocks, ends at another brick wall on the other side of Schuetten Avenue." I pulled the truck tailgate down then tossed Father a dry bath towel from a metal footlocker, took a towel for myself. "The wall's about the size of a small billboard and fully exposed from the other side, at the bottom of a hill. You can actually see the wall from the road. It's where Schuetten Avenue sits atop an above-grade bend, before it snakes its way into Philly. As a matter of fact..."

I grinned before I got serious again. Father looked at me, asked, "What's so funny?"

"The wall *is* a billboard, Father. It's a sign, painted directly on the brick. The one that greets everyone entering Three Bridges from the south. You seen it?"

"I think so. It advertises a new restaurant."

"Exactly."

Until the storm sewer had been rerouted it ran both above grade and below it, as in a fully exposed stream in some spots and a tunnel in others, through a 100-plus-acre property that hooked up with the Wissaquessing River downstream, the property not worth diddly before the rerouting. Might take a few more thrusts like what just chased Father and me up the ladder, I told him, but mounting pressure from the rerouted wastewater would knock out most of them painted bricks in the billboard wall I was describing. Sometime in the next hour was my guess, if it hadn't happened already, with the sewage left to drain into those 100-plus acres that had become a cow pasture in the valley area below Schuetten Avenue. Then we'd have Hugh Volkheimer, scofflaw tannery owner, meeting Hugh Volkheimer, cattle rancher, I said to Father. The same Hugh Volkheimer who expected to use the prize beef from his ranch to make hamburgers for his first-ever "Black Angus Volkburger Restaurant," due to open next year, right here in Three Bridges.

One anonymous call to the FDA and it would be good fucking luck getting your beef certified, Hughie.

* * *

We were both toweled off and stepping into extra coveralls I kept in the truck for emergencies. So I asked Father a second time, "How did you know where to look for me?"

This section of the old sewers was so close to the Conrail tracks that, when they built the row homes that replaced the shanties, this strip had been left empty. At two in the morning, the only things moving out here were the rats and the stray cats that chased them. Still, much as everyone around town recognized my old Willys truck, for Father to have found me out here, he would have first had to know I was out this late, and second, the general vicinity to look.

"You could say I got a phone call," he told me, snapping the fasteners on the front of his dry coveralls, "but the truth is I was asleep, so I only dreamt there was a call, from a boy who sounded a lot like your young friend Leo. 'Wump needs help, near the train tracks' is what I heard, which startled me awake." Father dropped his muck-stained clothes inside the truck's tailgate. "So I jogged alongside the tracks until I saw your truck."

Father leaned over to look into the open manhole. I did likewise, saw nothing but darkness, but we could still hear the rumble of running sewer water. I was for sure certain he hadn't heard from no talking dead babies, else it would have come out with his dream right then and there. A few nudges from my soggy work boot and the manhole cover clanged shut, snug inside its iron ring.

"You think maybe Leo is, ah, you know, tele-whatchamacallit, like them Indian swamis?"

"Telepathic?"

"Yeah."

"I think he's an especially sensitive kid, Wump. And I think you and he have a very special bond. Beyond that, only heaven knows."

17

Wednesday morning; Sister Magdalena's funeral today. Spent parts of yesterday in a doctor's office for Viola's arthritis. That, plus she'd developed a hefty winter cough that wasn't letting go, so she had some tests done. We spent the rest of the day at our house getting ready for the Easter holiday. Viola made me dig out her cardboard ducks and posters and ceramic bunnies from the basement so she could arrange them around the house and decorate the front lawn like she did every year. I tried talking her into leaving Harry's Easter basket packed away but she wouldn't hear of it, so three baskets sat on the dining room table, ready for the Easter Bunny, making like this year was no different. They say the first year after a person's death is always the worst for the survivors, each holiday a reminder that the person is gone. Viola being so Catholic, and this first holiday being Easter, well, this made it a little tougher.

Our Lady of the Innocents Church holds about six hundred people. Today it was full up, standing room only for the sister's funeral Mass. Viola and me were in the third pew, sitting with the parish sisterhood, with nuns from other parishes in pews behind us. She was knee-to-knee with Sister Dymphna, their rosary-beaded hands intertwined with each other, their fingers pressing each bead for the moment it took to finish another Hail

Mary before moving on. Behind us were the grade-school kids, St. Jerome's orphans included, the ones in wheelchairs at the end of each pew.

Leo and Raymond were side by side in pew and aisle. It was good seeing this, knowing how sick Raymond had been lately. It wasn't so good seeing Adam, back in the last pew of school kids, whispering and cracking smiles with the eighth-grade boys. Must have been easy come, easy go for him when it came to mothers. Behind the kids was the rest of the congregation.

In front of us in the first and second pews were monsignors, priests, and sisters from other parishes, plus a few diocesan big shots. The cardinal didn't come, a bit too frail to attend in person. I admired the cardinal; took real balls to replace Monsignor Fassnacht with Father Duncan as the bishop's acolyte for Sister's funeral today. The congregation knew no better, had been told Monsignor Fassnacht wasn't assisting because he was still too sick. Amen to that, in spades.

The interior lighting of Our Lady's church always reminded me of those dancing water fountains people see in newsreels on the Las Vegas casinos, where the water was lit from underneath by colored spotlights that exploded upward against a dome of darkness. The church's smooth plaster walls curved near its rounded ceiling, their white giving way to a soft sky-blue. Paintings in flowing reds and yellows and peaches showed saints ascending to heaven in firecracker starbursts, ushered north toward the pearly gates by tiny winged cherubs in swaddled cloth, the gates guarded by large archangels robed in silver and gold.

Back on Sunday night, with Father Duncan and me sitting in my truck before we left each other's company, the two of us in clean coveralls but both still smelling pretty ripe from the sewer, Father knew how upset I was. About the tannery, and the baby skeletons, and Sister Magdalena's death. He'd promised me he'd find some answers, then told me he learned something important the past few days.

"It has to do with those newborns," he'd said. "I think all of them were boys."

* * *

Sister Magdalena's service was over, her graveside cleared out except for me and Father Duncan, her casket suspended above its final resting place. I looked to where Father was pointing.

"The section of the cemetery back in there," he said, pushing the palm of his hand out like he was opening a swinging door, "and farther on up the hill, is where every Catholic from this parish who died during that period was buried."

The mourners trickled out the cemetery gates on foot, in cars, some in small school buses. My Viola waited patiently in our truck, her homemade angel food cake on her lap. Our last stop would be the parish convent, where the mourners had been invited for coffee and tea. I'd leave soon, as in soon as I could get a grip on what Father Duncan was explaining to me, and at the moment he had me looking out over a rolling sea of crooked old cemetery headstones.

"What isn't back there," Father said, "are graves for the infants noted in the death announcements you showed me."

"From Mrs. Volkheimer's Bible?"

"Yes. No record of their funerals either. There are only records of prayers offered on their behalf, with 'Male Baby' noted in place of a first name. I found prayer offerings for a number of other newborns with the same first-name notation, bunched into the late 1870s, '80s, and '90s, all who died the day they were born. It's as if a plague had the town in its grasp. A plague affecting newborn boys only."

"A plague manufactured by the Catholic clergy, Father."

"C'mon, Wump," he said, frowning. "Ease up on the Church, okay? We're on the same team here."

"Yeah, but what they done back then—"

"Look, we don't yet know what happened. You're speculating based on fifty-year-old childhood memories. There's a lot of room for interpretation."

"Fine, Father." But I wasn't wrong, and I was sticking to my guns. "So how many was it who died the same day they were born?"

A light gust of a warm wind pushed the hair off Father's forehead, a break in the cooler weather we'd seen so far this April. The weatherman said it would get hotter through the rest of the week, maybe set some records. Father answered me. "There were prayer offerings for one hundred and twenty-four children in less than twenty years. That's a lot of prayers for dead children for a town small as this one was back then." His eyes went distant; they narrowed as the wind brushed us again. "Yet I found only fifteen grave markers for them."

Had to be the ones who died from natural causes and made it to the graveyard, which we agreed on. I didn't need to ask where the other one hundred and nine went; we both knew. One thing I did need to ask. "So how about their baptismal records?"

Father's head bobbed a few times. "I asked myself the same question. The fifteen buried in this cemetery," he spoke as he watched the last car leave through the gates, a chauffeured black Cadillac, the bishop in its back seat, "were all baptized in this parish. I could find no baptisms recorded for any of the others anywhere throughout the diocese."

No Catholic baptism, no burial in a Catholic cemetery. That was the rule, no matter how good a life a person led. Abe Lincoln, a friggin' president of the U.S. of A., and the man whose religious ideals I lived by, couldn't have been buried here; he wasn't Catholic. Hell, based on this reasoning, Our Lady of the Innocents, the Blessed Virgin herself, wouldn't have qualified either, and it was her church.

"You find it odd, Father, that all them infants died before they could be baptized?"

"I can't speak for the times back then, Wump. There could be some practical reasons why a child with Catholic parents might not have been christened, although to not christen them—"

"Yeah. To not christen them," I said as one baby came to mind, my insides suddenly turning, the echo of long-ago and not-so-long-ago screams ringing my ears for an instant. "That pretty much slams the gates of heaven shut right in front of their little faces, now don't it? Or so the Catholic religion teaches. So I've got a new theory for you, Father. Want to hear it?"

"I'm open."

Viola was giving me the cold stare from the truck. I needed to be quick. "Here it is: the Church refused to baptize them."

I let Father chew on this for a moment, except what I got from him was pretty much a poker face. I continued. "I figure the crazy monsignor pastor back then thought there was something wrong with all them infants, so he refused them the sacrament. Might also be why Sister Irene and him didn't get along."

I checked on Viola again. She faced forward now, knew I was looking at her, was giving me her profile only. "I've got to get Viola over to the convent, Father. This theory make sense to you?"

"I think it fits too easily with your contempt of the Catholic clergy, Wump. Again, speculation but no hard evidence."

"Evidence? The Church, I figure, knew all about the lunatic monsignor and kept quiet. Except for, like I said, Sister Irene. She had run-ins with him all the time. Maybe she had the goods on him. I got to get going, Father. See you at the convent?"

Father reached through a separation in his vestments, into his pants pocket. "I hope to be there. Here, take this. I have a favor."

It was a folded piece of loose-leaf paper. I opened it, saw a column of hand-printed names with dates next to each of them.

"These are the names of the fifteen infant boys who are buried back there—the ones who did get baptized. Look them over and let me know if you can tell me anything about them or their families."

18

A convent was normally a dreary place to be most days of the week, for me at least, but only because it was too quiet. Plenty of times I been here fixing things, hammering this, tightening that, where some of what I was working on didn't cooperate, so I'd let go a little swear word or two because I couldn't help myself. Cripes, you might have thought I cursed out God in church with a mouthful of hamburger at three o'clock on Good Friday the way those nuns would come at me, wagging their fingers then blessing themselves so I wouldn't burn in hell.

I was in the convent's long dining room, could see Viola in the adjacent kitchen, a flowered apron on. She was slicing up her angel food cake and putting it on paper plates, helping the sisterhood serve the funeral-goers who'd stopped by to accept their offer of hospitality. Been maybe forty parishioners come through already, give or take.

Funny thing about poor Sister Magdalena: she never threw stones. There was this one time I let go a granddaddy of a curse when I was working on a second-floor toilet. I stuck a screwdriver in my finger trying to hammer out a stubborn rubber flapper inside the tank. It drew blood and cracked the toilet porcelain at the bottom; no way the tank could hold water after that. What came out of my mouth was a real showstopper, something like "holy fucking Mary fucking Mother of God." I hadn't realized Sister Magdalena, rest her soul, was passing by in the hallway. The swearing stopped her in her tracks outside the open bathroom door. I figured I was in for a good scolding and pulled my bleeding finger out of my mouth to deliver an apology, but she'd already done an about-face and returned to her room. It happened one Saturday morning, I recall, because it took me most of the day to replace the toilet tank, and the whole time I worked on it, Sister stayed put behind her closed door. I felt horrible about it and was first in line for confession that afternoon.

"You look very nice today, Wump," Sister Dymphna said. She was complimenting me on my black church-going suit and my combed hair. "Would you like a refill?"

Sister took my empty cup and saucer, returned in a few minutes with a serving tray. Fresh cup of coffee for me, some steeping tea for her, and two pieces of Viola's cake. We moved to the parlor and sat.

"She's finally at peace," Sister said. "Peace, thank heaven, for her tortured body and soul. God in his infinite wisdom will have mercy on her."

Sister shocked me with this comment. Just to make sure I'd heard her right, I gave her a chance to change her words. "You mean tortured like in some kind of mental illness, right?"

Sister gave me a sly look and returned her cup to her saucer, looked left then right before answering me in a low voice. "He played with her faith, Wump, and counted on her vow of obedience, and her willingness to sacrifice herself on its behalf. He also convinced her of something else that, on the face of it, sounded so utterly ridiculous, but to a young Venezuelan novice who spoke and read little English when she first arrived in the States—a person who had vowed to dedicate her entire life to Christ and the Church—it was more like a dream fulfilled." Sister shook her head. "He convinced her the Second Coming of Christ was imminent, and she could be the Mother of God. He even showed her passages from the Bible where he claimed this was written. He's mad, you know."

Monsignor Fassnacht. You sick, sick bastard.

"So our young Sister Magdalena became pregnant, with twins," Sister said. "Adam and Ruth were delivered by cesarean section, the procedure arranged as a favor, then kept quiet by a doctor at Nazarene Hospital. Then

Sister gave both children to me, to care for them in the orphanage. Over time her depression grew, pushing her toward her own madness."

"But Sister," I wanted to say this gently, in case she didn't know, "I think Sister Magdalena, ah, that is I think she and the monsignor were still, ah…"

Truth was, Sister Magdalena went back. I seen it, on a regular basis. The same as what Father Duncan and me seen yesterday with Harriet the postulant leaving the rectory. Mrs. Gobel's radio, blasting that rock 'n' roll music so the old cook couldn't hear what was going on upstairs, and Sister Magdalena taking out the monsignor's wash afterward, same as Harriet did regularly now. It had begun again, this union between Sister and her tormentor. Went on for months; didn't stop until around the time Harriet showed up.

"Yes, they were together again, I know," Sister said, lowering her voice some more. "It started back up as a kind of blackmail, you could say. Monsignor is on the orphanage's adoption approval board. The last hurdle for clearing prospective parents interested in children at St. Jerome's. Adam's and Ruth's adoptions were in Monsignor's hands. There aren't many chances left for children their age to find a family."

"Blackmail? Like in the movies?" This was pissing me off. It was going on between priests and sisters—*holy* people, for Christ sake—in a convent and a rectory. Places you'd expect were protected from crap like this. "So you're saying Sister started back up with the monsignor because he threatened to reject the adoptions?"

Sister Dymphna put a finger to her lips to quiet me down then she stared, sizing me up like she was deciding which way to answer. "On the contrary, Wump," she said finally. "Sister did what she did because the monsignor threatened to approve them."

Back when I was a kid, getting adopted meant you had at best a fifty-fifty chance at a better life, but that was decades ago. Nowadays there were jobs enough for everyone, and money enough, too, for raising families. The country was loaded with optimists, all wanting to see the USA in their Chevrolets. So it had to be hands-down better for an adopted child to be raised in a new family instead of in an orphanage. Just *had* to be. "Why wouldn't she want them to get adopted?"

Sister Dymphna took the last bite of her cake; I hadn't touched mine yet. "Sister did want them to find adoptive parents," she said, "just not the parents being considered. They're wealthy Europeans. Old country German, actually, and new to the US. They were highly recommended by Monsignor. She saw something sinister in that. As for me, I came down on the side of knowing it was the last chance for the two of them. And as smart as Adam is, he'd surely get a good education with this family."

I agreed with Sister's logic, except it made me feel worse about Sister Magdalena's state of mind as she neared the edge. "Any idea what Sister would have done once she got out of Three Bridges with the children? Desperate and, you know, as depressed as she was, and them on the run? As needy as Ruthie is and as nasty as Adam can get, it would have been real difficult for the three of them."

"No, I don't. But I must say I think you're too hard on that boy, Wump," she tsk-tsked. "Adam's a born leader who's going to make a real difference. His prospective parents think he's entirely engaging and mature beyond his years. And they also believe they can be of developmental assistance to Ruthie, too, as she gets older. Look, I agree Adam may be a little emotionally scarred by all these goings-on, but with the right encouragement I expect he'll straighten out. Which brings me to another topic: Have you gotten those things together for us for Good Friday?"

I caught a glimpse of two smallish hands reaching for the last two paper plates of Viola's cake on the table in the dining room. I craned my neck to see who had spirited them off, but I was too late. "Sure, Sister. It's all in the anteroom next to the church sacristy. Play swords from the five-and-dime, some old broom handles I fitted with spear tips I made from cardboard; the centurions are pretty much all set. And I nailed some scrap wood together for the cross, so all the props for the Stations are ready. The cross should be light enough for a small kid to carry."

"We won't be pressuring any of the younger children with that burden, Wump, but I'm sure it will still be fine. Thank you for your help."

"My pleasure. So who's playing Jesus then?"

"We thought it would be a fitting gesture," she said, eyeing a new mourner entering the parlor, "for Adam to do the honors, since he's an eighth-grader and he's leaving us."

Adam? As the crucified Christ? I wanted to say "It'll be your funeral,

Sister," but for once I kept my mouth shut. Sister excused herself and left to greet the new guest.

I took my cup and saucer over to the dining room window to finish my coffee and work out the Adam-playing-Christ scenario in my head. Outside on the convent lawn was Leo, a paper plate full of Viola's angel food cake in his hands, leaning over Raymond in his wheelchair. Leo broke off small pieces for his buddy, fed them to him and took some for himself. Raymond still looked peaked, but the past few days his cheeks had started showing a touch more color. The two boys finished up their cake, Leo pushing the last few crumbs into Raymond's mouth.

19

Father Duncan's list of the fifteen infants buried in Our Lady's cemetery in the late 1800s had a number of surnames I recognized. Common German family names like Schmidt and Huber and Werner. The phone book was loaded with them and so was this town, but I was in luck. The list also had the name Goode on it, and Three Bridges had only one Catholic family with that last name, so I wouldn't need to waste any more of my Wednesday playing detective. I was plenty busy otherwise, getting the church ready for Easter.

The Goodes lived one blacktopped street and one concrete alleyway away from Viola and me. There were two kids in the family: the parish baseball team's little shortstop Sonny, twelve, and his younger sister whose name I couldn't remember, but I knew was in the first grade. It was four-thirty in the p.m.; prime after-school playtime for the kids in the neighborhood.

I traipsed down the middle of the doublewide cement alleyway that separated the back yards of one street from the next. A purring car engine approached me from behind; I moved to the side, the car creeping by so close the driver could have picked my pocket. That was how these row homes and alleyways were set up, block after block of attached brick and stone houses, two stories of living and sleeping space above ground level

concrete basements and built-in single garages. Waist-high black iron rail-
ings separated the backyards, each yard with a narrow patch of grass side
by side against rectangles of cement driveway no wider than the family car.
Mrs. Goode was rescuing her wash from the tangles of her spiderwebbed
overhead clothesline. Little Sonny and his slow cousin Teddy Agarn sat
cross-legged underfoot of Sonny's mother, not far from the garage door.

Mrs. Goode threaded her way around them while she pulled her bed
sheets off the line. She folded the last one as I entered the yard, placed it on
top of the other clean wash in her laundry basket. With the sheets and
Sonny's mom out of the way, the boys raised themselves to a knee on the
hard driveway. It was a pose I recognized: they were flipping baseball cards.
The one with the closest flipped cards to the garage door got to keep both
cards. Teddy's card pile was larger than Sonny's.

"Got a minute, Mrs. Goode?"

The sun had dropped below the flat roofs of the row houses, but was
still half visible over my shoulder. She shielded her eyes like she was
saluting me; I stepped to the side so the sun was out of her face. "Mr. Hozer.
What brings you by today?"

"Sorry to bother you, ma'am. Our Lady's new parish priest sent me
over."

"Father Duncan? If this is about Sonny skipping baseball practice,
Father will need to talk with one of the sisters. He was asked to stay after
school with a few of the other altar boys. He's serving the High Mass for
Easter this year."

"It's not about that, ma'am. Father wanted me to ask you something
about the Goode family tree, if you don't mind."

"The family tree?" Her eyebrows tented. "You'll need to come inside.
I've got a casserole in the oven. Now why on earth would Father be interested in the Goode family tree?" she said to herself, me tailing her into the
basement entry.

The laundry basket stayed in the basement. I followed her up the
narrow steps into her kitchen, where she pulled a bib apron off a hanger in
a small pantry closet, looped the front over her head, and tied off the
middle around her waist. She grabbed her oven mitts; the casserole came
out of the oven, was left to cool on the range top. She craned her neck

toward the screened double window over the kitchen sink. "Sonny!" she called to her boy in the backyard. "Let me know when your father pulls in."

Mrs. Goode wasn't much taller than a bar ledge in a taproom, a fair bet why little Sonny was called Little Sonny, since his father was near six-foot. One thing about her son's genes, though. They gave a good account of themselves in the arms, wrists, and hands department. I seen this kid throw and hit a baseball. Amazing. The rest of his body would hopefully catch up.

"My side of the family hails from Reading," she told me. Some strands of her chestnut-brown hair dropped into her eyes. She blew them out of the way, went after a bobby pin not doing its job above her forehead, then spoke with the pin clenched in her teeth until she'd gathered her hair up and reassembled it. "But the Goodes have a long history here in Three Bridges. As far back as, well, I don't really know when. Since before the Revolution, I think. So what's got the new Father interested in the Goode family's ancestors?"

"Your husband's parents—they still alive?"

"Just the elder Mr. Goode. He's in his late sixties. What's this all about?"

So far so good. Now for a little fib.

"Father Duncan's been looking at the oldest parts of Our Lady's cemetery, checking to make sure every grave is still properly marked. How many brothers and sisters does your husband's father have?"

"Hmm. My father-in-law. It was a big family. Let me think." There was noise outside coming from under the kitchen window, Sonny calling to his mother.

"Okay," she said, ignoring him. "I think this is right. He had six older brothers and two older sisters." Her finger tapped her lips. "Wait..."

More noise from the back yard. *"Mom!"*

"I hear you, Sonny," she called at the open window. Her nose crinkled. "Now I remember. It was eight brothers. Six were older, making Gramps lucky number seven, then there was an eighth. Two of them died young— the first and the last—the first one, I recall him mentioning, born the day President Garfield was shot. Only three of the family's ten children are still alive, Gramps and his two sisters, who all live in Conshohocken."

"MOMMY!"

"Pipe down, Sonny. Dinner's ready," she called out the side of her mouth. "Get in here, and bring your father with you."

"It's not Daddy, Mom," Sonny said in a cracked, little boy's voice. "It's Uncle Dwayne."

Mrs. Goode slammed her wooden spoon on the counter, pulled open a closet door and grabbed a straw broom. "Not up for any of his antics this afternoon," she said. "Sonny's uncle got pink-slipped from the tannery. Now he's drinking all day." She hustled down the steps to the basement and out the back door, me on her tail.

Dwayne Agarn had his large son Teddy by the scruff of his neck, hauling him out of the Goodes' driveway, baseball cards slipping from the boy's hands. Teddy was the same age as Sonny but size-wise towered over him. Teddy was also maybe an inch taller than his old man. Heavier, too.

"He's eating with us tonight, Dwayne," Mrs. Goode said. "I already cleared it with his grammy. Let him go."

"You'll be needing to clear things with me, not his grandmother, from here on in," Dwayne said, slobbering some. "The boy's got chores. I said let's go, Teddy, you lummox, you."

Little Sonny ran up next to his cousin and tried to slip Teddy's baseball cards into his chubby hand. His uncle wheeled and clamped onto his nephew's wrist. "Get lost, Sonny. Go eat your momma's dinner."

Sonny ignored him, moved the cards from one hand to the other, strained while trying a second time to pass them to Teddy, and now the three of them were moving in fits and starts in a circle, looking like a dog chasing its tail. Then Sonny's knees buckled. Dwayne was applying more pressure to his wrist.

"Owww, Uncle Dwayne. Teddy's cards...!"

Enough of this bullshit; someone was going to get hurt. Mrs. Goode and I reacted at the same time, quick-stepping toward them. Little Sonny dropped to one knee, cards slipping through his fingers. Mrs. Goode closed in with her broom as Dwayne hovered over her son. Sonny stretched his reach, a few cards still in his hand; more pressure to his wrist. He squirmed, then suddenly—

Dwayne's arm was whipped behind his back and bent upward, toward his shoulder; he squealed like a woman in labor. The oafish Teddy closed his big chubby hand around his father's fingers, pushed them and his arm in a direction they shouldn't go, up into the shoulder blade.

"No hurting Sonny, Daddy," Teddy said grimly. Dwayne's face started losing its color.

Sonny got to his feet, quickly collected the scattered baseball cards. Teddy released his father's arm, and Dwayne cradled it up near his shoulder, doubling over some at the waist, trying to catch his breath. He coughed then spit onto the alleyway cement. When he straightened up, his eyes were wide and round and terrified, like a nightmare had spooked him. The expression on Teddy's face was near the same; the crotch of Teddy's tan chinos darkened. Sonny handed him his cards. Teddy disappeared in a hefty trot up the alleyway, around the house at the end of block.

"Just so you know, Agarn," I said, the boy's father still recovering, "I taught him that move. Wasn't none of your son's doing. It came from me and me only. Taught him it just so he could handle them school bullies who been picking on him. You get a burr in your saddle about this, you see me, not him, understand?"

Dwayne Agarn was still coughing, the back of his hand swiping at his lips to clear them of spit, his other arm limp at his side. He steadied himself on feet spread for balance.

"Stay the fuck away from him, Hozer," he said through a raspy breath. "You're as loony as he is, teaching him all that senile old John L. Sullivan–boxing bullshit. You stay away from him, you hear?" Agarn staggered away, down the alleyway, same direction as his son.

It weren't from no boxing lesson was what I wanted to say, but I didn't. Pure Saturday afternoon Gorgeous George wrestling was all it was, something Teddy must have picked up from the TV. But it was better for Teddy that his father thought I taught it to him. Much better, for the both of them.

Mrs. Goode checked out her son's wrist then nudged him in the direction of the back door. "I've got to get back to my dinner. What I told you about Sonny's grandfather's brothers—is this what the cemetery records show?"

I fumbled inside my pocket for the list from Father Duncan and made a quick sweep of the names. "Yeah, I think that's right. Thank you for your time, Mrs. Goode."

* * *

I'd lied to her. President Garfield was shot in 1881. We just got through hearing all about him and President Lincoln again this past November when our beloved John F. Kennedy was assassinated. Father Duncan's list showed a grave marker for the last of the Goode brothers, the one who died in 1899, but nothing in 1881 for what would have been the firstborn.

Hell, there it was again. 1899. The last Goode boy was born the same year as me. And the same year the orphanage was rededicated, according to that old photograph of Sister Irene and Rolf Volkheimer and his wife.

Hold on.

I stopped in the middle of the block, dug deep into my workpants pocket to pull out Father's list of grave-marker names, snaked it out without losing any screws or nuts or hardware receipts. The wind kicked up a notch, a summer-like gust from the warming trend Viola told me was coming; made me hold the loose-leaf paper with both hands.

Mrs. Volkheimer was pregnant with her first child in that old photograph. Born in 1899, died the same day according to them German death announcements she kept with her family Bible. But her baby's name wasn't on this list, which meant there was no grave marker in the cemetery for him, either.

Jesus. Two firstborns, from two very Catholic families, neither buried in the parish cemetery. Wait—make that three. The Zerhoffer infant. Had he lived, he would have been the older brother to the boy with frostbite who Sister Irene and me rescued. No marker for him either.

Viola would have to put my dinner in the fridge tonight. I needed another visit with Mrs. V.

20

Daylight saving time changeover was Sunday after next; we'd be springing forward. Even now the afternoons were getting a little longer, the sun not setting until six o'clock, near what it was now. I pulled my truck into the circular front driveway. A burst of orange sunlight greeted me from behind Mrs. V's turreted Victorian roof. It set off the house in a jagged silhouette, like it was pushing the old place at me.

Her cook opened the front door but didn't offer to let me in, instead kept a full three feet away from me, the screen door between us. I wasn't sure if she was sizing me up or was afraid of me. I never done nothing to her, yet still she acted this way.

Who was I kidding? It was me who croaked her employer's husband. That was plenty.

"She's not here," she said, her round cheeks full of food. She swallowed most of it. "She was taken to Nazarene Hospital this afternoon."

My heart skipped a beat. "For what?"

Her face softened; the screen door opened and I stepped inside. "Heart palpitations," she said, her tone more even now. "She's not in any immediate danger. Just can't get excited. All this rigmarole about finding her husband's body is what did it. They want her to rest in the hospital a few days. No visitors."

Horst her gardener husband joined us in the hall, wiped his mouth with a napkin. I thanked his wife for the information and turned to leave. Then I turned back.

"Look," I said to them, "you two and me didn't get off on the right foot those many years ago. Not sure why, and not sure what I can do to change it, but please, just get a message to Mrs. Volkheimer and her family to let them know I'm thinking about her."

I made for the screen door, was surprised when Horst offered his hand while leaning past me to open it. "We're thinking about her, too," he said, his long face showing its age, his forehead a washboard of worry lines. "We'll deliver the message."

His shake was firm and honest. Mrs. Volkheimer had touched a lot of people during her lifetime. Old folks felt a kinship at times like this, watching other old folks get closer to death. It didn't make sense to hold grudges, for real or imagined slights. Maybe this was what turned these two around. Either way, I was touched by it.

* * *

If I located more families on this list, I figured to get the same answer but not with any of them knowing they had this in common: firstborn infant sons dying at the hands of their parents. Real biblical-obedience bullshit, courtesy of the nineteenth-century Catholic Church.

Biblical. Now there's a word I hadn't used lately for sure.

I decided I would call Father Duncan in the morning. Figured me and him maybe ought to stop by the orphanage to do some thirteenth-century Bible reading.

* * *

It was about eight a.m. I didn't get an answer when I phoned the rectory looking for the father, so I decided to take a walk.

It was supposed to be warm again today, in the low eighties. Tomorrow, Good Friday, it could reach ninety. Light-jacket weather now, short sleeves later. Hadn't seen an April this warm around here since I was a kid.

Something told me Father knew all about them families already, the Goodes and the Schmidts and the rest of them, and their nineteenth-century babies, too. Something told me he already knew what I'd learned yesterday, which was those infant boys in the sewers were all firstborns. Probably had a hunch about it, but wanted me to chase the information down anyway. Something told me all this because he never said nothing yesterday about visiting the orphanage this morning, yet here I was walking half a block behind him, which he hadn't noticed, the both of us headed to the same place.

Hell. Could be he was here on some other priest business, not to do any reading from a devil bible. Maybe I was just overreacting.

I'd picked up two escorts this last leg, Raymond in his wheelchair and Leo pushing him, on their way back from a grocery store errand, a brown Food Fair bag sticking out of the wire basket beneath Raymond's seat. The three of us left the sidewalk and cut across the orphanage's front lawn. The wheelchair shook and hitched as Leo pushed it over the uneven grass until we got to the side of the property, onto a hardened clay footpath, the ride finally smoothing out. We followed the bellied path around to the kitchen door in back. Leo stopped at the tip of the special wooden wheelchair ramp I built for the orphanage's disabled kids; he resettled the red baseball cap on Raymond's blond head. Raymond's feet, snug inside a pair of beat-up red high-topped PF Flyers, dangled off the sides of their stainless-steel footrests, their canvas tops frayed white and torn in spots, a few of the silver eyelets missing. The tread on these sneakers hadn't suffered near as much abuse, looked close to new and always would, long as Raymond was the one wearing them. Leo resettled Raymond's feet inside the footrests and retied the laces.

He checked the leather straps across his buddy's chest and legs, making sure they were tight enough for the short trip up the incline. I grabbed one handle and Leo grabbed the other; we pushed the wheelchair up the ramp together. I brushed past them to get at the door, aware of Raymond's open, sightless eyes. They blinked a few times.

you're not overreacting

This thought stopped me. Except it wasn't a thought; it was a voice. I took my hand off the door handle. "You say something, Leo?"

"Nope. Wasn't me."

"What do you mean it wasn't you? Who else, then?"

He shrugged. "Maybe it was God. Or Raymond."

I let that pass. "But you heard it?"

"Yeah. Kinda."

"Kinda? Explain 'kinda.'"

"Kinda with my mind I heard it." He was studying me and smiling a small, goofy smile, one that hung around longer than it should have, betraying he was worried about my reaction.

Jeez-o-man, stay calm, I told myself. "Tell me what you heard, son."

"I heard someone telling you you're not overacting, something like that. Sounded like it was Raymond."

"Like Raymond? Really, now."

"Yep. Sometimes I watch him while he's doing it. His lips don't move and nothing comes out of his mouth, but I can hear him in my head anyway. Sounds like he's talking from inside a big seashell, next to the ocean." Leo's head bobbed up and down, looking for my approval. My squinty expression betrayed me.

His eyebrows drooped. "You don't believe me."

I placed my hand on his bushy noggin to pat his wild sandy hair, then I caught myself doing it and stopped. "I don't know what to believe anymore, son. What you said doesn't make much sense to me."

"Raymond says I can talk that way, too."

Leo looked at me like he was about to say *Hey, it's really true, and boy-o-boy, did it surprise me, too.*

hey it's really true and boy-o-boy...

The echo. It wasn't me. It was Leo's voice, but his lips—his mouth—nothing moved.

"Leo? How in God's name—?"

I was feeling real uneasy, staring first at him then at Raymond, slowly looking Raymond over in his wheelchair, head to toe and back, settling on his narrow, emotionless face, his lollygag head tilted to one side, his left cheek leaning on his shoulder.

I was sixty-five friggin' years old, for God's sake. Old soldiers like me had enough crap tricking their minds every day. I didn't need stuff like this making me doubt my sanity. "Forget it, I don't want to know. Just stop it, whoever it was."

we're sorry, Wump

"Raymond this time," Leo said. "He started talking this way a coupla months ago. Tells me not to be afraid even though he's getting sick. He's my best friend, Wump. Please don't make him stop."

Leo's eyes moistened up, and I nodded an okay, told him to ignore what I'd said. "You boys talk anyway you need to. Just do your best to keep this old man out of it." I put my hand on Leo's shoulder. "Let's get inside. Your school bus will be along soon."

The orphanage kitchen was cluttered from breakfast dishes and bowls and mugs piled high in the large sinks and on the counters next to them, all ready for sudsing and rinsing then drying and reshelving by the nuns, except no one was here, at least not in the kitchen. Leo left Raymond under the arch to the hallway, turned the grocery bag on its side on an empty part of the counter, and let the contents roll out. Some fruit, a few small spice jars, and an institutional-size can of Crisco. He folded the bag, stood everything up for the nuns to put away, then threw open the door to the Frigidaire. Out came a quart-size glass bottle of soda. He shook it hard with both hands then put it on the table; he carefully unscrewed the top. The excess pressure escaped little by little until most of it was gone.

Leo eyed me eyeing him. "It's okay," he said, grabbing a jelly-jar glass from a cabinet. "The sisters said it doesn't much matter if Raymond has soda this early in the morning. He likes Black Cherry Wishniak but only if there's no fizz. Not as much burping." He pulled a paper straw out of a drawer, carried it and the glass of soda over to his friend. Leo held the glass and straw steady while Raymond eagerly sipped. The straw circled the bottom, searched and found the last few drops.

Leo pushed Raymond down the hallway and left him outside the library. A few cranky doorknobs turned, the last one the knob to the orphanage's front door. Leo squeezed himself outside with a book bag slung over one shoulder, then pulled the door shut behind him. Now it was real quiet, like on those early mornings when I lived here. Maybe quieter. Midnight quiet.

I heard Raymond in the library. No, it couldn't be, because what I was hearing were voices. They were down the hallway and across from the library, in the parlor. Children's voices. As I got closer, I heard a woman's voice, too.

"Don't you look handsome in those knickers, young man. Handsome indeed.

"Here's a new bonnet for you, child. Oh, aren't you a beautiful sight this morning. You'll be the prettiest young lady at the Schuetten town fair."

The town hadn't been called Schuetten for more than fifty years; what the Christ was going on? "Hello, Sister?" I called down the hall. "Who's there? Hello?"

"Don't be raising your voice inside, Johnny. Go wash up. And your potato sack better be out back, not inside. I don't want to be smelling it in here."

I hustled to the end of the hall and whipped around the foot of the stairs to face the parlor. "Now see here, Sister, what's all this talk about—"

I was talking to no one; the parlor was empty.

Raymond—where was he? "Where'd you get off to, son? Raymond?"

More noise, coming from behind me, across the hall, on the other side of the library's closed pocket doors. A clap-a-tap rapping that sounded like wood against wood. It started out slow and soft, but now it was louder and faster. I felt a rush of air blow against me. It pushed me back a step, away from the library, where from behind the doors it now sounded bad as a Midwestern twister ripping into a cluttered soup kitchen, with so much knocking and banging that the pocket doors shook and snapped their edges against each other but somehow stayed closed.

My ears popped; the chaos got louder. They popped again; louder.

Pop, louder, pop, louder. "Owww..."

I covered my ears and turned weak-kneed away from the doors. This noise—it needed to stop, felt like it was shredding my eardrums—

The air suddenly retreated. The racket dwindled, the painful pressure in my head disappeared. I dropped my hands to my sides and slowed my breathing. Nose-to-nose with the closed doors of the library, I knew how terrified I was, could smell it in my own body odor. Still, I had to face it down.

I cozied up to the doors, cupped my hand around my ear, put it next to the polished wood and concentrated. Nothing moving inside far as I could tell; all quiet. Dead quiet, like a hospital morg—

The door I leaned against rumbled open so fast its beveling nearly took my ear off—*THOCK-K-K-K!*—the doors then slamming into their pockets. I had my arm coiled and my fist cocked except I was left staring at...what?

The archway was empty.

I stepped inside the library. No sunlight showed through the windows. I checked the parlor with a glance over my shoulder; still was a sunny day. A straw-colored lampshade, its bottom rim curved under like a rice paddy hat, covered a dangling light bulb, the bulb socket's length of black wire disappearing overhead, into the dark near the ceiling. It felt close in here, unsafe, like the rubber hose room at the cop precinct or a boxing ring, two places where pain could come at you unexpected and from any angle, or in the prison hallways where you had to keep your eyes on everyone's hands, or on the farm, where a leather strap settled everything. Or worse, where the gripping, gruesome agony in the room was not your own, but rather your defenseless, dying son's.

The shade and bulb swung slowly, silently, like a clock pendulum. They cast a shaft of yellow light onto an opened book on a card table in the middle of the bare oak floor. I stilled the light with my hand then tipped the shade up to get a better look at the library.

Wow. The furniture was all jammed up unnatural-like against the ceiling and windows and walls like twigs in a bird's nest, only the nest was upside down and close enough overhead to make my scalp tingle. Grade school desks, their wooden lids cocked and twisted off their hinges. Paintings and mounted photographs clawed from their fractured picture frames. Arts-and-crafts papers, some shredded into strips and hanging, others ripped into tiny pieces of confetti sprinkled overhead like stars in a midnight sky. Books, their pages pulled from their spines, the bookcase shelves they once sat on snapped and crushed. And attached to the ceiling, the steamer trunk, big and black and sturdy enough to hold a car engine, gaping like a screaming mouth. Inside the trunk its contents hung there, frozen in place.

Get out, my mind shouted. *Go.*

I wiped my palms on my trousers. That's when I noticed it, on the wall above the fireplace. Two floor lamps, their shades gone, their long brass poles slapped against each other. Into a cross.

My blood pounded in my ears. My eyes centered on the book on the card table. I could hardly breathe. I leaned over it.

The Devil's Bible. My nose filled with the reek of attic must and cat piss.

Creak.

I jumped. A wheelchair rolled out of the shadows, slowly, each plank of hardwood floor groaning as it crossed it.

"Raymond." I held my hand to my chest and exhaled.

I strained to look at his face, at those open, unfocused, other-way eyes, and I listened, waiting like a fool, somehow hoping to have this orphanage library bedlam explained by, how was it Leo put it? A voice from inside a seashell?

Raymond stirred, his weak, chicken-bone chest rising to catch a full breath. He lifted his head off his shoulder, his eyes widening but still vacant. His chin rose. Then he laid his head back down, exhausted.

"You should go," I said. "So should I." But my eyes were drawn to that Bible.

I told myself it was just a book. With a trembling hand I reached under the heavy front cover, its leather binding strips cracking from age. I closed it then opened it again.

A maze was on the top half of the first page, in reds and blues, a circle working itself outward from its middle. The German started right in, written in a flowing hand beneath the circle, the first few words large, including *Der Heirlige Bibel,* or "The Holy Bible," then smaller, *Am Anfang,* or "In the Beginning."

What I knew about the Bible could fit inside a comic book. If there was anything in there worth seeing, like—well, like maybe something that could explain all them infant skeletons—I'd need to translate the whole book to find it.

the back

I glanced at Raymond, swallowed hard, and turned to the last page.

Inside the heavy back cover was a brown envelope newer than the book, more like a businessman's small portfolio than an envelope, with an accordion bottom and leather shoelaces tied around its middle. I unwrapped the laces and shook the contents onto the card table and spread them out.

Maybe a hundred or more old death notices, flimsy and yellowed and in different sizes.

I tried to remember what Father said. How many newborns died back then and didn't get buried in Our Lady's cemetery? A hundred and, ah, what was it, one hundred and—

one hundred and nine

I pushed them into a pile then squared them off. First card showed a drawing of the Blessed Virgin with a short supplication for the dead under it. It was for a Baby Warner, no first name, born October 17, 1879, died the same day. Second card had the same drawing of Our Lady, same prayer, was for a Baby Gunther, who also died the day he was born, November 2, 1879, again no first name. Third card, Baby Hochmeyer, January 21, 1880, same story. Aside from the names and the dates, each card looked the same, all showing a black and white sketch of Our Lady and carrying the same prayer for the dead that ended with the words "...some shall die so that all will live."

Wait a second.

March, 1880—April, 1880—May, 1880—

I turned through the pile of cards, slow at first then faster, stopping once to take a swipe at sweat on my upper lip. Some of the notices ripped as I turned them over, they were so flimsy.

Sonovabitch.

They were in order. By month, day, year, oldest to newest. But they came out of the envelope in a sloppy pile, upside down, some even turned over. All I did was push them together. Just how in the Christ—

Something moved, above me, on the wall. I snapped my head up, heard a scrape, metal on metal.

ignore it

I shook the noise off. Here was the last notice in the pile. April 20, 1899.

take it

I stuffed it into my pants pocket.

The book suddenly slammed shut, scattering dust in my face. I cleared my eyes with my fingers and palms, not sure of what I seen. My shoulders were in a knot, and the hairs on the back of my neck prickled. I told myself it's only a book, damn it. I stepped in closer.

The cover flipped open. The first page rose by its bottom edge, its top corner dragging down lazy-like and sounding as scratchy as sandpaper on wood. My wrinkled hands balled into fists so tight I could feel my fingernails biting my calloused palms. The first page settled flat against the inside of the front cover. The second page lifted itself the same teasing way, moved in slow motion, right to left. Then the third, and the fourth.

I wondered what would happen if I touched it—

The old pages suddenly flipped by my face in a wind-whipped, tan blur that halted at a page near the back of the book, the air above it shimmering like summer heat rising from a city street's blacktop. The overhead lamp pulsed yellow then white-hot then yellow again. The pages settled into a mild flutter then finally flattened out. The cone of lamplight now swept across them, slowly, each pass like the creak of a rocking chair. Then, like a magnet, the pages pulled the light steady again, centering it above them.

Hell, I should have guessed.

The book was open to the leering little demon Father showed me before. Clawed hands, long, red, and sharp groping fingernails. Lunatic smile. I leaned in, looked into the demon's eyes. Black. Crazy.

"All them dead babies in the sewers," I said to it, my voice raspy. "Why?"

I waited for a response, a sign, anything, swallowed hard, then waited longer. I burrowed my eyesight deep into the demon's face. "C'mon, you little fucker, tell me, damn it—"

I froze. Something was on my leg, lightly crawling up the back of my thigh. It moved softly, felt big, like one of them hairy tarantulas. It tugged at my shirt.

I grabbed it and felt fingers.

"Raymond!" I was breathing hard, about to crucify this kid.

yes

I released his fingers, lowered his long bony arm into his lap.

read the book, Wump

"The *what*?"

the page facing the picture. read it

I lingered, looking over this young man and his long, thin body. A body of not much use to him his whole life and failing him even more now that he had the leukemia. His mind—maybe it was making up for all the other parts of him that never worked. I turned back to the book, to look at the page Raymond said to look at. Nothing was on it. Or—maybe there *was* something, real faint, like a shadow, showing through its back.

I turned back one page. Still blank. Yet when I turned it back again the shadowy writing was still there.

It was on *this* page. It only looked like it was on the other side because it was slanted the wrong way, like it had been written—

yes, backward

read it from the other side

I tilted my head and leaned in, almost flat to the book, concentrated on seeing the handwritten words against the light and through the paper, on its other side. I squinted. Now I could make them out.

"Ich wurde von ihm herausgeschmissen,"

I was banished from him,

"wird wieder geboren,"

will be born again,

"der erste aus zwei..."

the first from two...

"jungfrauen,"

virgins,

"ihm gewidmet."

avowed to him.

I lifted my head up. "Sounds like crap."

keep going

"Mein kind folgt seinem,"

My child follows his,

"ein tausend mal zwei,"

a thousand times two,

"schreckliche ende fuer seine diener,"

vile ends for his servants,

"ein neues Universum. "

a Universe new.

Above me I heard a long, tortuous scraping of metal. I snapped my head up, saw the crisscrossed posts of the two hanging floor lamps moving, sliding against each other, slowly grinding out silver-gold sparks from the contact, the sparks spraying the clutter on the wall and ceiling, the lamp posts twisting, shifting from an upright gold cross into a throbbing, glowing, red X. It sizzled like a branding iron as it hovered. I stepped back.

"Out. We need to get out—"

I grabbed at Raymond's wheelchair from the front, both my hands on its arms. The chair was stuck. "The brake! Where is it—?"

Flames from the X exploded over my head. I stumbled backward, hit the floor, felt the heat—

Raymond. God, help me help him.

I strained to reach the brake lever, twisted it to free the back wheel, stood and quickly backed the chair out of the fire's reach, toward the library archway, toward the way out.

The library doors slammed shut in our faces. I looked back, saw the blazing cross, heard its ferocious roar. Another fire blast exploded like a stoked flamethrower, shot across the card table, tickling the pages of the demon bible. I draped myself over Raymond, watched in panic past my shoulder as something took shape in the center of the flames.

Out thrust the face of the demon, its skin charred, its lips parting, its lazy eyes opening. The lips separated into a smile, showed silver-white dagger teeth drenched in spit. The smile became a leer.

I was way past fear. My mind quickly entered a place I'd seen other soldiers go when the horror of the battlefield had closed in on them, where adrenaline took over, and the soldier's own life didn't matter. I straightened up, turned to face the demon head on, Raymond to my back. I leaned forward, my chest broadening, leaned into the heat, no turning back—

"Open these doors!" I bellowed. "Open them! *Now!*"

I inhaled a breath, my lungs filling up in a fiery agony. I quickly exhaled. The air leaving my mouth felt scorched, like I was burning from the inside out. My mind was overcome by images of lungs on fire and arteries igniting like long fuses, their red-hot trails coursing through my arms and legs then sizzling their way back through my veins and into my heart, my beating, fiery, unsacred heart, charring it tar-black. Now I knew what the fire was after. It tickled a wafer-thin inner sense of my being, my inner tabernacle, my pure—

The demon's leer was now a booming, scorn-filled laugh...

—and everlasting—

The laugh ricocheted inside my skull.

HAHAHAHA!

...SOUL!

YES, YOUR IMMORTAL SOUL!

FUCK WITH ME, OLD MAN, AND I WILL BURN *IT!*

The blast-furnace flames on the cross immediately retreated, sucked back inside the cross, whole. With a hiss, the devil-head disappeared. I hugged myself, saw and felt no burning flesh or fiery blood vessels, aware my heart was working overtime but still on the job.

Raymond.

I turned to him. He was unharmed in his wheelchair. He hadn't broken a sweat from all this commotion. But his eyes...

They were still an ocean-blue beneath narrow blond eyebrows but somehow, in some way, they were different.

They were focused. On the wall. Focused on the lamp-cross now throbbing with a red glow, the cross again suspended in the nest-like debris hanging there. His eyes were focused and doing what? Staring? Like a sighted person?

His eyes fluttered and all at once, the stare I thought was there was gone.

The glow of the cross dimmed until the polished yellow-gold of its plated brass returned. I unclenched my fists, the tidal wave of adrenaline in my blood beginning to retreat, but still...

We needed to get out. I tried separating the doors. Useless. I swung around, looked for another way, got ready to scream at the lamp-cross again except now I noticed the cross was dripping water.

I took a few slow, careful steps around the book on the card table. I raised my hand, tapped a finger against the brass; it felt cool. I tapped it again, saw the lampposts were sweating. The water droplets pooled onto my fingertip, ran past my knuckles into my palm, soon became a trickling stream. I stepped back as the stream changed color, a sparkling crystal turning cloudy until—

It erupted, became a baby-shit-brown waterfall that gushed from the crossed lampposts, stinking like a rain-swelled cesspool, and it was then that I saw it. Another shape, forming from a glob of head flesh, with thumbprints that became eyes and a small gash that turned into a suckling mouth, and—

Out of the sewage waterfall leaped the vision of a baby's face, its eyes and mouth closed, its cheeks puffed like tiny pink balloons. The infant's head was shaking, struggling, its only noise a fierce grunting as it fought to keep its eyes closed and its lips sealed. The cheeks deflated and the lips parted, the mouth now gagging furiously as it gulped in the sewer water, the eyelids pressing down hard until they couldn't stay shut any longer. The eyelids opened, and I seen in the newborn's face a deathly terror, a terror that came from not knowing cold, not knowing pain, and not knowing what it meant to drown.

21

"Wump." A female voice startled me. "You're as ashen as a tombstone. Are you all right?"

Sister Dymphna hovered as I regained my bearings, only half hearing her speaking. I was on my rump on the library's hardwood floor, everything around me out of focus. Father Duncan leaned in front of my face, studied me, then tugged on my upper arm. The two of them got me to my feet. I needed a few deep breaths.

"Can't rightly say I remember ending up on the floor, Sister. I—"

I got a jolt. The devil head, the drowning infant, fire, gushing water— these images made me wince as they jammed my senses then were gone. My heart was thumping again. I raised my head and turned around, slowly, Sister and Father each clamped onto an elbow. I kept turning, made it a full 360; I was awestruck. "What happened to it? The library. It's..."

"It's what, Wump?" Sister said. "What happened to what?" Her eyesight followed mine, ending with the empty space above the fireplace.

Everything was as it was, same as when Father and me were here a few days ago. Framed paintings, the photographs, the artifacts and other Sister Irene keepsakes, all of it sitting on tables and chairs and against other furniture, and all this furniture down, on the floor, where it belonged.

"There was fire, and water, and it was like a funnel cloud came through here, everything whipped up, raised eye-high around me. The furniture; them brass lamps. And there was a card table—"

Sister and Father traded glances. I knew how this sounded, like old Wump was sprawled on the boxing canvas, reaching for the ring ropes. "Raymond," I finally managed. "He was in here. Where's Raymond?"

"Over there, Wump," Sister said. "In the corner."

Raymond was in his wheelchair, next to the arts and crafts supplies and an old mahogany secretary's desk. His hand twisted the tuner knob on a small table radio, stopping every few seconds to listen.

"Ask him," I said to her.

"Ask who?"

"Raymond. Go ahead and ask him. He'll tell you what went on in here."

"But, Wump," Sister said, resting her hand on my shoulder, her head giving me a patronizing tilt. "Raymond's mute, remember?"

"He can talk. Not with his mouth, but with his mind." They looked at me like I had three eyes. "I know it sounds crazy, but I heard him."

I brought this up to Father Duncan before, but he'd passed on it; maybe this time he'd believe me. Father said nothing at first, but I could tell he was working it out in his head.

Father turned to Raymond. "Raymond. Is this true?"

Nothing.

Father crouched next to the wheelchair. "It's a special gift if you have it, Raymond. No need to feel embarrassed. Is Wump right?" Silence.

"Please, Raymond," I asked. "Show them. Please."

Raymond stirred. His right hand left the radio tuner and settled onto an armrest, firmly gripping the padding on the chair arm. Then his neck muscles tensed and his chin rose. His lips slowly parted, and through a string of slobber they opened wider and wider until—

BURRRP.

Sister and Father stifled smirks, and the three of us watched Raymond as his body relaxed, his blond head rolling lazy-like until it leaned against his shoulder again. Like a tired child at the circus, his eyelids fought to stay open until they finally closed, and he was asleep. I smelled cherries.

"Black Cherry Wishniak," Sister said when I mentioned it. "Raymond's favorite. Sometimes the sugar can get him really animated." Her comment was out there as much as an explanation for what I thought I'd heard as it was for Raymond's burping. "He'll nap now, until lunch."

Raymond slumped in his chair in the corner, began snoring like a soldier back from a weekend pass. "Please," I said. "You need to believe me. I know what I seen in here."

I gave Father and Sister a rundown on my "visions," which was what Father had taken to calling the demon's head and the infant's drowning face. The funny thing was, he'd stopped looking goofy at me. At the end of the library's long table, where the old bible-book was still open to the devil picture, he leaned down like I did and put his head level to the table top, his ear almost flat against the paper. With his thumb and forefinger he cautiously lifted and steadied the page with the backward writing on it, studied it like I had, from the other side. When he straightened up, I tried to read his face. For a moment he looked excited. Then the color drained from it.

"This," he said to himself, so low I nearly missed it, "is the one."

"The one? The one what?"

I waited for an answer. He stayed quiet, stepped over to the huge steamer trunk and peeked inside. Out came the strongbox the devil book was in, and in a moment the hefty wood container was resting on the table, next to the book, the box lid open. He flipped the devil book's cover closed. Dust scooted from between the pages, spreading out like car exhaust on a cold day. Father ran his hand across the smooth cover, his face solemn.

Still no answer from him. He slipped his fingers under both sides of the book and lifted, about to put it back into the strongbox.

He needed to answer me, damn it.

I slapped the palm of my hand down on the book and pressed. It slipped out of Father's grip, returned to the table with a thud. There was a yelp from behind him, from a surprised Sister Dymphna, who I now noticed held a book of her own, thin and black and square as a record album, and near as large, like a ledger. I didn't apologize for scaring her. "Tell me what's going on here, Father. Now."

Father's lips parted to say something, then he changed his mind. He exhaled, said finally, "Those families I asked you about—the ones whose babies are buried in the church cemetery—what did you find out about them?" His hand dug inside the vest pocket of his black suit jacket.

"I learned it was probably all firstborn boys who got tossed into the rivers and sewers. The other infants, the ones who died naturally back then, they got buried in Our Lady's cemetery. What's your point?" I had my eye on Sister, too. She was spooked, clutching the book she'd entered the library with against her white bib, holding it near as tight as a mother did a baby when there was danger about. Something was real familiar about the book she held, but it wasn't coming to me.

Father retrieved a brown envelope the size of a small Christmas card from inside his jacket. He handed it to me. "Open it."

The envelope was unsealed, had a return address in the corner that read *Coroner's Office, Phila., Penna.,* with no other writing on it. I opened the flap, slipped out a piece of paper. It was stained brown and crinkly, like it had gotten wet then dried out. The words on it were hand printed and in German, some of them circled in pencil. It didn't take long for me to figure out what they said, and it sent a frigging chill through me. Same words as the ones written backward in this Bible. "Where did you get this?" I asked him.

"It was tucked inside the blanket of the dead infant the cop pulled out of the river," he said. "Kerm our coroner friend asked me to translate it."

I read the circled words again, tried to reason this through. *Will be born again, the first from two virgins...I was banished from him...my child follows his...*

Beneath the paragraph, printed in a shaky hand in German first, then English, was *God forgive us.* Finally it sunk in.

"You're saying these people—these 'virgin' parents of the dead infant fished out of the river—they threw away their newborn son as a *precaution*? But that's just crazy. And all them infants from before, them babies in the sewers, their parents were—"

"Yes, Wump. Just doing their part. Making sure a certain unholy child whose birth was deemed imminent had no chance of survival. It's not considered crazy if the Church tells you to do it. To most Catholic folks, it was more like getting a directive from God. To not obey it would have been religious heresy, in this parish at least. It's not unusual for a panic like this to survive a few generations by, you know, word of mouth."

"But, Father," I said, the evidence back inside his vest pocket, "this word of mouth came from a book written by a hermit monk more than, what, six hundred years ago? All them babies died because of some dead monk's words?"

Father wrestled with the size of the massive devil book until he was able to deposit it inside the strongbox. "It's a proclamation," he said finally. "One the church leaders believed could come true." The strongbox lid closed. He twisted the crossbar of a small metal latch on its front to secure it. "I'm not saying I agree with them, but I can tell you their reasoning.

"There were numerous versions of this phenomenon in different European countries, where a priest or a monk or some other cleric was told to copy the Bible as penance, each of their works supposedly completed around the same time—as I mentioned before, the same night, if you believe the legend—in the thirteenth century. It's rumored there were as many rewrites as there were languages in the civilized world. They showed up for sure in France and Poland and Holland. The Church tracked those books down and acquired them." Father rested his hand on the strongbox. "Each has a hand-drawn picture of the Devil in it. Same picture as this one."

"But why would the Church want to track them books down? They were just copy jobs of the Bible, like you said, written as a penance."

"Because, Wump," Father answered, "one of the books was rumored to have the Devil's own writing in it, telling of his return." Father laid a hand on the strongbox. "This may be the one."

That statement made me look more seriously at the box. Still, this was the 1960s, and we were in the U.S. of A., the best damn country in the whole world, and these were the best of times. There was no room for stuff like this to happen. Then again, what about them visions I just had?

"The Devil's return? Return to what?" I asked.

"To the big leagues. To prominence here on earth. He's always been about pleasure, Wump. Pure and simple, decadent, personal gratification. Except he's been relegated to that sneaky little voice in our heads that most of us have to deal with. The tiny, sexy whisper that says, 'Go ahead, do it if it feels good. Who cares if someone gets hurt?'

"He wants equal time and doesn't stand to get it as long as the firmament's current administration is in place. He also wants to avoid going head-to-head with the Almighty, since he lost that battle once already. So here he is, looking to cash in on a known tenet of Christianity, and Judaism, and countless other religions. Who is everyone waiting for? The Messiah. Whether it's his first visit, his second or his tenth, it doesn't much matter. The world awaits him, expects everlasting life from him. So the Devil intends to trick us into thinking he's the one who will give us what we want, when we want it. Or so the legend goes."

"So then the deal is"—even as I said it, it sounded dumb—"he shows up pretending to be Christ?" This whole line of thinking—religion in general, a real-life Devil—sounded dumber than a bucket of spit. Always had, always would.

"That's the concern, Wump. Now, and last century, and probably every century since Christ's death and resurrection. Concern that a false Christ will appear. Someone who will lead us into and out of the Apocalypse, because this is what we expect from the real Messiah. Where would he try to take us? No one knows. But if it were to happen, it won't be to a good place. And when would this be? Don't know this either, of course."

"A thousand times two, Father," I reminded him, "is the when, according to them words."

"Yes, Wump. The proclamation seems to bear this out. A hundred and nine dead babies in a twenty-year period. Those deaths indicate the monsignor of this parish at the time thought our current century, the twentieth, would be the one. The timing would have been right. A birth back then would let the child grow and mature, place his emergence as an adult in the 1930s or '40s. During the Second World War. And my, oh my, how the Church had a field day with that speculation while the war was going on."

There was a pause in his explanation while he let it sink in for me. Finally it clicked. "You mean Hitler?"

"Yes. Do you know when he was born, Wump?"

"No."

"April 20, 1889. Same month and day as you, my friend, but ten years earlier."

Good grief. Hell, maybe I did know.

"Of course no one can speak to the age the false Christ will be when he actually shows himself. Will he be an adult, around the age Jesus was when he started teaching? Will he be a child? An old man, maybe? Will he even know who or what he is until it's time for him to act? And showing himself —announcing his true identity—that could be key, too, from the Almighty's perspective at least, since the Church figures God won't intervene until He's sure we're dealing with the real thing. Then, let's just say, we expect there'll be a rebuttal."

"A rebuttal?"

"Yes. Like the last time they met. When God banished him from Heaven. It wasn't a pillow fight."

He meant Lucifer, the fallen angel.

Father Duncan went silent on me as if this was all sinking in for him just now, too, and Sister, she hadn't said a word, deferring to the father. The quiet was broken by a loud snore from the corner, Raymond's nasal intake making him flail some in his wheelchair. Sister resettled him, but only after she dropped the book she'd been holding onto the desk in front of him.

Thin black book, on Sister Irene's polished red mahogany desk...finally I remembered. It wasn't a ledger. It was the first logbook for St. Jerome's Home for Foundlings.

"Is your truck outside, Wump?" Father asked, looking the strongbox over.

"Huh? No, it's back at my house. I walked. Why? This Bible going somewhere?"

"Yes. I'm taking it to the archdiocese's offices in Center City, Philly. After the cardinal sees what's in it, I expect he'll want it to go to the Vatican."

Father tented his dark eyebrows, waited for me to say I'd get my Willys to help him transport this thing. My eyebrows crept down, near my line of vision. I was still deciding.

"Look"—he sensed my doubt—"what I said to you a few days ago, about the Archdiocese sending me here because of Monsignor Fassnacht's behavior, it wasn't the only reason. Magdalena's declining condition was the catalyst. The sisterhood wants this Bible removed, had never under-stood the original direction Monsignor gave them years ago when they rediscovered it, that the Archdiocese said it should stay at the orphanage.

Turns out the monsignor never reported it to his superiors, only said he had.

"This proclamation—I paged through the book a few times looking for it, or anything like it. For something Monsignor might have used to persuade Magdalena; I found nothing. This was a great find on your part, Wump. Truly a great find."

A great find on Raymond's part, but I wasn't saying nothing, else they'd think I was even more confused.

"Fine. I'll get my truck."

22

Took me fifteen minutes to walk home, drive my truck back, and park it curbside in front of the orphanage. I hustled back into the library.

Father acknowledged me with a nod, sidled up to the end of the long table, positioned himself next to the strongbox; he reached around both sides. I shooed him away from the side nearest me. We each grabbed a handle, raised the box a few inches off the tabletop and scooted it over to the edge, then lifted. Damn thing was heavy, more container than it was book. We settled it on the hardwood floor to rest a moment and to reposition it for the longer walk out the front door to my truck. I bent forward slightly to stretch the muscles in my back. This put me nearly face-to-face with Sister Irene's old mahogany desk, Raymond snoring next to it.

Father had rested long enough. He reached for the handle on his side of the strongbox and lifted.

"Hold on a second, Father," I said, straightening up. I wiped my palms on my pants then shot a curious look at Sister. Before they found me on my duff talking crazy in here, the father and Sister Dymphna were upstairs in the attic, and what was it they brung down with them?

"Is this book on Sister Irene's desk what I think it is, Sister?"

"What it is," she said, her voice reverent, her dimpled chin a hardened white knob, "is a record, in Sister Irene's own handwriting, of the comings and goings of St. Jerome's children from the first day the orphanage opened its doors."

Like I figured, Sister Irene's logbook. I turned back to Father Duncan. "Father, you mind if I—"

"Go ahead, Wump. Take a look, but please make it quick."

I studied the book's cover. Black, made from a pimpled hide of some sort. The top and bottom edges on the side that opened were protected with smooth, three-cornered leather patches the color of clay. I opened the cover.

The pages were hand-lined with rows and columns, each row half an inch high, maybe ten rows per sheet, the column headings labeled in longhand. Leftmost column had children's names, next column was labeled *Birth Date*, next one *Adoption Date*, the next one *Adopting Parents*. Rightmost column wasn't labeled. With all us orphans having "St. Jerome" as a surname during our stay at the orphanage we were guaranteed, the sisters had told us, that there'd be at least one saint looking after us. About three-quarters of the way through the book, I found what I was looking for, the handwriting striking in an inkwell blue-black. My twelve years as a St. Jerome's orphan on one row, in four entries.

Name: Johannes St. Jerome
Birth Date: April 20, 1899
Adoption Date: October 19, 1911
Adopting Parents...

I knew the names of them bastards already, stifled an urge to spit on the entry. I turned a few pages farther back, toward the front of the book, then a few more, then all the way back to the beginning. Sister and Father watched over my shoulders as I worked my way forward, a few pages at a time.

It seemed almost none of the earlier group of orphans, the ones who came to St. Jerome's in the late 1880s, got adopted. Notes in the last column said some "left at maturity," anywhere from their sixteenth to eighteenth birthdays. Some "ran away." A few died, their dates and causes of death noted. I paged forward, reached the entries on kids born a decade or so later—late 1898, early part of 1899 and after—and...well, lookie here. The *Date of Adoption* column had lots of entries in it, orphans getting adopted left and right, many at older ages, same as what happened to me. Except all these adoptions didn't start until—

"You know when the old monsignor died?" I asked Sister. She didn't respond, looked puzzled. "I'm talking about Our Lady's pastor back then, around the turn of the century. The one Sister Irene didn't like."

"Oh. You mean Monsignor Krause. Let me think. He was the parish pastor, I believe, from 1875 until his death in..."

Sister scoured another pile of memorabilia on the couch behind her, moved some of it out of the way and flipped around a large picture frame so it faced front. It was a portrait of the old Monsignor, him sitting in an arm chair wearing a black cassock with red piping and buttons, a purple sash, and a black skull-beanie sitting above his chubby, stern face. The brass plate below the painting gave the dates of the monsignor's birth and death. "He died in 1911," Sister said. "July twelfth."

"Now ain't this odd," I said to the both of them. "Look at all these adoptions so soon after the monsignor's death. Close to twenty of them over the next three months. Weren't twenty adoptions the whole ten years prior. Seem odd to you, Father?"

I gave Father some room. He ran his fingers down the page the book was opened to, his eyes bouncing back and forth between the *Date of Adoption* column and the *Date of Birth* column. What was also odd were the entries for the adoption dates. Some of the handwriting was different.

"Here's one," Father said. "A boy named Arno. Arno was about fourteen when he was adopted. Here's another adoption, for a boy who was thirteen. And another one, for another fourteen-year-old." He turned a page, said, "How about you, Wump? How old did you say you were?"

Suddenly it hit me why the writing was different. My stomach lurched; I was close to tasting this morning's oatmeal all over again on its way back up. For one sickening moment, I was completely drained.

One entry, nothing to do with me, was the reason, for a boy whose name I couldn't read on account of my eyes were so moist. The entry started out in a steady hand, then ended in a large blot of ink in the middle of the word *July*. To the right of the inkblot, *July* got written a second time, but in someone else's hand.

This was the moment Sister Irene died.

"Wump?"

I remembered how hard her death hit us, and now a real sadness washed over me. My eyes spilled over a bit; I took a swipe at them. "I was twelve when I was adopted, Father."

"You all right?" he said, leaning in, his head turned up at me.

"I'm fine," I told him, exhaling as much of the sadness as I could.

Father returned his attention to the book, sneaked an occasional peek back at me. "There were adoptions of younger children, too," he said, turning backward, forward, backward again. "But—"

Now he saw the sense of it. "You're right, Wump. Out of the blue, beginning late July that year, there was a flurry of them. Right after the monsignor's death."

And the short burst of adoptions continued for some time afterward, even beyond when Sister Irene died. The good Sister popped into my head again. I could picture her sitting at this desk, pictured her gasp, the nub of her quill pen staying pressed against the paper, and pictured her grabbing her chest. I pictured her face thudding onto the open logbook. Pictured her gone. I choked back the tears again.

"Ah, excuse me, people." A stern, schoolmarmy voice from the hallway startled the three of us. It was Sister Marie, the tiniest nun I'd ever known. Four-feet-eight today, the aging process making her something less than that tomorrow. Sister held a black phone receiver that looked as big in her small hand as a stage prop on Uncle Miltie's TV show. She spoke to us out of the side of her mouth. "Father Duncan." Her words were quick and hard, sounding like they came from a duck that was tread on. "Important call for you."

Father straddled the space between the library and the hall, listening at the receiver, tiny Sister Marie gone. Sister Dymphna and I went back to the logbook.

So who was doing the adopting, I wondered.

The bigwig citizens of Three Bridges was who. Except Sister Dymphna wasn't old enough to recognize any of their names. She read a few out loud for me.

"Arno St. Jerome," she said, "adopted by Herman and Hannah Silberbauer on July eighteenth."

"The Silberbauers were former owners of the old Schuetten Inn," I told her. "They each came from old, moneyed European families. They went to Mass every day."

"Oskar St. Jerome. Adopted July twenty-second by Willem and Gertrude Schultz."

"Willem Schultz made bicycles, also assembled parts that went into horseless carriages. Owned a lot of property. My first two-wheeler was a donation from his shop."

"Gunnar St. Jerome, adopted by Judge and Mrs. Gergen Ortmann, August first."

"I remember Gunnar." I stifled a fond smile. "We poked fun at him because the adoption made him an instant big brother to the judge's ugly twin daughters a year younger than him. Gunnar had the biggest ears I ever seen. Howdy Doody size, from what I recall. Real flappers. Funny thing was, they looked like—"

whose ears did they look like, Wump

I shot a glance at Raymond, still asleep next to us, in his wheelchair. He hadn't stirred, except I knew it was him in my head just now. "Ah, they looked a lot like..."

WHOSE EARS WERE THEY, WUMP

Jesus. "The judge's. And his daughters. Looked just like theirs."

A chill came over me, my skin tingling as pieces of a broken, long-ago world tried to reassemble themselves in my head. "Now that I think of it, them other two boys whose names you mentioned, they had features that made them fit in real well with their adopting families, too."

Sister Dymphna's hands, at first clasped together under her bosom, loosened their grip. One moved to cover her mouth as she nervously sucked in her next breath, the other went for the crucifix on the chain around her neck. The breath escaped through her fingers. She said it first while blessing herself.

"Mother of God," she whispered. "They were adopting their own children."

Sister murmured a Hail Mary. I was paralyzed.

It made sense. Their families put their firstborn infant boys in an orphanage teeming with forgotten kids, hiding them rather than kill them.

Then the old brimstone-preaching prick-bastard pastor of this needy immi-grant parish died, and the panic behind the devil-book proclamation died with him, so all them rich families wanted their kids back. The poorer families...hell, they'd been like chickens made to dance on a hot plate; no real choices. Weren't nothing could be done, for them or their dead babies.

My head was spinning, searching for other confirmations but, hell, this was fifty years ago. Weren't many of my childhood memories left to draw on, least not many I could call up on demand. Still, seeing the names of these and other boys in this logbook shook loose a few. Glimpses of faces, some older, some younger, of kids with wavy brown or curly red or straight blond hair, with flat and wide or long and thin noses, and with short and squat or tall and skinny bodies. Those rich folks had kept their firstborn boys in St. Jerome's all them years—why in God's name not rescue them earlier? If any of them looked too much like their real parents, well whoop-dee-god-damn-do-and-shit-me-an-apple, so what? Who could have proved anything? Instead they let them live a lie in an orphanage. Only thing the kids had going for them was Sister Irene, taking care of them, watching over them.

Watching them—that was it. *She* was the why. Sister Irene, providing for them, but at the same time keeping a vigil, their parents trusting her to look for tendencies, or indications of evil behavior. And now, thinking harder on it, I realized one St. Jerome's boy had a real bad one.

We called him Donkey. A long-faced six-year-old with a wide mouth of separated baby teeth. When he laughed he sounded like a jackass getting his balls squeezed. What happened to him made a lot more sense to me now.

Donkey had a speech impediment so bad, he could have been a martian for all us kids knew. Was dim-witted, too. But his biggest problem was he was a firebug. Liked torching outhouses. Actually, it was only one outhouse he set on fire all by himself, but when us boys heard about it, we got him more matches and prodded him to do it a bunch more times. Some of the local folk caught him on their properties while their commodes were still in flames, stick matches in his pockets, his laugh loud and annoying. Rest of us kids, we—

Jeez, now that was weird. Weren't no other kids now that I thought back on it, just me and him. Anyway, I always got away. After each outhouse fire, there'd be a complaint made to the orphanage, but since Donkey was so young, Sister Irene had always managed to talk him out of trouble.

Then late one fall night there was another fire, a huge one. A silo full of harvested grain ignited—a real spectacle that one was, start to finish—and the laughing half-wit wouldn't leave with me so he got caught again. Far as I knew, no formal complaint ever got filed about it. But soon afterward, miracle of miracles, Donkey got adopted. And soon after that, God rest his soul, he was found a little south of here, face down in the Wissaquessing River.

Us boys got told he'd slipped off the bank and cracked his head on a rock. Such bullshit, I knew now. It was his parents who'd offed him, just cleaning up after the mistake they thought they'd made six years earlier, when they let their firstborn son live.

Christ, what in the hell did they think they knew? Only thing Donkey was guilty of was being too simple.

I was dancing around something else that tugged at me through all these memories. A question I hadn't asked, because I wasn't sure I wanted to know the answer. I scanned the log again.

Sister Dymphna, still beside me, followed my eyes and finally said what we were both thinking. "I'm wondering the same thing, Wump. About your adoption. Were they your real parents?"

I didn't look nothing like them. Not back when I was a kid, and not now. Sure, I had a bull of a body same as Mr. Hozer did, which was something him and his wife had figured was good for farming, but nothing else matched. Not eyes or hair or nose, and definitely not ears, his the size of pocket watches, mine twice that. Besides, I hated the Hozers so much I couldn't have been blood-related. When their grain silo sparked up the night I left their farm, it was all I could do to keep from spreading the fire to their farmhouse with the whole damn Hozer family still inside, sleeping. Got close to making it happen. Real close. Can't tell me a natural-born son would have hated his real family that bad.

"Won't never know, Sister," I said to her. "Either way, it was one adoption that didn't take."

Father Duncan was off the phone now with news of some sort. "That was Mrs. Gobel. Nazarene Hospital phoned the rectory. It's about Mrs. Volkheimer. She wants to see a priest. Can you take me over, Wump?"

I was stunned. "But she's only there for observation. What happened?"

"A coronary," Father said. "Happened overnight. She's stable and awake, but she's asking for last rites. We'll take the Bible with us."

Last rites. Extreme Unction. Hearing Mrs. Volkheimer's name, I quit with the self-pity and made myself focus. But I managed one final look through the last few pages of the orphanage logbook. In the *Adopting Parents* column, I didn't see the name Volkheimer anywhere.

23

We made a quick stop at the rectory, so now I had my truck parked in a space facing the rectory's kitchen, waiting for Father to pick up what he needed. My fingers tapped the steering wheel nonstop like an assembly line full of trip hammers, just me and the devil book in here.

Yep. Me and the Devil. The Devil and me.

Hurry up, Father.

I opened the truck door; I had to get out.

After a few long minutes, the snap of the kitchen's wooden screen door made me look up to see Father hustling toward the truck. I caught some movement at a second-floor window, above the kitchen exit. Two slats of the window's closed Venetian blinds separated as someone sneaked a peek at Father leaving the rectory. Monsignor Fassnacht's bedroom; the man was like a phantom anymore. The slats sealed themselves back up.

Father climbed into my truck with a black leather bag. I got back in behind the wheel, a sick feeling engulfing me. I'd seen other bags like it many times, working for the parish long as I had, one bag in particular, carried by someone I now despised.

"Your own bag, right, Father?" He knew what I meant.

"Yes, Wump. Mine and no one else's."

Most recent was when my boy died. I had the hospital summon its priest on call, long as he was from any parish other than Our Lady's; I wouldn't let Monsignor Fassnacht near him.

In the bag would be Father's diocesan-issue sacrament-of-the-sick gear: a prayer book, a crucifix, some anointing oil, a prayer stole. The bag joined him on the passenger side of the bench seat, his hand on its wide handle. This left me and the big devil-book box together on the left. I put the truck into gear.

Nazarene Hospital was fifteen minutes away, just inside Northeast Philly, where it was a lot more populated. We kept to ourselves for the ride, me grinding through the truck's gears from city block to city block, first-second-third, first-second-third, happy with the repetition and how it kept my mind blank. The Father, I couldn't read him, but his stillness made me tense. First, second, third gear...

The truck chugged into the hospital parking lot. It was near noon, visiting hours in full swing since ten o'clock. We parked a distance from the hospital entrance, no spaces open any closer. Father looked down his nose at the Bible strongbox before he climbed out.

"Precious cargo," he said, rolling up his window. "Anything in the back you can cover it with?"

We'd just left Three Bridges and we were barely inside the Philly limits, not in some roughhouse section of its inner city. There was no real crime around here. Still, so Father could feel better, I dragged out a small canvas paint tarp from the back of the truck, draped it over the box, then tucked it under the box's corners. We locked the doors.

"She's on the third floor. Intensive care," the desk clerk said.

We exited the elevator, Father taking the lead down the bright hallway, his bag held firm in his large-knuckled hand. It was like the parting of the Red Sea the way nurses and orderlies and patients with bottles on wheels all hugged the walls to let him pass, me in his wake. We pushed through a set of swinging doors into intensive care and bumped up against the nurses' station just inside. Father was cleared to see Mrs. V, and I got cleared because I was with him.

Intensive care wasn't much more than a wall of light blue floor-to-ceiling curtains pulled around beds on wheels, plus medical equipment we could hear but couldn't see. The unit was full of beeping and humming and wheezing pumps, and snoring and coughing and mumbling patients. The shoes visible between the curtain hems and the white speckled stick-tile floor belonged some to nurses and some to sniffling, nose-blowing visitors. We headed where the nurse directed us, to the bed at the end of the row. The curtain wasn't drawn, and it was the only bed in the unit with access to a window.

One of the bed's chrome-plated pull-up safety bars was down; the bed was empty. We both stopped short.

"Over here, fellas."

Her voice came from the side of a pink vinyl wing chair turned away from us, facing the window. We circled to its front. The tiny Mrs. V sat upright; she'd been able to see our reflections in the window glass. A drip bottle hung on a stand next to her, and trailing it was a thin clear tube that led to an IV needle that disappeared under white tape stuck to the back of her hand. A second connection, a black wire, led from somewhere under her gown to a machine with a gauge like a clock, a busy red needle inside it. Her white hair was combed back into a thick braid with its dark brown vein threaded through it, the braid brought forward under her chin, resting beneath her weathered but perky face.

"Another wonderful day, isn't it, fellas?" she said, not taking her eyes from the brightness showing through the window. When me and the father stayed quiet, she answered herself. "Such fine, warm weather for April. No accounting for my garden, of course, which is in desperate need of a good rain."

"You shouldn't be out of bed," Father said, looking her over, the hem of her flowered nightgown visible from beneath a baby blue cotton robe. Her Easter-yellow slippers didn't reach the floor. I figured Father was doing what I was doing, which was sizing up what it would take to put her back into bed without tangling her up in the hospital tubing. "I was told you had a coronary," he said. "Look, why don't you move back over—"

"You hush now, Father, I'm fine where I am," she told him. "It happened a little after midnight. I thought it was just the hospital food keeping me up, but the darned equipment I'm hooked to said otherwise. My doctor says it was a mild one, so it'll be one more day here in intensive care as a precaution, then another day or two in the step-down unit for more observation. They'll release me, God willing, in time for Easter."

She lifted her right hand from the chair's armrest, not very high, but enough for her to curl every finger into her palm except for her pointer. She delicately aimed her finger in my direction. "And don't either of you figure on trying to carry me over to my bed. I'll get back into it in a minute. I just want the sun on my face."

It didn't look like she was in any danger at the moment, and listening to her defiant little speech made a person think she could live forever. I found a chair for Father and placed it next to hers, nodded for him to sit. He accepted and set his bag on the slate windowsill. "I'm here to administer the sacrament of Extreme Unction," he told her.

"Of course you are, dearie," she said, her blue eyes brightening to go with a small, sly smile. "And to hear my confession." She told Father she sent her family home this morning so they could get some sleep, then had a doctor make the call to the rectory.

Father opened his bag and removed his orange-and-gold prayer stole with swirled red embroidering, kissed it reverently, and placed it around his neck. Mrs. V waited with her age-spotted hands in her lap, her fingers stiff and cupped some from arthritis, and narrow as twigs on a dead tree. Father placed her one hand atop the other, then took them both into his own. His glance at me said I should leave. I wandered off toward the nurses' station.

The adoptions, the devil bible—I was pretty much all stoked up from the past few days. I paced the floor, hands behind my back, one work boot in front of the other, a slow march back and forth in front of the nurses.

A riveting tension started in the back of my head, spread to my neck and shoulders as the hate welled up in me. My upper back sizzled, my brain scatter-gunning its way through memories and events old and new, trying to resolve who the bad guys were.

Old Monsignor Krause. As the parish's nineteenth-century patriarch and a German immigrant, he had started the hysteria. Some called him a visionary. Few other than Sister Irene knew him for what he was, a doomsday prophet who shepherded a flock of frightened, poor, and all-too-faithful immigrants.

And all those murdering parents who, at the monsignor's direction, drowned their firstborn baby boys, the parents convinced, as he'd been convinced, it was something needed doing.

The parish's current pastor, Monsignor Fassnacht. A predator and borderline lunatic.

Religion itself. Too often it was about human sacrifices done out of reverence for the Almighty. "Tests," God called them, with people killing other people just to see if they'd do as they were told. As lame as a plough horse working a rock quarry, this kind of reasoning was, and I wouldn't never buy it.

And my adoptive parents. Only people worse than them abusive bastards were my real parents, whoever they were. Screw them. Screw them all. Maybe it *was* time for a change at the top. Maybe it was time to give some other supreme being a shot at making sense out of all the shitty cards so many of us been dealt, maybe even have him reshuffle the whole goddamn deck.

Calm down, old man, I told myself; you're talking nonsense.

I gave Father Duncan ample time to hear Mrs. V's confession and perform her last rites. As I neared her bed I heard her shooing Father away, her pleasant tone gone, replaced with what? Anger? Despair?

"You have to leave," she said, her eyesight dropping to her fidgeting fingers and the rosary beads wrapped in them. She wouldn't look at neither of us, tears forming on her blinking lashes. Behind the tears, I saw confusion.

"Go. The two of you. Get out. Now."

* * *

"What got her so upset, Father?"

We were at the end of the hospital floor, in front of the elevator. I leaned past him and pushed the button, seeing as how he was too preoccupied to do it himself, the wind gone out of his sails.

"You should know better than to ask that, Wump. I heard her confession then administered last rites. You can take your pick which bothered her more."

I figured she was mentally prepared for the unction, seeing as she was the one who asked for it. And confession was supposed to make a person feel better afterward. Clean slate and all that, once you did your penance. Had to be something else.

I settled on what it was.

"You told her about all them adoptions, didn't you?" I asked him. We got off the elevator, headed toward the hospital exit. "You told her there were a lot of them real soon after the old monsignor's death. Couldn't resist, could you, seeing as how she was alive back then. Wanted her perspective and all. Am I right?"

"Wump," Father said, pushing through the hospital entrance doors into a spring sun that was throwing off heat like it was high noon in midsummer, "give it a rest. Let's focus on getting the old Bible downtown to the Cardinal."

Father shielded his eyes, looked for the faded red of my truck cab among the cars in the parking lot, pointed it out for himself at the far end, then said, "This is the end of the line for our detective work. All the loose ends are tied. In my book, anyway."

We were in the middle of the steamy blacktop when I stopped him short with a hand to his bicep, pulling at him so he faced me. "Here," I said as my fingers reached into my shirt pocket. I slapped a yellowed prayer card into his palm. "In my book," I told him, "there's still a loose end or two."

Father looked the small death announcement over.

"This card," I asked, "was for her son, right?"

"I suppose, Wump. Look, there's no need—"

"Tell you where I found it, Father: in the back of the Devil's Bible. Except unlike most of them other infants whose prayer cards were back there with it, Mrs. Volkheimer's son didn't drown, in the sewers or the river."

"You don't say." He held the card out for me to take it back. I left him hanging.

"Yep. The old photograph of the rededication of St. Jerome's, the donations Rolf Volkheimer and those other wealthy town folk made for the renovations, these things make sense to me now."

"Stop, Wump." Father resumed his walking. I followed on his heels.

"Rolf Volkheimer was readying the orphanage for his own son, wasn't he?" My voice trailed him but he could still hear me. "His wife was pregnant with their first child, but he didn't want to believe the devil-book proclamation. So he hedged his bet by giving their son to a nun, so she could observe his behavior as he grew. Who better than a priest or a nun to recognize demonic behavior, right, Father? Except"—Father retrieved his hanky while we walked, ignored me while he wiped his sweaty neck— "except Rolf died, from a freak accident caused by yours truly. A few months later the old monsignor—the parish's crazy pastor, the reason for the devil-child scare—he died, too. Old age. So one by one them firstborn infant boys who'd been made to live as orphans rather than be destroyed by the hysteria—the older ones, all of them watched real close by Sister Irene as they grew, just in case the proclamation was true—they started getting adopted, with Sister Irene and their parents the only ones who knew the real story. Then something unexpected happened. Sister keeled over at her desk. Heart attack."

"Wump—"

"Mrs. Volkheimer was so very obedient, wasn't she, Father? Just like most all them other misled parishioners of Monsignor Krause, all part of this fine German town of Three Bridges in this, the parish of Our Lady of the Innocents. Appropriate, huh, Father? The parish's name, I mean."

He abruptly stopped in my path, the nostrils of his right-turn nose flaring like he was about to take a poke at me. "I said that's enough, Wump, and I mean it."

"One last observation, Father, then I'm finished. As devout a Catholic as Mrs. Volkheimer was, Rolf couldn't trust she wouldn't rat them out and spoil the plan, so he kept the truth from her all those years. I'm right, ain't I?"

Father lowered his head, resigned to a truth that seemed larger than the both of us. He looked at the prayer card again then unclenched his teeth. "I did say something to her about those adoptions. It was to take the edge off the guilt of the decision she'd made those many years ago, at age nineteen, to destroy her own child. So young, so barely out of her childhood, carrying this burden for so long, and not able to confess it until now. So to answer your question, Wump..."

Father raised his head, and I knew this was a good man, because I saw in his eyes the suffering of his flock, and his frustration at not being able to ease it. Father said finally, "I've only succeeded in having her trade in one kind of guilt for another. Yes, she never knew her child might have survived."

The announcement back in my pocket, we both walked. I wanted to go to her now, but knew I couldn't. I wanted to go back into the hospital and sit with her, put my arm around her fragile shoulder, tell her it was okay, that what was done was done. Tell her she'd had little choice but to follow her faith, duped by a scare manufactured by some religious fanatic who probably wouldn't have recognized the devil from John F. Kennedy. She'd decided on what had to be done, and to offset it, her husband, Rolf, had done likewise. And if God was anything like these religious leaders painted him, he'd forgiven her.

Father slowed his pace and stopped. His jaw slackened and he let out a low, kick-in-the-pills grunt, one that pulled me back into the here and now. So deep in the muck of all this bullshit, I hadn't realized we'd arrived at my truck. Father groaned. "Goodness. For the love of Christ—"

The passenger side window had been busted in, a jagged edge protruding like an iceberg from the deep. Broken glass crunched under Father's wingtips as he moved closer to the window. He twisted the now unlocked handle on the passenger door, and I unlocked the door on the driver's side. The devil book was gone.

24

One thing we learned from the lady at the hospital information desk when we went back to question her: soon after Father Duncan and me showed up, another priest had asked for Mrs. Volkheimer.

"Older than you," the woman said to Father. Then, looking my way: "Around your age but with black hair. A full head of it." She told us the priest had gotten into an elevator but came back down quickly, within minutes, then left the hospital.

* * *

I turned off the truck's ignition. It was near two o'clock. Father and me were a few car widths away from a squared-off layer of windblown trash and leaves that took up nearly a full parking space behind the rectory, the trash settled and fused together after months of sitting undisturbed under a car. From sometime in early winter and up through yesterday, Monsignor Fassnacht's tan Chevy Impala sat on top of this trash. Now the car was gone.

Father climbed out of the truck, shaking broken glass crystals off the seat of his pants in the process. "Just so you know," he volunteered, brushing off his hands, "when I speak with the Cardinal, I intend to tell him about your part in discovering the message inside that Bible, Wump. As long as you don't mind."

Big fucking deal. Like there'd be a prize or something for finding it. I said fine, it was up to him, but I knew things like this didn't never see the light of day again once the Church finally got hold of them. Of course that assumed we could get it back. "I suppose you and him got a whole slew of things to talk about," I added.

Things like visions and infants dying and infants orphaned, and how it seemed like God hadn't much cared about the welfare of this little town back then, not to step in and fix it all.

"I suppose I do," he said. "But I wish I had something to show for it." He leaned back inside the passenger side window, his hands folded, the underside of his jacketed forearms pressed against the ledge. A broken glass chunk still attached to the chrome window trim snagged his sleeve. He pulled the glass piece off, placed it on the truck's front seat, and asked if I needed his help replacing the window. I was thinking a plywood insert would handle it, followed by a trip to the junkyard for some replacement glass after Easter, so I told him thanks, but no. His eyes lingered a moment on the empty space next to me on the front seat.

"It'll turn up, Father," I offered. "Something tells me we ain't seen the last of that book."

"Hope you're right."

Me, I didn't share the sentiment. Sometimes a person needed to be careful about what he hoped for.

* * *

I entered the church through a side door near the rear, let myself into Our Lady's sacristy. One large room, nearly square, brightened by light oak furniture and oak wall trim, all the wood lacquered, the place brightened even more by arctic white wall paint on every other paintable surface. The room had a heavy feel to it, loaded down by plated gold and silver accessories and bulky furnishings: a grandfather clock with an embossed moon face, its three brass weights near as big as gym dumbbells, the weights attached to the ends of thick chains; an antique oak desk with wide legs, its clawed brass feet the size of lion paws; a prayer missal resting on a spindly book stand, the stand seeming too flimsy, the chunky prayer book the size of a large photo album with a thick letter-and-symbol title on its red cover embossed in, lo and behold, still more gold.

And plenty of crucifixes. Some sat on the tops of polished yellow-gold scepters each as tall as a shepherd pole, all kept in a stand in the corner, used for special occasions like High Mass. Another crucifix extended like a paperweight across a pile of papers on the oak desk, was maybe the size of a kid's school ruler, and contained a relic of a German saint. Four other twelve-inch crucifixes were in plain sight, centered on each of the walls, metal-on-wood crosses leaning slightly forward as if Christ's body was ready to bleed on anyone standing directly in front of it. After the vision I seen at the orphanage, I kept my distance from all of them.

On the wall separating the sacristy from the church's main altar were twin oak armoires side by side. Two parish priests meant two wardrobe closets with two sets of vestments, plus any other personal belongings the monsignor or Father Duncan wanted to store here. I told myself the reason I stopped in was to make sure them Stations of the Cross props and costume items Sister Dymphna and me gathered up were where we'd left them, in the room that mirrored this one on the other side of the church altar. Truth was, I wanted to look around.

Last two places I poked my nose into were the wardrobes. First one I opened had a red sweatshirt hung on a hook on one side, and on the flat bottom a leather catcher's mitt and a pair of Converse sneakers. The barrels of two upright baseball bats were visible behind the vestments hung on the armoire's cross pole.

"Bet your baseball locker looked like this too, huh, Father?" I said to no one before a little chuckle escaped my piehole. Just to make sure, I ran my hand around the bottom of the wardrobe, deep into the back, figuring there was no telling where the devil bible might turn up.

No such luck.

I pulled on the wooden handles for the front doors to Monsignor Fassnacht's wardrobe, but they didn't budge. I pulled harder. The doors weren't normally locked, so what the hell was the problem—

Pop. The doors were just stuck. I poked around inside, high and low, but there was nothing incriminating in here either.

* * *

To quote them Saturday afternoon TV cowboys, the kind of day I'd had made me feel like a horse that had been rode hard and put away wet. And I was hungry.

Viola's keys and handbag were on the small table next to our front door. This wasn't normal, Viola being home now in the middle of the afternoon. Also wasn't normal to see her things left out like this neither, seeing as how she scolded me when I did it.

"Viola, honey, where are you?"

No Viola in the kitchen or basement. I went to the upstairs steps, called her name again, made the climb. She was in bed, the covers up to her neck, eyes closed, hair in her night bonnet.

"You feeling okay, sweetie?"

"Just very tired," she said, her eyelids heavy; she'd been asleep. "The Sisters said they would finish my chores. Would you like me to make you some lunch?"

I told her no, of course not, I'd fend for myself. "Get some rest." I climbed in bed next to her, stayed there until she drifted off.

I called her doctor, told him I didn't like what I saw. This wasn't like her, sleeping in the middle of the day. And what about them blood tests, Doc?

"Relax, Mr. Hozer," he said. "Folks are entitled to naps as they get older...No, no answer on those blood tests yet, maybe tomorrow. You mustn't worry..."

I stayed home the rest of the afternoon.

The flu or maybe an intestinal virus was what she had, me and her decided, since half an hour later she was hugging the hopper, vowing never again to eat breakfast scrapple or Lebanon bologna cold cuts or chicken noodle soup, her three meals for today.

Viola slept fine overnight. Got up only once, which was at least three times less than usual. Me, I didn't fare so well with all the crap I'd seen yesterday. Spent a lot of the night awake, thinking some about Viola, some about this town.

I choked down a bowl of corn flakes and milk rather than ask her to scramble eggs for me. She gave me a peck on the cheek, said she'd be fine, and pushed me out the front door, reminding me the church needed me, today being Good Friday and so close to Easter.

25

Warm apples and cinnamon grabbed my sniffer soon as I entered the rectory's kitchen. Mrs. Gobel's old country strudel, from scratch. I told her I'd have some soon as I finished shoveling up the trash the absent Monsignor's car had been protecting in the parking lot. I asked if no car meant there was still no Monsignor.

"Ja. No Monsignor Fassnacht," Mrs. Gobel said from her seat at the kitchen table, a hot tea steeping in front of her. "I checked his room, ja. The door vas unlocked. His bed was still made from yesterday."

Her tired smoke-blue eyes lingered on mine as I took a seat across from her. They were smaller today, her eyes, deeply inset, and her cheek sagged. She seemed sad.

"You okay, Mrs. Gobel?"

"Ja. But Monsignor Fassnacht, he's not okay, ja?"

"He's having a hard time. It might just be because him and the new Father don't get along."

"Ja, that's for sure, but it is more. He is..." She paused, lowered her eyes to her teacup.

"He's what?"

"I think he is leaving," she whispered.

"Leaving?" I said, whispering back at her like most folks did when whispered to. Then, in a normal voice, "Leaving what? The parish? The priesthood? What?"

"Both. The religion maybe, too. There is writing on his mirror."

The writing was in the soft marking-pencil red teachers used to score tests, crushed into the floor-length mirror hung inside the monsignor's closet. It said, *On the quadrillionth day the Scorned One rose to scar the creator's splendor. Third Testament, Metamorphosis 1:1.*

And beneath it, *Duncan, thou shalt rot in heaven.*

Mrs. Gobel waited for me at the bottom of the steps. "Has Father Duncan seen it?" I asked her.

"Ja. He's on his vay to tell the Cardinal about it."

Her eyes turned sadder. "Your vife just called. She is looking for you. She needs you to come home right away."

* * *

We cried together, Viola and me, and for a long time. Now the only one still crying was me.

We sat on our couch, Viola dressed in a housecoat, the collar tied up neatly with a small pink bow, her covered arm feeling gentle as a sparrow's wing on my shoulder. *What a loving, wonderful arm this is,* I thought. If only it could stay there, on my shoulder, forever.

I leaned forward, my elbows digging into my knees. I lowered my head into my hands.

My Viola. My wonderful, wonderful Viola.

I'd gotten home by the time her doctor arrived, and in a voice as tired as an old priest giving absolution, he told Viola and me the results of her blood test. She had leukemia, and it was going to kill her.

Viola smoothed out both suspender straps on my shoulders, fussed over me the way I liked her to. "There's a comfort in knowing how the end will come, Johnny," she said, patting my shoulder again like a mother does a hurt child. "And I have my faith. I am truly not afraid. You mustn't be afraid either, my dearest."

But I was.

* * *

The clock. Last time I glanced at it, on the wall above the hi-fi cabinet, it was nine-thirty; now it was nearly two in the afternoon. I heard the phone ring a few times.

Viola's affairs were in order, she'd already told me. So, too, had been Harry's, ready for when the time came. Mine were as well, but none of it had been my doing. See, around this house I always did what came natural to me, which was use my hands. If something needed building, I built it; when something broke, I fixed it. Viola, she handled everything else; the shopping, the cooking, the cleaning, everything about the family. Including the affairs of the sick and dying, like our insurance, and our wills, and our burial plots. Some parts I didn't have an interest in or the patience for, others, the stomach. No matter now. When the time came, she would rest next to Harry, and me next to her, the three of us in beautiful Bountiful Gardens Cemetery, which was next to the parish cemetery, both graveyards on the edge of town.

I was cried out. Tomorrow was Saturday and Viola's doctor had hours in the morning; we would see him then. For now Viola had left the house, said she was going for a walk and planned on doing some shopping up Schuetten Avenue. It relaxed her, shopping did, so much so she wanted to stay out as long as she could, even if it tired her. She made me promise I wouldn't miss the church's afternoon services if she didn't get back in time. Knowing how much she liked shopping on the Avenue, and how much I loved her, I agreed.

26

As far as handling personal affairs and settling scores went, some had been added to my list that my dearest Viola wouldn't have stood for if she'd known about them. Out of respect for her, I let things run their course and controlled my temper the best I could. But when the time was right, God help the SOBs at the tannery who'd done this to her.

It was near three p.m. and I was in Our Lady's church, sitting by myself in a pew in the second-story choir loft, there only because Viola had made me promise to go. But right then I couldn't have given a constipated cat shit about any of it. Easter, Good Friday, and least of all a reenactment of the Way of the Cross by kids in dress-up. If not for Viola, I'd have told God to his beautiful disease-free face to take a flying—

Jeez, clam up, old man, I told myself. I needed to stay in control, for Viola's sake.

The church was filling up; Stations started in fifteen minutes. Lots of older folks in here, women mostly, their heads covered with scarves tied under their sagging jowls, or with lace doilies bobby-pinned onto rinsed silver-blue or white or ebony hair, their feeble wrinkled hands tangled in rosary beads. My hands were folded and hanging over the choir loft ledge, the church organ to my left, me with a high, end-zone view of the congregation, each station a miniature sculpted scene fixed to a small ledge that was in turn fixed to the wall. Fourteen stations in all, seven on the right, seven on the left, all lit at bottom by flickering red votive candles. I smelled the burning wax laced with a lingering odor of incense, the incense a holdover from a funeral procession. It was good the loft was empty; I wasn't feeling up to being cordial.

Giggling young voices reached me from below, followed by an older voice who spoke low but in a stern enough tone she might as well have been shouting: "Quiet, people," the sister demanded. "You're in church."

Four columns of uniformed children appeared, Our Lady's fifth through eighth grades, two columns of boys, two of girls, all carrying their Maryknoll missals. They walked up the aisles, a sister leading each column, the ragged march looking like a lengthening pitch fork, its prongs leading to the pews at the front of the church, where the grade-schoolers began filling them in. There was a break in the stream of children, the aisles empty for a moment until a second set entered, the ones who were handicapped but could move under their own power, some who I knew from St. Jerome's orphanage. They dragged themselves up the outside aisles, their leg braces and crutches and canes scraping the marble floor, then banging against the wooden kneelers as they filled in more of the pews. The ones in wheelchairs entered last and were parked, or parked themselves, one each at the end of a pew.

My mind. I couldn't stop the hate. What did Christ really know about human suffering? Did he ever let himself feel pain, or did he just say he did? As the Son of God, he had the power to turn it off, so why should we believe he let himself feel any of the agony? To impress his father? To redeem our pathetic human asses?

Far as I was concerned, he felt none of it and still couldn't. He couldn't feel the pain of these handicapped children, else he'd do something for them. He couldn't feel the pain of the living dead neither, the physical and mental agony that came from the total, endless sucking of life from the body of a person with a terminal illness. The agony my Viola would endure until the leukemia finally took her. I knew this pain already, watched it kill my son. I knew it, and I felt it, and God couldn't, and I wanted to know why, damn it.

but He does feel the pain, Wump

In my head, that ocean breeze voice…

I looked past my hands, past my fingers clamped so tight on the lip of the loft's wooden ledge their color was gone, then I looked down onto the congregation a full story below and scoured the faces of the children in the wheelchairs. Someone was missing, yet I knew he was here. I waited and listened for the rest of him to show.

—*EEeeEEeeEEeeEEee*—

The last wheelchair rolled out from under the choir loft, up the left aisle. It was Raymond with Leo pushing him, Raymond's baseball cap in his lap, his blond hair swept behind his ears. "The axle on his wheelchair needs grease," I said to myself, realizing I'd always have a need to repair things. Raymond spoke to me again.

I feel Him, Wump, can feel Him, feeling my pain. He's here with me, and I am grateful for it

Leo pushed Raymond up the aisle, and Raymond didn't stop speaking to me the whole way. Told me wonderful, loving things, in comforting, wind-carried whispers, about how God gave his worn-out body real strength, a strength he never knew he had, the strength to endure, the strength to love those not afflicted like him. The strength not to hate. I felt a settling, peaceful warmth come over me. It lasted only a moment, but it was enough to melt my tension. My hardened hands released the ledge, and I resettled them loosely against its varnished finish. Leo left Raymond at the end of a pew, squeezed past him into a seat. The church grew silent again.

Ring-a-ling-a-ling, ring-a-ling-a-ling.

The congregation stood. A tiny altar boy took a few short, nervous steps up the middle aisle and stopped just beneath me, his handheld bell pulled in tight against his white surplice, the ringer now in his firm but shaky grip, keeping it silent. A priest in orange and red and gold vestments drew up next to him. No mistaking Father Duncan. Broad shoulders, that large right-turn nose. The congregation faced inward, toward the center aisle where the procession was gathered at the rear of the church. Father patted the altar boy on the back then guided him forward with a touch to the boy's shoulder. The procession moved up the aisle.

Except for the altar boys, the children in the procession were all eighth graders, each a Passion Play character in a makeshift costume. Pontius

Pilate was in white, a bedsheet wrapped and tucked inside a rope waist, the toes of a pair of forest-green Hush Puppies shoes peeking out from underneath. Mary, mother of Jesus, had her bedsheet gown draped over her hair, the sheet a royal-blue cotton above the light blue of her wool school uniform. Simon, who would be made to carry the cross, wore a tan peasant smock and brown chinos. Veronica's folded hands gripped the cloth she'd use to wipe Christ's face, her gown arranged like Mary's, but in pale yellow. The Roman centurion tugged at his neck, his clip-on tie looking uncomfortable under a dime store gladiator chest plate, his other hand carrying a broom handle spear. And Adam. Dark, tall, and unmistakable as Jesus, his crown of thorns a jumble of Popsicle sticks stained brown and glued together, the handiwork of the fifth grade. Sister Dymphna followed a few steps behind him.

The procession stopped, turned to face the first station; Father Duncan bowed. His tiny acolyte wobbled into a genuflection.

Father raised his head and addressed the quiet congregation in his pulpit voice. "We adore thee, O Christ, and we bless thee." He then read from his missal, told the congregation their response should be "Because by Thy holy cross, Thou hast redeemed the world."

"Because by Thy holy cross," they said, my lips moving with them, "Thou hast redeemed the world."

Pilate, his arm across his waist to keep his gown from unwrapping, stepped forward to deliver his line. "M-m-my conscience…"

I had trouble hearing him, he was talking so low. Sister Dymphna leaned in, said to him in a loud whisper, "Speak up."

Pilate responded in a cracked voice, "My c-conscience says you are innocent, but the people say differently. Jesus, I condemn you—to death."

Jesus, in front of Pilate, tilted his Popsicle-sticked head a degree or two up, meeting Pilate's eyes. It was then I saw Adam's lips move; Pilate flinched. One thing I remembered about the Way of the Cross: whatever lines Adam had in the play, they weren't this early.

Father Duncan finished the first station by launching into an Our Father while young Pilate retraced his steps down the center aisle to the back of the church, just like in practice. The Our Father was followed by a Hail Mary, then a Glory Be. Plenty enough prayer for the boy playing Pilate to come back up the right aisle, find the pew where his classmates were, and elbow his way into the end of it, also just like in practice, except none of this happened. It was then a voice echo faint as a heart murmur reached me, on instinct making me look right at Raymond, and again on instinct making me wait for the next message. When the second echo hit, I realized it wasn't in my head, that it was coming from the bottom of the stairwell leading to the loft. Sounded like a boy, whimpering.

I descended the stairwell and here was our Pilate underneath the steps, bent over toward the wall, his forehead pressed against the marble. His cheeks were lined with tears.

"What's the matter, son?"

His puffy eyes were focused on his hands as he nervously picked at his fingers. "I'm going to die," he said, drawing on stunted breaths, his sobs ringing the stairwell, "in a rice paddy, in another country, with my throat cut. He condemned me. Jesus condemned *me!*"

"Take a deep breath," I told him, laying a hand on his shoulder. "Adam's having a tough time. Just ignore him. He doesn't know—"

"He's not Adam!" he sobbed. "His voice, it was like a full-grown man's. When he whispered, I—it was like he really was Jesus!" Young Pilate spun from under my arm and untangled himself from his bedsheet, revealing his plaid school clip-on over a flyaway-collared white shirt.

"I didn't want to be Pilate. Pilate was a bad guy. I'm sorry, Jesus!" He rushed out from under the stairwell and pushed through the heavy exterior church doors. I followed him outside before the door closed, called for him to stop, but he'd sprinted halfway down the block already, running toward a late afternoon sun beginning its disappearance into evening twilight. Except—

Out here, the sun—it was too low in the sky for this time of day. It was April; the days were supposed to be getting longer. It wasn't even three o'clock, and what I saw on the horizon was an dusky-orange sun trimmed in half by a block of row homes, the sun looking tired like it did in the fall, just before it gave way to the bleakness of winter, rather than the way it should be, primed and ready for spring. Its normal fireball color, a burning brilliance that could sizzle a person's pupils, was paling before my eyes, taking on the flat, dead pewter of a midnight full moon. I stared at it, viewed it head on without blinking, because for some strange reason I could.

I thought about Viola, that I should look for her.

"You're an old fool," I muttered, then told myself to cut the shit. Could be there was a simple explanation. An unexpected storm front. A rare eclipse maybe; one that came once every hundred years or so. Or a new phenomenon the weathermen would get to study on for decades. I headed back inside knowing only that something wasn't right. I closed the door behind me and stood there with my back to it.

The congregation was on its feet. The pews closest to me in the deepest part of the church, farthest from the altar's artificial lighting, drifted into darkness, the older parishioners squinting at prayer books they now needed to lift closer to their faces. The interior lighting—I needed to switch it on.

I took to the shadowy right aisle under a wall of stained glass windows set back in alcoves two stories high. At this time of day on brighter after-noons, these windows would be brilliant, overpowering, their thick mosaic panes forming shafts of light that looked like spun cotton candy, the rainbow kind. Sitting in their warmth, Harry told his mother he felt such an unmatched comfort; said it was like God's smile, so radiant as it warmed his diseased body. But today, at this moment, the panes were the dull color of the walls, a so-what blend of black and white and ash. Single votive candles lit the foot of each ivory-carved station like torches in a medieval castle. Scenes of torture in miniature, these stations were, fitted into marble half-shell inserts between the windows and the floor. I stopped on the fringe of the second station's squirming, shape-shifting orange candlelight. In the middle aisle Father Duncan's procession stopped and turned to face the second station as well.

From across a bobbing sea of children's heads, I watched this pious priest again recite words that, for him, I figured were more fulfilling than the oath of President.

Father Duncan: "We adore thee, O Christ, and we bless thee."

The congregation: "Because by Thy holy cross, Thou hast redeemed the world."

Sister Dymphna trailed the procession. She retrieved my makeshift cross from the last pew, placed the scrap wood creation onto Adam's shoulder. The procession moved on. On cue at the third station, Adam dropped to one knee.

"Jesus falls for the first time," Father Duncan told the congregation, then, "We adore thee, O Christ, and we bless thee."

"Because by Thy holy cross, Thou hast redeemed the world."

Adam rose to his feet, the cross still on his shoulder.

Inside the utility closet just off the baptismal chapel I pushed up two switches then backed myself out to see the result. Forged, clear-paned iron lanterns big as old-fashioned streetlamps now illuminated the kneeling congregation; the parishioners lowered their prayer missals to arm's length. I stepped back into the utility room and threw two more switches, peeked out again into a church now as bright as it was for midnight Mass on Christmas Eve, the domed ceiling fully visible from the spray of spotlights at the base of its upward curve. Again the beauty of this church impressed me, its ceiling a burst of saints and angels in a celestial sky below a mural of God the father, the mural studded by specks of white-paint stars that twinkled from reflections of the spotlighting beneath them.

The procession swayed its way up one side of the middle aisle then down the other, stopping across from each station's platform for Father to deliver his prayers. At the eleventh station, Father raised his head and announced soberly, "Jesus is nailed to the cross." He offered the prayer, "We adore thee, O Christ, and we bless thee."

"Because by Thy holy cross..."

He read once more from his Maryknoll missal. "The executioners throw our Lord onto the cross. His arms and legs are extended. Hammers fall, and His body is nailed to the wood. The cross is raised for the whole world to see. The weight of His body tears at the nails. Rivulets of blood make their way to earth. Cramps and suffocation set in. Every nerve of His body is taut with agony. The King of Heaven and Earth willingly lies helpless."

Sister Dymphna removed the cross from Adam's shoulder. Adam rose to his full height, tall, lanky. His forehead looked wet from gleaming sweat as it drained from under his crown of Popsicle-stick thorns.

Except it wasn't sweat. The consistency, the color, they were both wrong. Too thick and dark. On cue Adam lifted his arms as if to mimic the outstretched Christ on the cross. He tilted his head slightly, turned it in my direction and raised an eyebrow, seeming to see me over the heads of his classmates. The brightness of the lighting glinted off the syrupy trails on his wet forehead, and for a few swollen moments I was again on a midnight battlefield in France, hugging dirt in a foxhole, shells screaming overhead, bomb-fire in my path, my soldier buddy from Tennessee fifty pockmarked feet of earth away from me, me and him wondering how we looked to each other, our fearful eyes granted fleeting black and white snapshots of ourselves from the shells busting up the ground around us. A hellfire blast ripped off my helmet, left globs of blood-tinged sweat on my temples and brow. I stared blindly to my left, into the battlefield darkness, waiting for the next bomb-burst glimpse of my GI buddy, waiting and listening while arcing rockets ripped holes in the air, and found their marks in distances from us which shortened with each exploding descent. The next flash revealed what the first blast had done, my buddy's helmet gone, his scalp gone with it, his face and ears a mask of dark, drippy red molasses, this young man from Tennessee only seconds away from a death I wouldn't see.

I blinked again at Adam and took an instinctive swipe at my forehead, now realized it was me who was doing the sweating and Adam who was doing the bleeding.

He was no longer a boy playing Jesus. I was jolted instead by the image of a battered man, a halo of blood creeping down from the crown of his head. I blinked hard, tried to clear my eyes, but the gore-soaked Jesus was still there. His eyelids were open only part way, and when his head again swung in my direction, he nodded. It was a signal; I was sure of it. Something a back-alley gambler on the con gave someone else in the trade who may have been on to him; my stomach lurched in response. There was a buzz in the congregation, and my wonder whether others saw what I was seeing was confirmed. Some began raising their voices in panic. Others showed tears of joy, said they saw Christ, and it was a miracle.

To hell with you, Adam.

He smiled at me, still in his pose, his arms stretched out from his sides like a doll on a stick. Then he raised his head toward the domed ceiling. I followed his eyes, and I was awestruck.

I felt my face redden. My ears tingled, my nerves, my whole being, snapped to a frightened, electrified attention. I watched as he watched: one by one, each of them twinkling stars on the ceiling dissolved.

The church lighting sputtered, on the walls and ceiling both. A final power surge was followed by the screams of terrified children and adults, all of it making me realize this wasn't some shell-shocked, faraway battle-field vision, this was real, and it was happening now. The altar candles and the votives that illuminated the Stations of the Cross all snuffed themselves into smoky trails. The church plunged into a gray-black din.

My eyes adjusted as I lifted kid after sprawling kid by whatever parts of their clothing I could grab, pulling them off one another at the end of each bottlenecked pew, then standing them on scrambling feet that all hit the ground running. The nuns barked orders to their charges to remain calm while adults led the kids and each other to safety through the back and side doors, the old folks among them rapidly blessing themselves over and over, their frenzied fingers crossing their chests but never really touching any part of their bodies in the process.

Weren't two minutes went by before the power was suddenly back on, the church still half full of chattering parishioners, some now breathing cheek-filled sighs. Their exit turned orderly until the noise level rose again, a few of them looking up, noticing the same thing I noticed only a moment ago.

The silver-and-gold-embossed mural of God the Father, which graced the highest point of the domed ceiling, was wearing away before our eyes, losing all color and definition. The few remaining parishioners screamed again in panic. Within seconds, the mural faded into nothingness.

Father Duncan stared at the empty space in the ceiling, his jaw slack, his face in awe, his head craned while he did a slow pirouette, as if a better angle would give him a different outcome. The last few parishioners stumbled out the exits and into a midafternoon darkness that figured to confuse and frighten them even more. I searched their faces as they left, caught Father doing the same. There was one face I was looking for: Adam's.

27

I followed the quickened footsteps of a frantic Father Duncan as he pushed through the curtained passage in the front of the church, a red velveteen entrance at floor level to the left of and next to the church's elevated altar. A few steps inside the curtain was an east-west hallway behind the altar, the passage running the width of the building. A left turn led to the sacristy. The door was open.

Inside, Father was ripping off his vestments, whipping each piece into his armoire, grunting because he couldn't get them off fast enough. Peeled down to his cassock and panting, he finally noticed me in the doorway.

"Wump," he said flatly. His face was pale, his dark hair mussed and forgotten. "It seems the Church's two thousand years of vigilance"—he moved to a desk, picked up the cradled phone receiver—"may be about to prove its merit."

There came a time when a player had to take full stock of his cards. Could be the cards were drawn as the stakes were raised. Or it could be he'd been lying to himself all along, denying he'd ever been in the game, and when he finally studied his cards, he could see with a sudden awareness that he was holding the perfect hand, dealt straight from the dealer's shuffle. Except for one problem: he wasn't so sure he wanted the pot, because it was loaded full up with family grocery money and home mortgages, and the proceeds from Sunday's widows and orphans collection. Still, at some point, his cards needed to be shown.

I spoke to Father Duncan with the soberest voice I owned. "I can't say I wouldn't welcome a change at the top, Father. Not anymore."

His finger hesitated above the phone dial as he studied me, almost like he was seeing me for the first time. He jerked his eyes away for a moment as he placed the receiver back onto its cradle. His eyes returned to mine. "You need to explain that comment, Wump."

"My wife just learned she'll die soon," I told him, "from the same illness that killed my son." I could feel my teeth grinding, my face changing color. "They never did nothing to deserve their fates, Father. So *you* explain to *me* where the Almighty's goodness is in all this, and why some other supreme being shouldn't get a shot at running this fucking rodeo."

My chest muscles tightened, the veins in my neck cording. A part of me said to take a bite out of the father right here, right now, for backing an entrepreneur who'd lost touch with his creation, and just maybe ought to step down.

"What I want," I felt my lips curling in anger, "is a God who cares about the people and things *I* care about."

Father's face wrinkled in a pained disbelief. "You're willing to trade the souls of every living creature who's ever inhabited—and will ever inhabit—this earth for one person's flesh-and-blood-only existence?" He blinked until his eyes narrowed, his body tensing. "Death is a condition of human life, Wump. Without it, there's no chance at the everlasting part."

"I don't know if the everlasting part exists, Father, and you don't either."

"Oh, but you are wrong, Wump. There are signs." His voice was almost pleading. "Miracles. Visions. They've hinted at its existence, hinted at an everlasting life which embraces all souls with equal vigor, but with far from equal final treatment. You've seen them, experienced them yourself. It's all we've got to go on, and for the rest of the folks out there, for all the people who hope to be with their loved ones forever in an afterlife but who've had to live by faith alone with no glimpses of the spirit world, it's been enough."

Tears. I felt them coming, squeezed them back. I wanted to believe him; I wanted this "faith." But all I knew was what I saw, and what I thought I was, and who I thought I was becoming. "Tell me this," I choked out, demanding of him, "who was it you saw out there at the end of Stations: Adam or Christ?"

"What I saw"—his mouth closed to a straight line, then reopened—"was what he wanted the congregation to see: Adam *as* Christ. What he is, I'm afraid, is an apprentice charlatan out to create a buzz while padding his resume with visions like these, taking his first steps at learning how to play to an audience. He is, I believe"—Father blessed himself—"the son of the Beast. The false Christ, still in training. And worry as you may, Wump, you, my friend, are not."

"How can you be sure about me, Father?" I said, straining, measuring this man from across the room. "Inside me—there's so much hate, so deep a need for vengeance. Against every person out there who's ever hurt me or my family. And against him, the Almighty. The Creator, who let this all happen while he 'rested.'" My teeth clenched, tight enough to tear the hide off a buffalo, or the flesh off a human being.

"I should have been tossed away like the rest of them, into the river or the sewers! I should have been drowned with all them innocent babies, their bones—*my* bones—spit up then spread out all over the morgue's concrete floor, like a dinosaur exhibit!

"It was *me* who was the bad seed at the orphanage. Me who was responsible for all them fires—oh, how I enjoyed them fires, Father—and me, who let some defenseless, sad-sack little kid take the blame, for Christ sake." My words were raspy, and I felt my lips quivering. "With parents who adopted him, then killed him, just to make sure he wasn't 'the one.' Killed him for something *I* did. The timing of my birth, the devil-book prophecy, the signs are there. They should have killed me, before I had a chance to do the things I did. The things I may be capable of doing. I'm a time bomb, Father, and now that I'm about to lose Viola." I felt my jaw shaking. "The fuse has been lit."

"Wump. Please. Settle down." Father's voice—it was soothing, understanding, the tone a priest used with a child whose sins maybe weren't bad enough to sit him in the corner let alone send him to hell. "You need to ask yourself one important question. If you're the false Christ, then who, or what, is Adam?"

"The real thing."

Father's mouth hung open a moment, and I could tell he was straddling a fence in his head, evaluating the whole frigging mess the two of us been exposed to these past few days. His downturned mouth showed he'd reached a verdict.

"The 'Second Coming'? No," he said firmly. "Absolutely not. You've got it all wrong, Wump." He lifted the telephone receiver again, wiped a sweaty palm against his pant leg, then poised his hand above the black-and-white dial.

"I've got it all wrong, Father? Really? So what is it you know about Adam and me that makes you so cocksure?"

"It's all about pedigree," Father said, rotating his thick index finger around the dial, manhandling each number. "Adam's pedigree matches what was written by the demon himself, and yours...well, yours does not."

He shot a quick glance out the crisscrossed panes of the sacristy window, grimaced at a darkness that had fully overtaken the midafternoon. "I'm calling the cardinal. He needs to know what we saw here today. What the whole congregation saw here today."

Father lost me. "My what? My 'pedigree'? What about my pedigree?"

There was a sound to my left, air rushing past us from an outside draft. It came from the vestibule alcove where a slanted shadow covered a second entrance to the sacristy. The brush of air was followed by a thud, something heavy that had been dropped flat onto the marble floor.

"Hold on a minute," Father said sternly into the phone's mouthpiece.

Like a chunk of split firewood tossed onto a frozen pond, a large book slid out from the vestibule, rotating as it crossed the floor's slick, marble surface. Once in the center of the room, friction slowed the book to a stop, one final twist slapping its cover open.

The pages of the Devil's Bible flapped themselves in a frenzied blur, Father and me on separate sides of it, until the crinkled paper settled itself. In the shadowy vestibule I now saw the bottom half of a cassock. It was red, not black, making me do double take because of the color. Finally the difference sank in.

Not black. Cardinal red.

"Father," I said, not sure if he was paying attention, "if you want to speak with the cardinal, hang up and turn around."

28

"Thank you for the introduction, Mr. Hozer."

This voice. I recognized it, and it wasn't the cardinal's. I squinted, trying to make out the man's facial features in the shadowy vestibule. He spoke again.

"Although I expect to be announced as 'His Eminence, the Cardinal.'"

Father Duncan hadn't turned around yet, instead strained with the phone to his ear while he spoke into the receiver, hard, right through frantic interruptions of the person on the other end who was so loud I could hear him from across the room. "Brother York! Calm down! Stop. Wait—" Father put a hand over his other ear to better hear. "Say it again, slowly."

Father Duncan suddenly stiffened. He turned in my direction, let the hand with the phone in it drift down to his side, then glanced at the demon bible on the floor between us. I nodded toward the vestibule. Out stepped Monsignor Fassnacht, his cassock the scarlet red of an ordained cardinal.

"Let me help you understand, Father Duncan," the monsignor said. With little effort he slid a tall scepter from a stand in the corner of the sacristy, the scepter's top end a heavy, hard-angled gold cross. He moved closer to Father, the pole end of the scepter resting lightly on the floor in between each step. Something wasn't right about his red cassock. The upper half, in the front. It looked to be two shades of red, the second more brown than scarlet, but only in spots—large, misshapen, brownish-red blotches, one of them wide, leading down from the neckline.

Jesus. The cassock was wet with blood, some of it already caking up.

"I suspect the Cardinal's assistant, that faggot Brother York," Monsignor said to Father, "has lost his stomach over what he's found in the cardinal's residence. Am I correct, Father?"

Terror lit up Father's wide, coffee-bean eyes. "He told me the Cardinal is dead," he said, Father swallowing hard. "He said his head was ripped off his body. It took a monster to do something like that."

"Let's be civil now, Father Duncan. Perhaps I was a bit, shall we say"— Monsignor wandered along the wall on my left, taking in the entire sacristy —"overly aggressive with him. But it was only because his snooping, through you, has made me feel more frustrated lately." He nodded his head, agreeing with himself. "Yes. Frustrated and threatened. It's like this, Father.

"My dream of advancing through the religious morass of Church politicos, well, it just never materialized. I've been mired in middle management, you could say, ever since they sent me here. But I toed the line, administered to a parish full of blue-collar, sauerkraut immigrants and their descendants for, how long has it been now? Oh my." His voice rose then fell in mock surprise. "It's been over thirty years! It took a while—more than half that time—for me to realize the only real currency in this business is, well, currency. Being assigned to a poor parish, one's advancement opportunities become a bit limited. That is, unless one is presented with a better offer. And I was."

Father Duncan kept a half-room distance from Monsignor, whose wandering took him past the long, windowed wall of the sacristy and closer to me. The monsignor stopped, picked up one sacristy trinket after another, examining then discarding them—letter openers, small plaques, a votive candle—returning each item to the polished surface of the credenza, his mouth turned down, looking bored. He lifted a paperweight, round, the size of a baseball but made of clear glass, with the Nativity scene inside. He raised it above his shoulder, faked a toss to the father. Father Duncan, deep in concentration, didn't flinch. Monsignor lowered the paperweight, let it sit in the palm of his open hand as if presenting it to us, then smiled while he closed his fingers around it. He crushed the glass and the figures inside until the paperweight was reduced to sand that ran through his fingers, onto the floor.

"Can't say I'll miss this place," Monsignor said. "Can't say I'll miss it one fucking bit." He raised an eyebrow as if he'd surprised himself.

"'Fucking,'" he said, his eyes twinkling. "How I've come to really enjoy that word, its sound so sharp, its spoken feel so abusive to the teeth and lips, so wonderfully violating, just like the act itself. *'Fucking!'*" he said louder, barking the word's hard-edged syllables while he passed in front of me. "Considering all the, ahem, fucking I've been doing lately, I've come to appreciate human behavior when it is at its crudest; how much fun it can be at its most primitive, animalistic level. Which brings me to you, Mr. Hozer."

Monsignor turned, stepped in closer to me. No way was I gonna move. Not gonna cringe one bit for this bastard. He sidled up and breathed into my face, and at this distance I smelled how sour his old-man breath was. Bad as decaying flowers on a gravesite after an animal's pissed on them.

"Lovable old Wump. What a wonderful name. 'Wump.' How perfectly it matches your personality and your mastery of some of the cruder elements of the English language." He sneered at me. "How stupid you are, Wump. It seems you need a lesson. About old books, and about translations of old scriptures. About how every word written, back when the written word was newer, meant something, and should never be overlooked. Last century the parishioners of this filthy, run-down tannery town, and apparently its clergy, too"—Monsignor chuckled—"had misconstrued a message. The message delivered by a very handsome angel whose only sin was his pride, and who fell from God's grace because of it." The monsignor suddenly turned, pointed the scepter at Father like a teacher in a classroom. "Father Duncan! Explain it to him like you were wont to do earlier. Explain what you meant by 'pedigree.'"

My fingers coiled into fists; something Father didn't miss. "Wump, don't do anything rash—"

"Duncan! Quit the bickering," Monsignor warned. "I'm not here to harm old Wump. I'm here to...Well, let's be honest about this. I'm here to harm *you,* you meddling fool. Now explain it to him!"

Father Duncan moved in front of his vestment armoire, stayed focused on Monsignor.

"'Avowed to him,'" Father said without looking at me. "The words he is talking about, which appear in the Devil's Bible—this phrase follows the declaration of how the false Christ will be a firstborn child; the 'first from two virgins.' It was misinterpreted by the few who had seen it, and when passed word of mouth from generation to generation, the phrase would have rarely been mentioned. Church dignitaries, New Testament scholars, and this parish's overly zealous monsignor from the last century, who forced his God-fearing flock to adhere to the same misinterpretation, making them destroy all firstborn sons from virgin relationships or face being shunned—they all got it wrong, too."

"Very good, Father," Monsignor said. "Now explain its significance."

"'Avowed to him,'" Father repeated. "Not simply to mean reverent followers of God, or those avowed practitioners of the Faith, but rather to mean clerics, or those who have taken the religious vows of celibacy, obedience, poverty. Specifically, the false Christ child would be the product of the ultimate transgression: carnal union between priest and nun."

Monsignor Fassnacht closed his eyes like he was listening to a melody, the cocky bastard relishing the moment—"Yes, oh *yessss!*"—and me, I was on red alert, my pulse quickening. This place, it was about to explode. I could sense it. Could sense an undercurrent, could feel the violence. In him. In me.

His eyes reopened, dreamy and relaxed. "And that, Father Duncan, is where I came in. Enter the unfulfilled cleric. Someone willing to forgo the vague promise of a joyful afterlife for the guarantee of a really great here and now. My prayers to God all those years...who'd have thought I'd hear from the competition instead? And with a better deal. *Ha!*"

Monsignor suddenly slapped the head of the scepter down hard against the top of the credenza as if the two of us had fallen asleep in class. He swept the scepter's crucifixed end across the flat surface, sending books and pens and other paperweights scattering. "He's really misunderstood, mind you. I'm speaking of Lucifer, the fallen angel, of course. The poor malcontent's just looking for some equal time. So I agreed to do something for him. Something simple. I agreed to talk the very young, very impressionable, and deliciously dark and sexy Sister Magdalena into thinking she could be the next virgin mother of Christ. And after I did what was asked, Lucifer, honest chap that he is, made the first installment on what he agreed to do for me."

Monsignor grabbed the inside of his thigh, up near his crotch. "Bulked me up like a steer on hormones," he said, shaking his package, "so all the women will crave me. But I had to agree to one other thing as well, of course: I had to let him take the inaugural spin behind the wheel of my new 'Caddy'"—he grabbed his crotch again—"while he fired the first salvo at Sister Magdalena. After all, this is the proclamation, right? Then lo and behold, a star was born. And as long as I follow the rest of the script, I get Lucifer's second installment on the deal: the Papacy, Father! Or at least a promiscuous equivalency of it! So tell me, Wump, you sorry old bugger, you..."

All this "old man" crap was pissing me off. Bastard was old as I was, goddamn it.

"Just what is it you would have done," he said, leering at me, "had you been who you thought you were? Huh, old man?"

"Who you calling old, jackass? You're crazy. I'm gonna whip you silly—"

"No, Wump!" Father cried then reached inside the armoire. "Back off!"

I hit the monsignor below the belt, a full-fisted delivery I hadn't used since prison, aimed with the cruelest of intentions, a punch reserved for wife-beaters and rapists and child molesters, and now the defiler of a young, defenseless nun. After the punch I tried grabbing hold of what I'd hit so's I could squeeze him into submission but—my God—the pain—my knuckles—they were broken. "Owww..."

Monsignor's powerful backhand flung me across the room, sending me crashing shoulder-first against the doorjamb. Through ringing ears I heard him curse me then laugh then curse me some more. I was dazed, defenseless, his blurred red outline walking slowly toward me while he raised the long gold scepter high above head, until—

THUMP. Monsignor's face lit up in surprise. My eyes cleared, and I could see him touch the back of his head with his hand, then turn wearily around. Father Duncan was standing on balanced feet, his baseball bat cocked, ready to deliver a second blow. For one fleeting, hopeful moment, I believed Father and me had a real chance.

Monsignor grinned; the moment dissolved.

"Part of the deal," he said, amused and no worse for either assault, "was I answer to no one. Guess I best stop fooling around with the riffraff and get to the business at hand."

He stepped back toward Father Duncan, raised the crucifix-tipped scepter shoulder high and parallel to the floor. The cross ignited. "You should have never come here, Duncan. You were too late." Monsignor took a swipe. Father dodged it, the scepter trailing fire.

"The dead babies?" Monsignor said, taunting him. "It's ironic how close to the truth the insane pastor was, but still, nevertheless, his was a wasted effort. This wonderful boy, my offspring, so to speak. Adam. He's such a joy, isn't he, Father? He leaves next week, along with his sister, to be reared by old-country folks who know Lucifer's ways."

A second swipe singed Father's cassock. Father ripped the cassock off, tossed it toward the middle of the floor where it billowed before settling on the devil book. Father again raised his bat, gripped it with both hands, gritted his teeth, and slammed the bat against the side of Monsignor's skull. The force of the blow jammed Monsignor's head unnaturally against his shoulder. He stutter-stepped and stopped. The swing should have killed him. Instead, his head slowly tilted back upright to face the father, and after a second stutter-step and a scowl, he was on the move again. Father connected with another full cut to the head, then another, but Monsignor continued to close in. Soon Father was backed into a corner, none of his swings having any effect. His breathing slowed until he calmed himself. He lowered his bat to his side.

"Father!" I yelled; I got to my feet. "No! Don't quit!"

"Wump, you listen to me," Father shouted. "Don't come any closer."

"How touching this is," the monsignor said, "and how close you two have become. What a pity though, huh, Duncan? The way things were before, you might have lived a long life, albeit as a pathetically nondescript cleric, and you would have never been the wiser. You might have grown old and died before seeing any real change.

"The display the church congregation saw here today? You were right, Father; the boy's in training. But you"—Monsignor raised his finger and wagged it at him—"you and the cardinal, you both thought you could interfere. And now you, like the cardinal, will pay the price." He spun in my direction. "Offer your respects to Father, Wump. And Duncan, say your final prayers. But fear not—"

Monsignor contorted his face then spread his feet like a woodcutter. With both hands he curled the scepter high above his head, ready to deliver a chopping, granddaddy of a blow.

"—I'm sure there's room for you in heaven, where you'll rot with the rest of the losers!"

The scepter descended with the crushing force of a battle-ax, but at the last second it dropped wide of its mark, landing lightly against Father's shoulder. The monsignor lurched forward, his eyes bugging out in a pain-filled wonder. Reaching up with shaking fingers he touched a foot-long crucifix embedded in the top of his skull. He turned on wobbling legs, his face and body convulsing, then he flicked out a desperate hand at his attacker, who stood flatfooted behind him.

"M-my son—"

His fingers caught young Adam's pants on the way down, squeezed then released them, and the monsignor collapsed into a choking, blood-spitting heap at the boy's feet. He exhaled his final breath, his eyes freezing into a dead man's stare.

All my senses were alive, fear popping and hardening my veins. I heard myself breathing, could see and hear Father emerge from the corner, his chest heaving, his steps tentative around the leaking head of the dead monsignor. Adam, his costume crown of thorns still intact, exhaled hard through his nose, but not as hard as Father did, who he was watching real close.

Father was awestruck into silence; he slowed his breathing. I reeled from the shooting pains in my right hand, not able to flex it and not wanting to, some, maybe all of my knuckles broken. Through my agony I heard something behind me, outside the sacristy, the tinny, annoying echo of a squeaky wheel as it crossed the marble floor of the church altar.

—*EEeeEEeeEEeeEEee*—

The color in Father's face was gone. He swallowed once, twice, his eyes never leaving Adam. Father struggled to speak.

"I don't know what to say, son, other than thank you. The monsignor was unstoppable. A madman. But truth be told—"

"He was lying, Father," Adam said, his juvenile voice cracking like it had just crossed into puberty. "Or maybe he was just mistaken. About one thing at least."

I squinted, unsure of what I saw. Rising above Adam were a pair of bare, olive-skinned shoulders caked in sweaty grime and streaked with scabby whip marks, and between them lifted the thorny, bleeding head of Jesus Christ. The battered form of the Savior engulfed Adam. "The deal he had, whether Monsignor realized it or not," Adam said, his voice deep, strong, no longer juvenile, and coming to us from his and Jesus's lips at the same time, "was he answered to no one except *me*." Adam and the form of Jesus squatted next to the body. "Step back, Father."

Adam's right hand reached in and gently—compassionately, like a chaplain on the battlefield—closed the monsignor's eyes. Still squatting, Adam and Jesus tilted their heads up, greeting our puzzled looks, then—

Adam's sober expression twisted, was overlaid by an impish, sneaky grin that said, *Just thought I'd keep you guessing*, and the hand that gently closed Monsignor's eyes now savagely gripped his chubby, lifeless face, and squeezed, crushing it like an overripe tomato. The embedded crucifix pinched out with a squishy *thlok* and slid onto the floor. Adam and Jesus wiped their bloody hand on Adam's pants. As the two of them glanced at the open vestibule door, the monsignor's bloated body lifted and was flung through it, disappearing into a windy updraft in the darkness outside.

Adam and Jesus, whose blood-spattered, murky faces now surrounded piercing and soulless black eyes, returned their amused attention to me. "Wump, you and I need to talk."

I heard the squeaky wheels again.

—*EEeeEEeeEEee*—

"But seeing as I have some business with Father, now is not a good time," Adam and Jesus said. "So I don't give a *schuetten* if you hang around or not."

I leaned against the jamb to steady myself, my limp broken fist cradled in my good arm. Long as Father was here I wasn't going nowhere no matter how much it hurt, or how terrified I got.

"When we last spoke, Father, about my mother's unfortunate accident" —Adam's young features were fuzzy, a glowing mist that shifted between a uniformed schoolboy and a grit-encrusted, half-naked, crucified man in soiled and bloodied bedclothes—"I guess I sounded like one really confused adolescent, didn't I?" His voice stayed strong, in control. "The train accident wasn't my fault, mind you, but I didn't care when she stumbled. Why, you might ask?" Adam shrugged. "Because she was clutter and needed to be eliminated." He approached Father's discarded cassock, singed and rumpled in the middle of the floor. Under it, the Devil's Bible.

"What have we here?" Adam said, leaning over, feeling the smoothness of the cassock's fabric. He lifted the cassock and tented it in his pinched fingers, tipped his head in Father's direction and hesitated, aware of his audience, then—

"Presto!" he said, pulling the cassock away. "Yes, it's still here, Father, awaiting study by the pompous, self-bestowed guardians of the religious free world, your Catholic Church. But frankly, Father—"

The book shook, began flapping like a flounder on a boat deck until it lifted and balanced itself on one end of the binding. The leather covers separated, and the book opened wide like a loose woman spreading her legs, its spine thrusting in and out at the priest. The pages suddenly ignited into a furious flame, the old leather cover squealing and popping, and the yellowed paper crackling, its embers spiraling to the ceiling.

"—what would be the point?" Adam said. "It too has outlived its usefulness, so it too must go. Just like the monsignor. He showed promise, was to get the Popehood he earned as Lucifer's proxy. Yes, Monsignor drank from the carnal cup and wanted refills. Fornication for the sport of it. How refreshing this was for Lucifer, at least in the beginning. Until Monsignor got impatient. And today he jumped a few too many spaces ahead on the game board."

With a wave of Adam's hand—"This should cozy things up a bit"—the sacristy lighting dimmed. The book was now a gas-pilot blue, burning evenly, efficiently. Adam and the glowing, misty form of Jesus retrieved the scepter and made the first move, taking lazy steps around the devil-book campfire, the scepter twirling slowly in their right hand. Father Duncan picked up his baseball bat and gripped it tightly, his jaw muscles stiffening. With a few clockwise steps, Father was able to keep his distance. It looked like he'd changed his mind about going without a fight.

"What? You're *afraid* of me? Come now, Father..."

Adam tossed the twirling scepter upward at the ceiling like a drum major at a football game. The ceiling disappeared before our eyes, revealing a starless black sky, the baton spinning as it rose until both ends burst into flames. It reached its peak and reversed direction, falling until Adam snared it perfectly in stride. He flashed a winning smile, the scepter spinning as he spoke. "I kept the monsignor from creasing your skull, didn't I? I saved your *life,* Father. Oh. I get it. You're wondering why."

Father reached where I stood, stepped in front of me. He spread his feet, raised his bat off his shoulder, ready to make his stand.

The freakish Adam now straddled the flaming scepter like it was a child's broom-handle horse. He clip-clopped a few steps closer. With a playful smirk, he mouthed off again.

"Sometime early in the next millennium, there will be—are you ready for this, Father? Maestro! Drum roll and cymbal splash, please! Ta-da! A nuclear holocaust! Thank you, thank you, you're so kind," Adam said, bowing. "I'll have reached my fifties, with a solid, widespread base of serious believers, many of them political. I'm bright, I'm likable when I want to be, and my childhood has been one that a campaign manager could only dream of: given away at birth, raised by nuns, and reunited with my mother who, alas, was then tragically killed in a train accident. And the ultimate showstopper: unexplainable but interesting things happen when I'm around. Like you said, Father, all padding on the resume. I'll mix religion and politics. I'll kiss the healthy babies, bless and heal all the rest, and they will love me. 'What, *me* be your president? Well, if you *insist...*'"

Adam and his scepter horse moved one clip-clop closer. "Nuclear winter, Father! Can't keep that busy little splitting atom in only one country's bottle. Once I get the chance, I'll make it go *boom*! Then *boom, boom, boom* and, oh yes, drum roll for the big finish, please—*KABOOM!* Tsk-tsk. It will set this poor planet back, what, thousands of years? Millions?

"Then, and only then, Father"—Adam gritted his teeth behind a raised hand with a pointing finger—"will the real fun begin, but this time it will be with a level playing field. For old Lucifer and me and, you know, *him*. 'The Almighty.' He draws strength from you, you must realize. Is so much stronger than us because of you and the millions of people like you. People who have followed him, pray to him, have faith in him. *Love* and *adore* him. Yuck."

Adam spit into the devil-book fire, the moisture sizzling, the fire doubling in size.

"Except all those people, all that love, will be gone. So then he, and Papa Lucifer, and me, and the other deities out there—trust me, there are more—we'll all get a second chance. And since Lucifer deals in immediate pleasure, and your Almighty offers only a hope there'll be some future, 'everlasting,' potential pleasure to be realized at an unsubstantiated later date—well, you know what they say about 'tomorrow.' It's one elusive little fucker, isn't it? So, given we get away with this planetary makeover, we expect all the love and adoration will get a bit more evenly distributed this time around.

"Look, all we want is a second chance at giving what crawls out of the ashes whatever it desires, so it will be beholden to and honor and adore *us*, not *him*."

Father glanced at me over his shoulder and nodded at the door; his message to get out.

"Ain't leaving you, Father."

"You're a witness to this, Wump. Go. You need to tell the Church."

Clip-clop, clip-clop went the scepter horse. "What, you think I don't hear you, Father? Sure, Wump, why don't you leave. Go speak with the church dignitaries. But before you do, I've got more fuel for your tannery pollution crusade, so while you're at it, why not stop in at Philly City Hall?

"It seems Ruthie, my mute twin, is speaking now. That's right. Her first words to me were: 'Hey Adam, look at this! If you spin in circles you get dizzy then fall down.' How profound. For a kindergartner, not a fourteen-year-old. Yes, Wump, she's a moron like the rest of them, and it *is* because of the water. But who's going to believe an old ground-pounder with battle fatigue? And what would it matter, even if they did? Go on, get out. I have no interest in you. But I do have an interest in Father here."

My feet were frozen in place, like in a dream where I knew I should run but couldn't.

—*EEeeEEee*—

The squealing wheel, behind me, so close.

—*EEee*—

The unlatched sacristy door bumped against my back and held there.

Clip-clop, clip-clop went Adam's shoes. His face turned charming despite its blood-caked, ghostly Jesus likeness. "So it seems, Father, what with Monsignor's recent, ah, dismissal, that we have a job opening. Let's call it Pontiff-in-training, with ascent to the throne guaranteed. Our man here on terra firma. Interested? You've got the experience. A former baseball player who became a priest. Odd combination, but it's one that caught Lucifer's fancy. You've sown your oats already, and you know what it's like to be pleasured, so unlike our most recent candidate, we know you'll be more discreet. You'll keep your extracurricular activities toned down and in your pants, not call attention to our little political movement. In return you'll be the most powerful being on earth. After me, of course. So whaddyasay? Feel like helping me rough up the Almighty?"

Adam squared himself in front of Father, the boy's face with an expectant look underneath his two black, impish cowlicks. "'Pope Connie the First.' Has a nice ring to it, doesn't it? C'mon, Father. It'll be *fun*."

Father lowered the baseball bat but kept it tightly gripped in one hand, his large forearm rippling under a white shirtsleeve, his grief-stricken look visible to me from the side. He nudged me a step farther back, then put on his game face and spoke:

"I am a believer of the one true God who is the Creator of heaven and earth, the father of Jesus Christ, Lord, God, and Savior of the human race." Father made a fist of his right hand, began pounding his way through the Sign of the Cross. "In the name of the Father, and of the Son, and of the Holy Ghost—"

He gritted his teeth and gripped the bat in two hands, raised it to shoulder height.

"—and if you bow your head and repent your sins, I will ask God to grant you absolution." He thrust out his quivering chin. "Confess, and God the Father might allow you to reenter the Kingdom of Heaven. Persist, and you will return to hell."

The devil-book blaze exploded skyward like a high school bonfire at midnight, and as Adam roared back at him in spit-filled anger, Father took a home-run swing at his head. A blurred flick of Adam's wrist put his free hand on the meat of the bat barrel before it could connect but Father didn't let go, instead tried to pull free while a sure-footed Adam looked at him, head cocked like a curious six-year-old watching an ant in the sun under a magnifying glass. Adam released his grip on the bat; Father staggered but regained his balance. Adam turned away from the panting priest, said in a low, disappointed voice as he walked, his head shaking side to side, "Father, Father, Father. You've made a poor choice."

Father raised the bat and took another run at him from behind. Adam suddenly spun, ramming the burning, hard-edged crucifix end of the scepter deep into Father's stomach, twisting it like a prison screw turns a key in a cell lock, then driving it up, under Father's rib cage, lifting the priest off his feet. Father's shuddering body rose, was held high, twitching like a fish on a spear. Adam then whipped the spear over the fire in the center of the sacristy, bellowing his disapproval: "Me, son of Lucifer, confess my sins? How *dare* you!"

Father's arms and legs ignited into winged flames, his chest heaving, his mouth spewing blood, his face contorting in tortured agony.

"Father!" I yelled, my voice ragged, trembling. "*Adam! No,* you *bastard!*"

Father's eyes drilled into me, held me back, and trying to speak, his laboring lips mouthed words through airless lungs: "...get out...now..."

The scepter swiveled out of the fire, slammed against the wooden credenza like a thundering sledgehammer, splitting the desk in two with Father, the hammer's head, still attached. Adam raised the scepter again, Father's blazing body now limp and lifeless as a skewered rag doll. The boy-monster brought the scepter down again and again around the sacristy, crushing piece after piece of furniture with the mangled and charred stump of something that no longer looked like it had ever been a human being.

Much as I wanted to cry for Father right now, and for Viola, and for Harry, and for the whole human race, this wasn't the time for it. I reached

behind me with my good hand, pulled the sacristy door out of the way and
backed up, trying to ease my way out. I didn't get more than a step before
something moved into me.

—*EEeeEEee*—

Raymond's wheelchair was against my leg, a wide-eyed Leo pushing it,
the chair's leather straps belted into place across Raymond's frail body.

"Back him out, Leo! Get him out of here. *Now!*"

"But Raymond wants to know if he said it," Leo said, standing his
ground, his face pleading.

I pushed on the chair arm, but it wouldn't budge. Behind me I felt the
heat, glanced over my shoulder, saw the fire that started as a burning
book now roaring out of control nearly two stories high, Adam's dark
silhouette standing fixed in front of it, the scepter upright by his side,
Father Duncan's torso no more than a smoky roast of meat impaled on its
end. I closed my eyes to this nightmare and turned back to the
wheelchair.

"Move, Leo!"

"But, Wump, Raymond says—"

"Move!"

Raymond's hand slapped onto my forearm in a death grip, and through
his long bony fingers I sensed something—impatience, or maybe seething
determination—until my subconscious was rocked by a bugling, wake-the-
hell-up scream:

DID HE SAY WHO HE IS

"What? *Raymond?*"

I heard a rumbling, and behind Adam a larger figure raised itself to
stand full upright, ten feet high, two pearly-white horns jutting from its
beastly forehead like bony handles, the horns curving down like a ram's,
curling around to frame the figure's charred face. Its form was human, its
beefy naked body the color of scorched pewter, its eyes yellow-gold, its
hands clawed, and its manhood so grotesquely large his legs were bowed
around it. With a single step toward us it, became one with Adam. The
room filled with an overpowering stench, like rotting flesh in sewage.

"Yes!" I shouted at Raymond, and in a flash I remembered Father
Duncan's words: God wouldn't intervene till he was sure it was the real

thing. "He said he's the son of Lucifer! The false Christ, damn it! And now they're one with Lucifer himself! *Go!*"

The beast let out an earsplitting banshee yell that dropped me hard against the floor. I pulled at Raymond's squeaky wheel for leverage, got to one knee and tried to stand. Raymond's hand dropped onto my shoulder, held me down like I was cemented into place until—

SNAP. The leather strap across Raymond's legs retracted like it was spring-loaded, slapped next to my ear like a fly swatter on glass.

SNAP. The wide strap across his waist recoiled the same way, ringing my ears, then—

SNA-A-A-PPP!

Raymond's strapped-in chest busted free of its restraint. His shoulders rose and fell, his chest heaving hard like he'd been holding his breath for ages. He filled his lungs, savored each gulp of air until his pale face and neck colored up to a healthy glow I hadn't seen on him as far back as never. I felt my eyes tear up, and I rubbed them with my good hand, because now I saw this diseased child with half-lidded blind eyes, and legs that been failing him all his life, step out of his wheelchair, and my, oh my if he wasn't simply so wonderfully and incredibly the most beautiful being I had ever seen.

He stood square in his PF Flyers, tall like I'd imagined, then put out a hand with his palm up, like a surgeon waiting for a scalpel, and I sensed a message pass from him to Leo. Leo retrieved a toy saber and the pretend billy club from the wheelchair's basket, placed the saber into Raymond's right hand, the club into his left, then threw the wheelchair's wide leather waist strap over Raymond's shoulder, letting it hang loose, and...

I couldn't recall ever seeing Raymond's back, him always in his chair. Now I saw it real clear from my spot on the floor, and my prior sense of how helpless he was before, so impaired and so feeble, so unfortunate and overlooked by God, all of this gave way to what I made of him now. The boy had a pair of wings the size of a storefront, and as they softly opened and spread out above me, covering the entire sacristy wall, there was this thing that came over me that I was for sure was really certain, and that I could embrace and believe with my entire being, and this one true thing was that now, without a doubt, we were gonna see a brawl of biblical proportions.

this belief of yours—this one true thing—

Raymond's soothing thoughts floated into my head like the aroma from a scented candle.

it is your faith, Wump

it has returned, and I am nourished by it

Raymond inhaled his deepest breath yet, and with a twist of his left wrist the small billy club grew into a top-heavy hammer bound with leather, its granite head the size of a building cornerstone. He flicked his right hand. The toy saber made of hard rubber and plastic became a double-edged sword tall as a lightning rod, its blade broad, long, gleaming. A dead ringer for something I'd seen elsewhere but couldn't place: a yellow mosaic sword set in two stories of stained glass.

The beast, now only Lucifer and Adam, with no trace of a masquerading Jesus, hissed at Raymond, Raymond's blond hair unfurling like a flag in a windstorm. With sounds more like grunts and clucks than a language, I heard the beast snarl and speak, and in my head I heard Raymond translate it:

"Be thou gone, Archangel, for this time my strength is multiplied, swollen by the minions of the damned!"

Raymond's sword—that was where I seen it. In every depiction of Michael the Archangel I could ever remember. Murals, the Bible, church windows...

yes, Wump. I am Michael, and I am one with Raymond

The beast motioned his open hand at the floor, where the gold crucifix late of Monsignor's head rested in a blood puddle. The cross was sucked into his clawed fingers where he gripped it by the short end, its long end lengthening then flattening out like it had been pounded by a blacksmith, becoming a sword twice the size of Michael's, his other weapon the scepter, the small lump of smoking flesh still on its tip. He raised the scepter like a sword swallower, stuck it in his mouth, then pulled it out again, slowly, between clenched teeth, the lump of flesh disappearing like cubed beef on a shish kebab. He chewed and swallowed, took a step toward us, and opened his dagger-toothed mouth; Father Duncan's remains were gone.

My heart sank, and the burned flesh foulness of the beast's breath made my legs weak. His meaty tongue surged at us from across the room, stopped short under Michael's nose where it danced, rising and falling like a whore's body, the tongue licking Michael's cheeks, one then the other, taunting him with its sexiness. Michael showed no reaction. The tongue slid back along the floor, the beast's mouth closed, and its wings emerged from behind its bare, lead-black shoulders like the raising of a circus tent. They were taller, wider, thicker than Michael's. They flapped, and Lucifer hovered.

Michael's wings raised him up, his weapons by his side, a no-never-mind expression on his face. He took up a position across the sacristy from the enemy.

This one true thing, my faith, it was badly bruised, yet I knew that, not far below the surface, it was still here. If faith was what you needed, Michael, then I had loads of it. Eat it up, big boy.

Michael dropped flat-footed to the floor. He nodded at me, his face showing nothing, his blind, other-way eyes still half-lidded and unfocused. He lowered his blond head and advanced on foot toward the beast. His steps turned into a determined march, and the airborne Lucifer's chest inflated until out of his mouth came a full-gutted, raging waterfall of fire. Michael trudged across the marble floor, the righteous sonovagun marching through the blast furnace flames unmarked, straight to their source. Leaving his feet he rose up eye level to Lucifer and clubbed his horned head with a sideways blow that sent the demon back and up like he'd been shot from a howitzer, his monstrous leaden body crashing through the front wall of the sacristy, into the deserted church. Michael followed, gliding slowly over the rubble through a jagged hole big as a bank vault; he set down on the other side. I stumbled through after him, and Leo after me. Inside the church Lucifer had recovered, was still airborne. He circled the ceiling, keen to Michael's entrance.

Lucifer dove like a kamikaze from the far corner, his crucifix sword raised, his scepter blazing, both ready to run Michael through. Michael waited him out, then with the speed of a featherweight boxer he delivered a short uppercut with his fisted sword hand, driving Lucifer upward like he was on a pull string, into and through two stories of shattering stained glass, and rocketing him out of sight deep into a starless, night-like sky.

Michael rose above the debris and drifted out of the church. Leo and me found a door and hurried outside in time to find him standing beyond the empty parking lot on the grassy slope leading down to the edge of the river. Michael's weapons were by his side, his chin raised, his head patiently swiveling back and forth patrolling the pitch-black heavens, his half-lidded eyes still unfocused, and looking no less blind than Raymond's.

The slope was deserted, so quiet it was unnatural. A dark, dead-air, Silent-Night quiet, but it was only late afternoon. No animals, no wind, no movement, no other people. No other witnesses. I blinked hard a few times, then stole a look behind me at the gaping hole that was once one of the church's stained glass windows, too real for me not to trust that it wasn't, other witnesses or not.

What started as a distant pinprick of light on a black sky canvas turned into a screaming winged ball of fire dropping like a meteor, its noise deafening while it swooped in toward Michael, its pitch stoked by pleading cries from what sounded like the millions of souls all damned to the bubbling shit-pits of hell, all speaking in crazy tongues but saying nothing, their voices instead climbing into one screeching bitch-fest jumble of earsplitting, chalkboard noise. Down, down, down, the dive-bombing Lucifer rocketed in for the kill from behind, Michael motionless on the grass like he was ignorant of his approach. A hundred feet from the target Lucifer raised his crucifix sword like a horseman bent on delivering a beheading, and it was then that Michael turned. With another blinding, crushing blow, Michael's hammer-club paralyzed Lucifer, pile-driving him down and out of sight below the surface, deep into the earth, with dirt and dust and smoke rising from the explosion.

Michael stood stiffened at the rim of the crater. Leo and me were side by side, and as we watched this thin blond angel man-boy of a warrior while he waited, him looking rock-sure as a statue on a mountaintop, I felt something wonderful, something powerful grow inside me.

It was a confidence coming from the mysterious feeling of knowing the outcome of a poker hand before it was played. This was Michael's faith, and Michael's confidence, and my faith in him became his faith in me, and this one true thing I needed to be sure about at this very moment now hit home: Michael, God's Archangel, was invincible.

Lucifer rose from the depths of the cave-in, lighted on his feet on the other side of the crater, began pacing like a caged animal that had been poked with a stick, scowling, hissing, growling, then scowling some more. Michael felt for the leather strap still hanging loose over his shoulder. He resettled it, then resettled his grip on each of his weapons. He turned, stayed earthbound and bent forward, and marched around the crater's edge, his noiseless PF Flyers tramping toward the enemy. Lucifer flexed then raised his weapons high while his yellow demon eyes rolled up into his horned head, and from the depths of the crater, from all those dark and pleading souls of hell he summoned it, summoned with one command all their hate, and their sins, and their grief, and their scorn for God—

"Bestow upon me—the fury—of thy damnation!"

—and guided it all into his monstrous winged body, and it was then I felt its draw, felt its surge of power as it groped at me, fueled all my doubts and my fears, of sickness, and of death, and of loneliness and depression, and of what my life would be without my Viola. Lucifer's head jerked in my direction, and with one final wrench at my core, he turned up the heat and stoked my pain, drawing it to the surface and feeding on it, making it his and mine together—

...Harry, his tired young body shivering, his last breath leaving his lips.

...Viola, lost and pleading and crying helplessly, her insides in the throes of shedding a life we'd created.

...Viola grimacing through a final, swelling agony, about to finger the last bead of her rosary, her voice fading to a whisper as she said good-bye.

I doubled over in agony—it was like my groin was in a vice.

"...unnhhh..."

Then words I never thought I'd ever hear slammed into me, overcame and took command of me: *"I will save her,"* Lucifer howled. *"She will live."*

I was spellbound, felt suspended, my eyes tearing up. The pain, it was subsiding...

"My Viola?" I mumbled, felt my face pinch, heard my voice quiver, not believing this possible. "You can help her? How?"

The demon roared like his long-shot horse just came in, and through a foggy numbness, I watched Michael break into a frantic run. A rejuvenated Lucifer got into a crouch, ready to spring to engage him.

"RENOUNCE THE ANGEL. RENOUNCE GOD! BESTOW YOUR FAITH...IN *ME*! CHOOSE ME, *AND YOU CHOOSE VIOLA!*"

The sudden might of Lucifer's backhand staggered Michael, dropping him to one knee on the grass, Michael looking smaller and weaker now, like a turtle with a cracked shell. A second backhand sent Michael flying, slamming him into the second story of the church's speckled granite wall. He slid down the wall to its bottom, dazed.

Viola's pleading face—I saw her in my mind, and instantly I knew her words, her thoughts, her outlook on her future: *"I have your love, Johnny, and I have my faith, and these are enough to carry me through to the end that God has planned for me."*

It was then I realized how very, very selfish I'd been, and it shamed me.

"Choose you," I shouted at Lucifer, my heart pounding, me knowing how empty this decision would make me, "I gain Viola's life, but—" Screwing up my courage, I ended the debate.

"Choose you, I lose her love. No deal."

Michael regained his footing and moved like he had radar, the beast striking at him again and again with slashing swipes and poking thrusts, but now Michael deflected each blow and drove Lucifer back onto his heels, pounding the demon's body with enough thundering, mind-drubbing power to separate starch from a sail, and the puffed-up pride from someone, or something, that had never earned it.

Lucifer's grip on me faded, and Leo and me brought up the rear, Leo first, then me cradling my arm and doing my best to stay close behind him. The smaller Michael attacked while not taking a backward step, pummeling the beast like a ten-ton punch press stamping out machine parts, pushing him away from the church, forcing the fight downhill, with Lucifer stumbling then recovering then stumbling then recovering, until they reached the bottom of the grassy slope where Michael stopped, lowered his weapons to his side, and waited. A winded Lucifer backed away from him, sized him up while getting his bearings, then finally realized where he was. He hissed, and Michael answered him through Raymond's subconscious voice.

your fate—

The earth shook as Lucifer's roar hit us like booming, snapping thunderclaps. Leo and I covered our ears while Michael continued.

is and always will be—

Lucifer teetered on the bank of the swollen river, its current raging. Upstream, the dam was open.

predetermined—

Michael dropped his club, slipped the leather strap from his shoulder.

you will reenter hell, and you will take your son with you—

Lucifer unfurled his wings, but quick as a striking cobra, Michael snapped the leather strapping around the demon's clawed hands, and as the beast struggled to lift his massive body, Michael pulled the strap taut and held his ground. With one gouging slice of his sword, Michael lightened Lucifer's load by about a hundred pounds, all from below the waist.

and you will do so without this

He tossed Lucifer's bloodied, coiled member onto the bank on the other side of the river, the butchered beast shrieking while Michael looped the other end of the leather binding around his beast-feet and drew it tight. Michael took to the air, and with a thrusting nosedive he slammed the hogtied demon underwater and pressed him down, steadily pushing him into the muck at the bottom of the river.

From the bank I saw the two figures that were one disappear beneath the surface, the ram-headed Lucifer and his drowning son Adam, bubbles rising from beneath them while Michael pulled back, the disturbed muddy sewage parting to reveal a round opening, a waterspout swirling downward, through the tainted river's floor, them both spilling into it and spinning out of sight, sucked into its depths like turds in a toilet bowl. Under our feet, the earth trembled and groaned until the toilet-bowl hole suddenly erupted, spewing a geyser of brown water and orange and yellow and white fire, and then, just as suddenly, only fire. Michael spiked the demon's coiled member with his sword, lifted and dangled it over the blazing hole. He rotated the blade in his hand, scorching the coiled gray meat until it was charred totally black, then released it and his skewer-sword, letting them both drop into the inferno. The fire belched, and with a small puff of smoke the blast furnace blaze sputtered and went out. The parted waters came together, covering the river floor again.

* * *

I was collapsed on the grass, the cynical side of me feeling like I'd just gone ten rounds with a gorilla. My serious side told me what I felt had mostly to do with my age. It was something that wasn't easy for me to admit, but it was time I owned up to it.

I let the cynicism resurface because it was easier this way, but it wasn't working. I seen and felt too much, was given glimpses of things seen only in Bible stories. I was humbled, but humble didn't seem near as big enough a word to describe just how utterly buck naked it made me feel.

you are wrong, Wump

"What is it I'm wrong about, Raymond?"

Me and Raymond were side by side, lying on a bed of soft new grass that sloped away from the church and ended at the river, and I suppose you could say we were talking. Leo was on his way down the slope with the wheelchair. Raymond explained himself.

about getting old, yes, you are right, but—

about fighting a gorilla

The wheelchair with Leo pushing it squeaked up alongside us.

in your prime the bout goes maybe three rounds, four rounds tops

I was too tired, too hurt, too upset to give the joke the laugh it deserved. I'd lost a friend today. Father Duncan, you, sir, were a hero.

I smiled at Raymond for his effort. "That's really rich, son," I told him. "But hey, you got too much faith in me."

one can never have too much faith, Wump

"Ready?" Leo said as he pulled up between me and Raymond. Leo engaged the wheel lock. I got to my feet, still cradling my wounded paw, feeling a bit dizzy now. I looked over my shoulder at the battered church, its pink speckled granite blocks twinkling in the sunlight, the sun back where it was supposed to be, low in the afternoon sky, but not ready to set yet.

"Help me get his arms, Leo."

"But, Wump," Leo said real sheepish-like, his shoulders sloped, his silly grin looking pained, like he was apologizing, "the wheelchair's not for him. It's for you."

The wings reappeared, and Michael, or Raymond, or whichever one of these two beautiful beings this was, helped Leo settle me with my broken knuckles and aching back and head into the seat. This wonderful being addressed me again.

I must do one more thing, Wump

it is something for you

"For me? Why for me? I don't need nothing."

Except...wait—

My spirits rose. Maybe there was hope.

"My Viola," I choked out. "Please. Please say you'll help her."

Michael laid a gentle, comforting hand on my shoulder, and as I peered upward at a face that stayed blank, emotionless, no different than moments ago while in the heat of battle, I waited for a response. Michael's heaving sigh told me the answer. I blinked through my tears.

that cannot be, Wump

I am sorry, but it is the nature of things

yet there is something else...

The magnificent winged creature who was both a frail, impaired boy and a princely angel rose up and glided out over the bank to the middle of the river, the water now calm, the dam sealed back up, the runoff from the spring thaw under control again. He was ghostly quiet as he floated a few feet above the water's surface, following the tree-lined river upstream toward the tannery, passing over two covered bridges and the remains of the third. He glided back down near the still water. I lost sight of him around a bend.

29

TWO MONTHS LATER

Sunspots. For weeks it was all we'd heard about. A bunch of them according to the weathermen, all doing whatever sunspots did, and all of them doing it back on Good Friday. Doing things like screwing up radio frequencies and interrupting the earth's electro-cosmic-magnetic force fields or some such shit like that. And causing the sun to look weak and pale, even creating the optical illusion it was setting at three in the afternoon.

Fine. It's all a load of crap, but fine.

Father Duncan, Monsignor Fassnacht, and Adam St. Jerome were incinerated when the church's gas heater blew. The explosion had caused a fire that destroyed the interiors of the sacristy and half the church, and took those three lives with it. I was blamed, me being Our Lady's lead maintenance person and all. Hogwash, I told them. They knew the old burner was a firetrap. I'd put it in writing last year with a registered letter to the archdiocese's top maintenance folks downtown, telling them what I had to do each month to keep the damn thing running. They all quit the blame game with me and backed off, the police included, when I showed them my copy of the letter and a postal receipt for it.

The Cardinal's murder. The city of Philadelphia was in an uproar because two months had passed, and no one had been charged. Kerm the coroner called to tell me they liked Monsignor Fassnacht for it. Much as I wanted to tell him they were barking up the right tree, considering the man had actually confessed the murder to me and Father Duncan, I stayed mum, and for a good reason. Only one of those four people, counting the Cardinal, was still alive: me, the one with the prison record.

So that was how certain things were explained away. Of course, the investigators had the cause and effect of the heater explosion all wrong. It blew up all right, but only after one hell of a spark had caused it and everything around it to go up, the spark coming from a burning six-hundred-year-old Bible torched by its demonic author. Outside of Sister Dymphna and Mrs. Volkheimer, and Leo, who was there but no one would ever believe on account of how slow he was, I had no one else to talk to about it.

Except, of course, Raymond, and my Viola, but by then it was too late. After a few weeks, when things had settled down, Raymond's leukemia took him. May 16th it was, in the morning. Raymond, in Leo's company, sipped some Black Cherry Wishniak soda, properly shook to remove most of the fizz, settled back into his wheelchair, burped, and was gone. Eight days later the leukemia took my Viola.

God's greatest gift to me, Viola's love was. For forty wonderful years she gave meaning to my life, a life so ready for the crapper by the time I'd turned twenty. My strength and my savior, and now she was gone.

The first two weeks after her diagnosis, I prayed to Father Duncan's soul every day, begged him to ask God to change his mind. The last two weeks, seeing her pain, I prayed for a different outcome, and this time my prayers were answered. She might have survived longer, a few more months maybe, suffering like she had but still here for me, talking with me, taking care of me, comforting me. But in the end, the only gift I had left to give her was to let go, and her final caring act for me was to die a happy woman.

These new shoes really pinched.

"I don't need you to carry me, Wump. Give me your hand and get out of my way," Mrs. V said, so I gave her the room she wanted. She swiveled out of the seat of my truck, stepped onto the running board, grabbed my arm, then planted both feet on the grass next to a wheelchair I'd set up for her. Around her house, her walker and cane still worked fine, but outside, especially on a grass lawn as uneven as this was, where the paths between the gravestones dipped in spots and were a little soggy, her wheelchair would be a must. She settled into it.

"Big day today," she said to me, beaming.

"That it is, ma'am."

I pushed her up to a gated section, about a third of an acre, inside Our Lady's Cemetery; we entered it in silence. This section contained the Volkheimer family's burial plots, and was surrounded by a low-rise ornamental iron fence with curled tops that could pass for candy canes, except they were black. I steered Mrs. V around the soft wet spots, careful not to get mud on my new Thom McAns.

New suit, new shoes. New birth, in a manner of speaking. Yessir, today was a big day.

It weren't no one thing that made Mrs. V and me decide about my "pedigree." It had been more like a smelling salts wake-up, where all of a sudden everything came into focus, with all this stuff pointing in the same direction, like iron shavings to a magnet. Didn't know who decided it first, me or her, but when I'd stopped by to see her the day she got home from the hospital, she looked at me real different, and I expect the look she'd seen on me was the same.

So we talked it through.

Rolf had always been extra nice to me. Made sure me and my kid buddy Heinie got apples or biscuits or something else wholesome to eat when we anted-up our sacks full of dog droppings at the tannery each morning. He'd lectured me when I got into trouble and he'd heard about it. He put up most of the money to have the orphanage rebuilt, paid the laborers extra to get it done early, which they did, finishing it in time for the birth of his and Mrs. V's first child. He kept a spyglass in the attic of their footbridge, sat real secret up there in a chair in front of a window with a full view of the orphanage's back yard, where all us kids played. And yeah, his son and me were both born the same day. The circumstantial evidence was overwhelming, for me especially, and for more than one reason, me knowing that a father I never thought I had, had been loving me all along as he watched me grow, and me also knowing it was me who took his life. Couldn't rightly say I'd ever get that one squared away, accident or not. Not in this life at least.

Sure, there'd been some changes for her and me. You could see them right here, in Our Lady's Cemetery. One newer grave, just recently sodded, for her husband Rolf, a plot that had waited for a body for over fifty years. Today we put some flowers on it, tomorrow being Father's Day. And now there were two other new graves, still mounds of dirt because they were only a few hours old. My wife, Viola, was buried in one, our son, Harry, in the other. I had them exhumed from the town cemetery next door.

See, right there, right under my nose, was something I'd never considered: my family's burial plots. All three were in the town's public cemetery, Bountiful Gardens. Viola told me she'd bought our plots there rather than in Our Lady's because the town cemetery had a breathtaking two-acre, township-tended arboretum in its center. Truth was, I knew now, she did it because the parish cemetery was for Catholics only, and since no one could prove I was baptized a Catholic, I wouldn't have qualified. Pretty silly when you thought about it, knowing Sister Irene had every orphan at St. Jerome's christened, even doing some herself right at the orphanage, including me, or so I'd been told. No less spiritually effective than a church baptism in God's eyes I was sure, but with no certificate. So there it was: no proof, no burial in a Catholic cemetery, yet with Viola loving me like she did, she never thought less of me because of it, never even questioned me about it. Her final resting place, she'd decided, should be next to her husband, regardless. What a lucky, lucky man I was to have had a love like that.

"It all gets fixed today, Viola honey," I said, looking over her grave, my empty plot next to it. I couldn't help but get choked up about this.

Mrs. V stayed silent while I dealt with my grief. When I finally blessed myself, she said, "Now let's go get you officially baptized, son."

We retraced our path back down the grassy incline toward my truck. The view was good from here. The river, the bridges, Mrs. V's property, and less than a mile in the distance, the tannery with its two smokestacks, the low-rise Wissaquessing Ridge as their backdrop. And right now, visible through the cemetery gate, was a flow of people on foot that got near as steady as the march of time. Many were Three Bridges German Catholics, but the past few weekends we'd been getting more out-of-towners, the cars on the street just like the people, all stop 'n' go and headed in the same direction. Been this way every Saturday and Sunday since Easter. One of a number of changes we been dealing with.

A second was how Mrs. V and me addressed each other. Guess you could say we'd worked it all out. I was still using "Mrs. Volkheimer" or "Mrs. V" or "ma'am," and she stayed mostly with "Wump." "Son" sneaked in a lot, a kind of compromise, but she wasn't really using the word much different now than how she'd used it before, except we both felt the difference when it was spoken. "Mom" hadn't entered the vocabulary yet. I wanted it to; I just needed more time.

Third, she'd asked me to move into her home. Maybe I would at some point, but it meant giving up the house where Viola and me had spent more than forty happy years together, and it was a step I wasn't ready to take yet.

Fourth was Leo, or rather Leo without Raymond. A terrible loss for him, and something that knocked him off kilter enough that I hadn't heard a telepathic peep out of his chatterbox head since. I tried to keep him busy, and what with me still nursing my busted paw, I guess you could say it had worked out okay for the both of us. I should say the three of us, since Leo had taken up with Teddy Agarn, a bull of a young kid but near as slow as Leo. The two boys were a great help with all the clean-up work needed while the diocese lined up contractors to repair the church, plus there was always other school projects, daily trips to the hardware, that sort of thing. And next summer, the three of us would rebuild the roof on Mrs. V's bridge.

Truth was I wanted to adopt Leo, but was told I was too old. Guess it didn't much matter, to me or to him. We were already spending a lot of time together, though for me it was never enough. The word around the Catholic Church was that kids who were slow like Leo couldn't sin, which pretty much made them perfect Heaven material. To know Leo was to believe this. Never realized how much I loved him until now.

Fifth and last thing I'd had to come to terms with was my own anger, including my need to personally crush my cousin Hugh Volkheimer's skull for what he, and the decades of contaminated waste generated by his filthy tannery, had done to my wife and son. The anger had blunted somewhat with all that happened on Good Friday and the weeks since, and with things looking like it was only a matter of time before Hughie's tannery went belly-up.

With Mrs. V safely tucked back into my passenger seat, I pulled the truck through the cemetery exit and waited for a seam in the throng of passersby on the sidewalk. It was amazing how fast the word had spread. Some walked with binoculars raised, some with their hands shielding their eyes while they squinted, all of them trying to get glimpses of it before they reached the edge of the tannery property, where you were able to see it best. Others, like the feeble and the infirm and the dying, rolled by in their wheelchairs, their heads down, their lips moving in prayer.

"I must do one more thing," Michael had said to me, and this one more thing he spoke of doing had been spectacular.

When the tannery was operating, which was Monday through Friday, its two round smokestacks got warm enough from by-product steam to take on a faint red glow, something akin to a sunburn. But on weekend days these red-bricked, side-by-side stacks were cooled enough to show a tan-white residue on their surface, a film that looked like they'd overflowed with oatmeal, the discoloration running the length of the stacks and tapering off down near, but not quite all the way, to the bottom. The tan residue had been visible for years, no one thinking any which way about the long, half-a-heart shapes, the stains mirror images of themselves. But the Wissaquessing Ridge behind the tannery was what pulled it all together, the ridge suffering a large rock slide from its peak to its base back on, yes, Good Friday. So now, when folks viewed the ridge from a distant rise at the edge of the property, they could see a natural phenomenon that defied their sense of reason: a forty-foot shape of a long-haired man on bended knee, his gown a loose-fitting mosaic of stratified rock layers, his jagged, protruding chin turned right and raised skyward, his body sized perfect to fit between the two tall smokestacks, with the stacks' oatmeal residue looking like feathery wings attached to his shoulders. Weren't no finer stained glass picture of an angel I had ever seen.

Like I said, word spread real quick, especially after all the attention the church fire got from the news folks. Except, also like I said, the wings were only visible when the tannery wasn't operating. So all them tannery workers, mostly second- and third-generation German Catholics, and every one as devout as an apostle, were calling for it to be a shrine while they looked for new jobs. I gave the tannery six months. Take that, cousin Hughie, you polluting bastard you.

But there was one thing that hadn't quite been wrapped up near as tight as these other events. It was what went on with Adam's twin sister Ruthie: her candy, her newfound voice, and her disappearance.

Easter Monday, early in the morning, I remembered sitting on the concrete steps out back of the orphanage while Leo was inside scavenging for my stray tools. There I was, tending Leo's wagon, my arm in a sling, my bum wrist cradled in a cast. His rusty red Radio Flyer was on the grass in front of me, weighed down by my toolbox. Our only mode of tool transport until my cast could be removed, Leo's wagon was. How my life had changed.

I remembered hearing the screen door snap shut and Ruthie tapping me on the shoulder, sleep still in her eyes, and I remembered how she'd greeted me with the first, last, and only words I'd ever heard her speak:

"Licorice whip?"

Her one hand offered me a limp piece of the strawberry-red candy. I accepted it, tucked into my shirt pocket. What her other hand held had caught me by surprise: a wooden spoon and a potato sack.

Dogshit Ruthie. I never had a clue.

Faded green pullover sweatshirt above worn dungarees. Long pant legs bunched against the tops of tan tennis shoes. Short, straight black hair and sleepy, Spanish-brown eyes. This was what I remembered of her as she left my sight around the corner of the orphanage, and it was the description I gave the police when they finally went looking for her. Ruthie hadn't been seen in Three Bridges since, nor anywhere else the missing-persons folks had searched. The old German couple set to adopt her, and her twin brother, Adam, were gone as well.

The thing is, I'd told myself the proclamation in the demon bible had read only one way. The same way the Catholic Church and so many German Catholic couples this century and last had figured it read, too. But try as Sister Dymphna and me did to recall its exact words, we knew we weren't really sure. Had it said firstborn son, or simply firstborn child?

We checked the hospital records and didn't like what we saw.

Adam St. Jerome. Date and Time of Birth: May 12th, 1950, 3:33 PM.

Ruth St. Jerome. Date and Time of Birth: May 12th, 1950, 3:33 PM.

The false Christ a woman? About as likely as a woman becoming president. No one would expect either, let alone if both got wrapped into one.

HIDING AMONG THE DEAD

Philo Trout:
Retired Navy SEAL.
Former bare-knuckles boxer.
Current crime scene cleaner.

"Couldn't pry me away...Bauer writes with authenticity...A knockout original story, with a host of equally original characters. Certainly not your typical crime fiction, and that's a good thing." —**David Swinson**, author of **Trigger.**

Philo Trout just wanted to start over.
He moved to Philadelphia to keep his past a secret. His new life as a crime scene cleaner is quiet—until he discovers that many of his "clients" are coming up short on their organ count.

As Philo tries to outrun his past, a coworker can't remember his own. Patrick was found brutally beaten, and is now an amnesiac as a result. When the connection between his coworker's history and missing organs begins to emerge, Philo is determined to solve the puzzle.

The trail of clues leads Philo into a dark conspiracy. A brutal organization will stop at nothing to protect their secret. And Philo's past as a fighter might be his only route to the truth...

If he can survive that long.

Get your copy today at
severnriverbooks.com/authors/chris-bauer

AUTHOR'S NOTE

The Devil's Bible, also known as *Codex Gigas* or "The Giant Book," contains the Old and New Testaments of the Holy Bible in pre-Vulgate Latin as well as other extensive religious writings of the first and early second millennium. The thirteenth-century manuscript was written as a penance in Podlazice, Bohemia, by a Benedictine monk who, according to legend, finished it in a single night by summoning the Devil to help him. It is currently on display in the Royal Library of Sweden.

ACKNOWLEDGMENTS

Terry, my put-upon wife, sacrificing mother, reluctant muse, and former social worker extraordinaire. Laurie Pascale, my first reader. The original Rebel Writers of Buck County: Jeanne Denault, Dave Jarret, Marie Lamba, Damian McNicholl, and John Wirebach. The many members of the Bucks County Writers Workshop chaired by Don Swaim, published novelist and former host of CBS Radio's Book Beat. Special thanks to novelist/short story writer Grace Marcus, whose insightful critiques left creative marks on this novel right up through the final page. St. Vincent's Home in the Tacony section of Philadelphia, PA, an icon. An orphanage in its previous life, St. Vincent's provided significant inspiration for this novel. Author Jonathan Harr, whose outstanding non-fiction offering A Civil Action gave me insight to the sometimes hazardous by-products of the leather tanning process. NYT bestselling and multiple Bram Stoker Award-winning novelist Jonathan Maberry, who made sure I received the spoils from a horror contest held by a non-profit writer's organization that, sadly, had already closed its doors. Any errors found within this novel are entirely the author's.

ABOUT THE AUTHOR

"The thing I write will be the thing I write."

Chris wouldn't trade his northeast Philly upbringing of street sports played on blacktop and concrete, fistfights, brick and stone row houses, and twelve years of well-intentioned Catholic school discipline for a Philadelphia minute (think New York minute but more fickle and less forgiving). Chris has had some lengthy stops as an adult in Michigan and Connecticut, and he thinks Pittsburgh is a great city even though some of his fictional characters do not. He still does most of his own stunts, and he once passed for Chip Douglas of *My Three Sons* TV fame on a Wildwood, NJ boardwalk. He's a member of International Thriller Writers, and his work has been recognized by the National Writers Association, the Writers Room of Bucks County (PA), and the Maryland Writers Association. He likes the pie more than the turkey.

severnriverbooks.com/authors/chris-bauer

Printed in the United States
by Baker & Taylor Publisher Services